Reckless Attraction

Hope Island Series

SK Mason

ISBN (EBOOK) 978-0-6452824-2-9
ISBN (PAPERBACK) 978-0-6452824-7-4

COVER ART BY DESIGNS BY LM
EDITING SERVICES BY KAT PAGAN FROM PAGAN PROOF READING
PAGANPROOFREADING@GMAIL.COM

To Grace,
Thank you for letting me use your amazing
personality to inspire this book. You rock! ❤

To K, the 'real' Avery,
I'll never listen to the Cranberries in the kitchen the
same way ever again. Your love of food will live on in
every page of this book. I look forward to more of
your recipes xoxo

Foreword

Reckless Attraction is based in Australia, and written in British English, there will be some terminology that might not carry around the world. For this reason, I have included a glossary at the end.

Chapter 1
Grace

The timer on my new industrial oven chimed every two seconds, like the melodic sound of a harp warming up for its most important recital. I closed my eyes, taking in the tune, my fingers tapping rhythmically on the pile of papers in front of me. Costings, a business plan, and the signed offer from the Queensland Office of Public Health.

A *signed* offer from the Queensland Office of Public Health! Okay, it might have been a preliminary offer, dependant on a thousand other things, but it was still better than I could ever have hoped for.

I did it. It's finally my time to shine.

My fingers traced the blue and grey logo on the front of the document. First, over the state-wide recognition. Then, the details of the offer. And finally, the cash agreement of five hundred thousand dollars, once I proved the worth of my project. High on adrenaline, I leaped to my feet and pressed my thumb on the menu pad of the oven, my finger stroking the shiny black glass. The words "Bon Appetit" scrolled down on the console.

Imagine how amazing it will be when there's actual food in there! Excitement coursed through my fingertips. Holding in my squeal, I threaded my fingers tight and brought them to my lips. What kind of oven offered seven tunes to pick from, greetings for every action, and the state-of-the-art definitions for temps and air flow?

The oven of the newest and biggest Queensland healthy lifestyle project, that is.

It wasn't just the oven that encompassed this incredible kitchen. It was the commercial fridge, the multi-gas plate stove, and the infinite storage space, as well as the bench length. If anyone was going to succeed with Nutrify, it would definitely be me.

Footsteps approached. Based on the shuffling of one set of treads, my pregnant best friend, April, was about to appear and finally see what the big fuss was about. It helped that we'd decided to combine Youth Legacy and Nutrify to market as Queensland's first and best wholeness centre. In a sense, this solidified us as family—more so than we already were.

April stepped in, her hand on her big belly, with her husband Jarryd and their adopted son Riley in tow. All eyes widened, scanning over every new inch in the building. "Wow, honey. This is *something* else," April breathed out as she settled on a stool by the breakfast bar.

Her tagalongs moved in different directions, Jarryd darting to the white goods and checking the installs, while the twenty-year-old beelined to the massive pantry. A frown of disappointment marked his face when he realised the kitchen was empty.

I giggled and settled next to April. "Kid, the tradies literally just left. Food and the rest will be delivered later today."

"This kitchen is the bomb. Can we raid it?" Riley cocked an eyebrow. "Or am I asking a stupid question?"

Jarryd playfully whacked him on the back. "Don't we feed you enough, buddy?"

Riley smiled, a hand smoothing his black hair into place. "Hey, I'm a growing boy." The young man kissed April on the cheek, then turned to me and said, "It's pretty amazing, Grace. I hope after I graduate next month, I get to be invited to whatever it is you're doing here."

"We already told you what she's doing here." April laughed as the door closed behind him. Turning towards me, she added, "In my defence, try explaining to a twenty-year-old and a two-year-old what Aunty Grace is doing. It's on the scale of grandiose." Her eyes shone with sisterly pride.

"Try saying Aunty Grace is amazing?" I chuckled.

Jarryd lifted a finger and continued. "More like Aunty Grace loves a mega challenge."

"No way. It sounds completely like Aunty Grace will be offered half a million dollars to design and run a healthy nutrition project across the state and change the way everyone eats around here." I narrowed my eyes as I teased my best friend's husband.

Jarryd sauntered over to April and stood behind her, his open palms on her shoulders. She placed her hand on his, her cheek briefly caressing his knuckles. "Don't listen to my hotshot, here. He's *only* a child psychiatrist. He wouldn't know a challenge if it hit him in the face."

A chortle brewed in Jarryd's belly until his laughter resonated in the room. Both April and I succumbed to the contagious giggles. He shook his head, his lips lifting into a cheeky smile. "OMG, no. Not at all. It's not like I am doing miracles with the kids we have. And, Jesus, their mother...

I'm a saint to have managed this woman for as long as I have."

April pretended to elbow him in the gut, her grin reaching her ears. Though, there was no denying Jarryd had done wonders with Riley since his court case over six years ago. The teen had been beyond lucky to get off with a warning, all while escaping the clutches of his drug dealer bio-dad. "It's true... what you did for Riley was short of a miracle." I sighed.

Jarryd squeezed April's shoulders gently. "What we both did. What we all did as a team, really. Finally belonging to a family made Riley who he is today."

The last few years flashed in my brain at high speed. Broad, tanned, and shrewd, Riley wasn't a kid anymore. Though the boy's father had been quiet since Jarryd's trial, we all lived in the shadow of the drug lord, and whether or not he would decide to storm back into their lives. I glanced towards the sliding door. When Riley was nowhere in sight, I asked, "Have we heard anything from the Cooper gang?"

Jarryd and April exchanged a glance. By the sudden appearance of the lines all over Jarryd's forehead, they had. "Hal Cooper returned to the area, just in time for his oldest son's release. I guess he might be hoping to locate and recruit Trey back into the family business."

I strangled my glass, the water shaking in the cup. "Does Riley know?"

"No." Jarryd lowered his voice. "And we would prefer to keep it that way for now."

April scrunched her face. "Being with us has given Riley a sense of purpose, and he's thriving." She carefully tucked a strand of brown hair behind her ear. "But he's only human. And his bastard of a father is relentless." In the background, a delivery truck reversed in front of the commercial kitchen, its lights and sensors snapping us from the conversation we'd been dreading. April smacked her hands on her lap. "All right, people, we've been fine for years. It's not going to change." Eyebrows wagging at me, she added, "And I'm not ignoring the topic at hand, Ms Lawson."

I rolled my eyes, laughing with her. "And speaking of, the first food order is being delivered."

I marched to the front door, signed the order form, and motioned inside. The delivery driver carted some of the containers into the middle of the room. I grabbed a few of the top items: two-minute noodles, chocolate biscuits, and a bunch of muesli bar samples.

I definitely didn't order these. As if he read my mind, the guy handed me a copy of the order form and added, "Freebies, lady. *Gotta keep the big, brand-new client happy*—my boss said."

Jarryd snatched two of the mini chocolate chip cookies and shoved them into his pocket. When I narrowed my eyes, the unspoken question burning my lips, he chuckled. "One for my little princess, and one for the big boy." Then, he kissed April and raised his hand in salute. "Grace, this is a great kitchen, a great project, and you are gonna kill it! Until then, I'm off to find my kids."

When her husband had disappeared, April leaned forward, head cocked to the side and belly touching the edge of the counter. "Come on, girlfriend, let's talk business now."

My legs crossed, I matched her posturing. "Okay, so we have provisional approval as of last night. The five hundred grand, the permits, and the business outline, as long as everything goes according to plan. On paper, we're ready to roll."

"But?" April grabbed a packet of Tim Tams from one of the crates behind her, opened it, and pushed the offering towards me.

"Thanks." I bit into a biscuit at the same time she did, picking up the chocolate crumbs with my index finger as they fell on the table. "I have to find a way to go beyond *another* type of diet. Nutrify isn't just about healthy eating. It's a whole redesign of how we eat and focuses on teaching people healthy habits. The last state campaign was all about swapping for healthier options, and it was good, but people still don't want to feel like they're going without."

April nodded before her eyes locked on the second chocolate biscuit in her hand. Her nose screwed up. "Should we put this back, then?"

"That's the point, right here." I laughed, my excitement building up. "I want to go way bigger than this. Completely change the way people are wired when it comes to good, old comfort eating and thinking that treats should be banned." My arms grew jittery. I crossed them. *If only I could articulate my vision better. Show the world that healthy doesn't mean boring.* "If all you had available *was* yummy food which happened to also be healthier, wouldn't you want to choose it?"

April shoved a finger in her mouth and licked it. "Is that even a question?"

"Right?" My eyebrows lifted. "So, imagine if suddenly, instead of telling people they had to choose boring and *healthy*—which, when it comes to popular belief, are often equivalent—all their choices, were both nutritious and appetizing? That's not even including the sad fact that junk food is cheaper than healthy alternatives." My throat tightened at the word *cheaper*, my belly suddenly feeling the ghost pangs of childhood hunger.

"I know you're a brilliant professional and you're passionate, but how do we go from A to B with this, Grace?" April said, a mix of worry and nurturing concern etching her face.

I took a deep breath and exhaled slowly. "Okay, so I clearly don't have all the details panned out, but I first want to host a major event for our local members of Parliament, where all the food will not only be to die for, but also dietetics approved." I linked my fingers, elbows leaning on the table. "If we can show our community, first-hand, that there are ways to completely change the way we feel about food, I think we could really make a difference."

April grabbed a notebook and pen from behind her and slid them towards me. For the last three years, my best friend and I had designed every initiative for her centre. And Youth Legacy had worked out. Better than worked out. The centre grew tenfold until it was one of the best in the state. So, when April threw me that piece of paper, I knew we were going to brainstorm until we were unstoppable and had it all mapped out.

We're in business, baby! My heart skipped a beat and a happy shiver travelled up my back. I relaxed my shoulders and grabbed the pen. April moved closer to me. She watched that marker like we'd watched it a hundred times before. Eyes wide. Lips parted. Filled with excitement and hope.

"Show me. Go through the basics first," she said, her tone focused. I wrote dot points, listing the stuff I already knew. *Healthy options, delicious options, no longer having to choose, affordable,* and *available as standard.* April pursed her lips, the twinkle in her eye glistening. "I like it. So far, so good. Show me step B, girlfriend."

"The next step is to promote the event as a state-wide trial, get it evaluated, and see how we can market it from there." *My own dream come true.*

"I reckon we need to think big here." April smiled. "The sky's the limit."

"Yes. That's the plan." I laughed, April's new enthusiasm driving mine even higher. "I think, with the right support, we could even market them as prepacked meals."

"You mean, commercially manufacture them?".

After three years of this, she and I knew how to make miracles happen together. "Yes. Taste and health don't have to be exclusive from each other."

"Oh, darling, I can't wait to try these meals," April crooned. She tapped her fingers over my scribbles on the page between us. "Just one question." The air grew thick. In the deafening silence, the clock above us ticked fifty times before April spoke next. "Who's gonna execute these meal ideas for you?" I froze, my jaw locking. When my heart skipped a beat, I forced a smile. Because, after all, this was just a little short-term problem, and we would find the solution in no time. "You have no idea yet, have you?" April cringed, her words presented more as a statement than a question.

I shook my head, my hair shifting with the motion. That query had plagued me for the last twenty-four hours. Whoever was going to partner with me in making these meals couldn't be any random Joe. It had to be someone with taste, initiative, professionalism, and a clear ability to share my vision. The whole thing promised to be an *out-of-this world* initiative. It would revolutionise how people ate and managed their relationships with food. It was going to change my professional life and the lives of those in our communities. Excitement increased until the buzzing in my head screamed louder than a KitchenAid on full blast.

All I needed now was to find an *out-of-this-world* head chef.

Chapter 2
Avery

M y phone buzzed on the kitchen counter. I ignored it. Instead, I turned the volume up on my speaker. "Zombie" by the Cranberries shouted in the background. As it should, since I was prepping for my *mind-blowing* Bolognese.

Proper chefs should have one classic tune per dish. No more. No less. My lips lifted, remembering Christian's words. God, I missed that son of a bitch. He'd taught me all there was to learn in the kitchen. Granted, a good decade had gone by since he'd tucked me under his wing. But no matter how many years passed or how many stars I'd earnt, I would always be a back-house chef, favouring homemade pasta sauce before any damn fucking caviar.

Slice. Cut. Dice. Within minutes, the smell of fresh herbs had spread through my apartment. First rosemary, then thyme and oregano. The perfect combination. I inhaled the tips of my fingers, pleased with the mix, before tossing the blend into the pan now heating on the stove.

The phone buzzed again. Hands deep in tomatoes, I glanced towards it. *Private number.* Warm air filled my lungs and I clenched my jaw, exhaling as slowly as I could while ignoring the annoying vibrations on my kitchen counter. On the wooden board, tiny pieces of red onions danced to the same rhythm.

"Will you just shut up?" I barely answered the phone for people I cared about. I wasn't about to answer some fucking unknown number.

Once the diced tomatoes were thrown into the boiling pan, the juicy mix quickly turned runny. The amber liquid spun in a wide circle with every turn of the wooden spoon. I stirred it slowly. A small blob of sauce found its way to my lips, and I groaned in appreciation.

Almost there, capocuoco. There was one thing missing, other than the shit-ton of salt and pepper I would add closer to the end. Wine. Red. Chianti.

No light was needed in the walk-in pantry. I could tell where each item sat, and God have mercy on the person choosing to move my spices around. My mind jumped at the memory of the last one-night stand I brought home. After waking up to my kitchen *rearranged,* I made sure she found herself on the veranda, purse packed and ready to go. What was her name again? Teagan? Reagan?

Reggie. Whatever. *You shouldn't have touched my fucking kitchen, Reggie.*

The cork of the Chianti popped, and I tossed the topper to the side. Then, I splashed the red wine into the pan, following Christian's teachings to the letter: *Don't be a cheap bastard. Pour it in.* The bottle gulped for five seconds, and when it looked about right, I sculled another few swigs down my throat. For inspiration. My body buzzed and warmth spread through my veins, my shoulders dropping. Content, I turned towards the kitchen island, where home-made pasta sheets were waiting. One by one, and with light fingers, each strand was lifted and shaped the right way until all the dough had been processed.

If this isn't perfecti—

A loud bang interrupted my thoughts, followed by a heavy commotion up the hall. I grabbed my Shun, my thumb running over the blade. A razor sting confirmed it was sharp enough to gut whoever the fuck that was. I just hoped I wouldn't have to. Judging from the number of footsteps stomping my way, it could only be one person, and he hadn't come alone. I counted the pairs of strides in my head.

Four. No, three. Three of them would be in my kitchen in about five seconds. I turned my sauce off and pushed the pan towards the cooling stove. *Three. Two. One.* I gripped my knife tighter, my knuckles growing white. Stance wide, I squared my shoulders and pushed my chest out, ready to pounce.

Deep-brown leather shoes entered my living room. I didn't even need to look up the Valentino pants to know that higher would lie the rest of the matching three-piece suit, his trademark ugly yellow tie, and above that, Hal Cooper's smug face.

Jesus... Deep breaths kept me focused. Hal Cooper and his two goons strolled in, meeting me by the island in the middle of the room. "What the fuck do you want, Hal?" I growled. My fingers loosened against the knife. Truth be told, if Cooper wanted me dead, I would be six feet under already.

"Is that any way to welcome an old friend?" Hal deadpanned, his eyes following the blade in my hand. "In my defence, I tried to have this conversation over the phone." The two thugs next to him closed in. I recognised one of them by the tatt on his wrist. A black tulip. The last time I saw him, he was sporting a matching black eye. The grin on his face told me he remembered how he got it too. I guess, today, he hoped to level the playing field.

I slammed the knife on the counter, before nodding at the gang leader. A sign of peace. Peace my ass, but I wasn't a complete idiot either. "I'm out, Hal. What do you want?" I said, keeping my voice steady.

Cooper ambled through the room, until he noticed the photo hanging on the fridge. His index finger drummed on the face. Then, it moved to her body and the Hawaiian necklace by the table. "How's sweet Sienna doing, Chef?"

I clenched my jaw, the taste of metal filling my mouth. It took every fibre of my being to stop me from launching towards the twelve-inch blade sitting between us. "Get to it, Cooper. You're not here for my sister," I spat.

Black Tulip snickered. "Avery always gets edgy when his baby sister's involved."

The second guy laughed before taking a couple of steps to lean over my pan. He stared at the orange liquid, now lukewarm, and dipped his fat, filthy finger in my sauce. He brought his hand to his lips and moaned while sucking on the coated digit. Something punched me in the gut, and going by the looks on their faces, they knew where to hit me. Without actually hitting anything.

Don't fucking react. Spaghetti sauce isn't worth dying over.

"Isn't pasta sauce supposed to be red?" he mocked, his finger back in my pot.

"Not if you blend it while the tomatoes are hot, you fuckwit." I pushed the pot away from him, sauce splattering over his white shirt. *That's going to be a bitch to clean.*

As if he remembered he was on a schedule, Cooper motioned for his goons to move back, and they sat behind the counter. Next to them, the bikie leader leaned against my marble top, his fingers running over the deep veins. "I'm guessing you'd like to know why I'm here," Cooper taunted innocently, like he wasn't a major drug dealer known for ensnaring kids into his twisted affairs. Kids like Sienna.

"I told you I'm out, Hal." I raised my hands in front of me.

"No, Chef." He snorted like a rutting pig, his laugh faker than his goon's online knock-off Gucci. "Not yet."

I narrowed my eyes, waiting for the punchline. 'Cause of course there was one coming. As fucking usual. "Spit it out, old man." I slammed my fist on the counter, my patience wearing thin. All I'd ever wanted was to be a chef in some small family restaurant in Italy. No crowd, no shady business, no having to pay for my sister's one indiscretion over and over for the last four years. I shook my head, my eyes rolling backwards in my skull.

How much longer do I have to pay for you roping a thirteen-year-old into one failed delivery that should have never happened in the first place? Air whizzed out of my lungs, and I crumpled on the stool in front of me. I ran my hands through my buzz cut a couple of times, my throat tightening.

"How many times are you going to knock on my door for this?" I twisted back and grabbed the wine bottle. I chugged the liquid. When I slammed it down, Black Tulip reached out for it. But I yanked it from his hand, and instead, tossed the bottle in the bin. "You can just fuck off." He cracked his knuckles, his eyes narrowed in response. "Tell me what you want, Hal." At that instant, I made myself a deal. Pardon or no pardon, after this exchange, Sienna and I were taking off. We were done. No more slavery to Hal Cooper. Italy sounded pretty damn good right now.

"I want information. That's it. Literally." Cooper stared at his manicured fingernails, his forehead smoothed out, pretending to be mighty angelic.

"Information?"

"Ya heard me. Just information."

Information, I could do. How bad could it be? "And this is it. Sienna's alleged debt is forgiven. Forever. And I never see your face for the rest of my kitchen days?"

"You have my word."

The word of Hal Cooper meant shit, but that's all I had. If that meant Sienna could continue living a normal life, and I could stop being Cooper's unwilling enforcer, then I would gamble on it. "What do you need?"

When Cooper nodded, Black Tulip passed him a stack of papers. The forms were pretty much filled out in scrawny blue ink. He slid them towards me.

Tender. Public health. Dietetics initiative. Grace Lawson. "What the hell is this?" I brought the forms closer to my face. I had to be hallucinating. Was Hal Cooper asking me to propose a tender to some woman from a youth centre? To cook?

The tender offered a hundred grand to a head chef willing to lead a transformative meal plan. Something about developing amazing food, all completely dietetics approved. On top of the outlined payment, they'd add a ten percent profit margin on any potential commercial manufacturing of the meals.

It has to be about the dough. "Let me guess. You're after the money?"

Cooper laughed, a deep insulting cackle, then looked me in the eye and spat, "You think I need a hundred grand?" The two bodyguards by his side joined in, snickering like I had asked the stupidest of questions. What was I missing? "No, Chef. I want you to cook your little heart away. Cook, create, discover, poison the crowds. No one fucking cares. What you'll get me is information."

I nodded, waiting for the other shoe to drop. "Okay?" My heartbeat increased until I could hear it between my own ears. I wiped my clammy palms on my jeans. "Information on what?"

Cooper smiled, the smile of an assassin. "Not what. *Who*. Ya see, there's this fellow. He works at this centre you'll be doing wonders for." He paused to clear his throat. "He stole something of mine. I'd like to get it back."

Okay, not so bad. "What did he steal?" If Hal Cooper was making me his bitch for the next few weeks, I wanted to know what I was looking for.

"Something very precious. That's all you need to know." His irises darkened. Whatever that guy had lifted, it had made a dent in Hal Cooper's major ego, and he was going to get it back.

"So, what information, exactly, do you expect me to procure?" I asked, wanting this whole thing over. *Now*.

"Simple facts. What's happening in that centre, who's visiting, names, details, just women's gossip. Nothing hard to get." Cooper stood up, signalling his sidekicks to do the same.

"Can you manage that, cook?" that second dimwit barked, right before he dunked his finger in my Bolognese for the last time.

I snarled, "Guessing it's all arranged?"

"Good guess," Cooper said. "Tender has been won by the woman. A *Grace Lawson*. You start at Nutrify on Monday, and half the money will land in your account a couple of months later." He slapped the back of my shoulder, which would have probably thrown me off balance if not for my size. "Don't tell me I don't look after you."

Black Tulip waggled his eyebrows. "Say hello to Sienna."

Against my better judgement, I lifted an arm between Cooper and the door. Sweat pooled down my spine, and the cyclone in my gut resumed. "I tell you what you want to know about this dude, and when the project is over, so is this little charade. Your word."

Cooper didn't even turn around. He threw his left hand in the air and kept walking. "My word."

Right before he crossed the threshold, I yelled out to him. I'd be damned if I went in blind. "Who's this guy I'm spying on?"

"A child psychiatrist. Dr Jarryd Williams." The words were mumbled in the distance.

Back inside my kitchen, I threw my sauce in the sink. It twirled like a tsunami down the drain, leaving amber stains all over the white porcelain. *A child psychiatrist? What kind of shrink gets tangled up with a bikie gang?*

Chapter 3
Grace

Nutrify was officially starting, and it was shaping up to be the most incredible, nerve-racking moment of my life. Partly because of the stakes and partly because, for some reason, the provisional tender had come with its allocated chef, right at the last minute. *While unusual, it was a small price to pay for 500K.*

The computer chimed as it turned itself off. The chair wheeled flush with the desk, I pushed the mouse against the wall and turned towards the back door of the main building. The lack of air-con in Jarryd's office was proving harder than I thought, but given I snuck in without asking him, I couldn't very well leave a complaint letter on his desk.

Focus. That chef should be arriving any minute now.

For the hundredth time this morning, I combed my hair through my fingers until my blonde bangs sat neatly on the side of my forehead. One would have thought that the amount of perspiration dripping through my scalp would have done the job.

Stop fretting... Sweat leaked through my foundation, and I'm sure I looked like a melting psychotic snowwoman.

My phone vibrated. With shaky fingertips, I unlocked the screen and loaded the message from April.

APRIL

He's already here! He came in the back way and asked to wait for you in the kitchen.

My heart skipped a beat, a mix of surprise and frustration filling me.

Who let him in?

APRIL

Not sure. One of the kids? Go get him, tigress! Haha.

I rolled my eyes, no longer hoping to staunch the river of sweat drenching the banks of my back. My throat scratched like sandpaper. I cleared it as I marched towards my brand-new commercial kitchen, my blood pressure rising with every click of my heels.

This was *my* project. *My* baby. *My* professional endeavour. No matter how brilliantly this guy came recommended, I didn't plan on watching the work unravel from the sidelines. I expected him to wait for me before moving in.

"Good morning, Miss," Oliver, one of the older youths at the centre, blurted out as we crossed paths.

"Hello, boys. Have you seen anyone new walking through?" I eyed the two juveniles passing me.

"Are you looking for the temple guy?" Oliver slowed his pace to answer. Based on how the kid locked his glare on his buddy, now ten feet ahead, he was keen to catch up to him.

Temple guy? "No, I don't think so. I'm looking for my new chef. I'm guessing someone dressed like Linguini from

Ratatouille." I shook my head, trying to dismiss the visual. "Minus the rat."

Oliver rolled his eyes. "Sorry, Miss Grace. The only guy today was the temple guy, and he definitely didn't look like that. Maybe he was the new gardener, 'cause he was carrying some pot plant thingies somewhere." Oliver scrunched his face in a brief apology before he raced away. He was gone almost instantly, leaving me no closer than I had been five seconds ago. I picked up my pace and headed towards the trade centre area.

I guess I'm about to find out if this guy really carries around a rat for luck... or not.

I'd worked with a few chefs in my time. Some great. Some terrible. Judging from experience, and given how recommended *Linguini* came, I'd guess he was one of the older, wiser options. Old enough to have been nominated Chef of The Year three times in a row.

A screeching ruckus snapped me out of my thoughts. The closer I came to the impressive white building, the louder the noise projected. Metal on metal. Cupboards being slammed. And, in the background, some light humming. My feet smacked the hard pavement, and daggers shot through my knees as I rushed towards the kitchen door. By the time I laid a palm on the handle, the chaos was in full swing: dishes being rearranged, fresh herbs sitting on the windowsill, and a small speaker playing some '80s pop music.

I paused in front of the doorway. My head tilted, I glanced at the half body sticking out of the pantry. Black pants, black sneakers, black socks. *Is this my new chef, or a ninja breaking in?*

"Hello?" I crept inside, my steps slow until I reached the end of the long melamine counter. Fingers trailing across the benchtop, I scanned the room for a weapon. A cotton tea towel made its way into my hands, and I pulled it by one end, ready to strike. "I know jujitsu."

Who are you kidding? A month of training with your brother when you were twelve doesn't count.

Black pants staggered from behind the pantry door.

"Hi?" I said, my tone weaker than I'd hoped. Who the hell did he think he was, barging into my kitchen like that? I huffed a big breath, then added, "Normal people wait to be introduced to their new work area."

"Guess I'm not normal." He turned around, showcasing a toned waist and broad shoulders.

Definitely not Linguini. I swallowed hard, my eyes wide. He sure didn't look like any of the chefs I'd ever worked with. That, or I'd been out of the commercial business for way longer than I thought. Above a grey Dickies t-shirt, which housed two massive biceps on each side, wide brown eyes glared back at me. I hoped the heat spreading over my cheeks didn't mean I'd turned crimson. But who was I kidding? Of course, I had.

I lowered my towel while I scanned the figure currently occupying my sightline. A good head taller than me, olive skin, short black beard, and strong shoulders. Shame took the reins when he caught me staring. "I didn't think you'd mind me decluttering some of the junk in here," he said, without stopping his rearrangement. Garlic cloves, onions, and saffron found their way where dried herbs used to sit —*those* now rested in the bin by his feet. Amongst a crap load of other stuff.

What's he calling junk? I narrowed my eyes, my hand gripping my makeshift weapon as I prayed to God I found the resolve not to fire him on the spot for the smirk growing on his face.

He pushed the basket of rejected goods towards me, his gaze dropping to my white knuckles. "Should I be worried? Is this death by..." He gestured at the cloth in my hand. "... tea towel whipping?"

"Nope. Not at all," I stuttered, tossing the towel on the counter and wiping my hands on my skirt. *Come on, girl-friend. Lead by example.* I forced a smile. "I'm Grace. You must be Avery. My new chef?"

A slight dimple emerged as he seemed to process the question. "Not sure I'm yours or anyone else's. But if you're asking whether I'm your new colleague, yes, I am." His tone wasn't amused, yet it wasn't annoyed either. It was some scary kind of neutral.

Oh my god, he's dead serious. I cleared my throat, waiting for the perfect comeback to manifest itself. When it didn't arrive, I offered a hand. "I'm sure we will work out our roles in this project soon enough, but for now, it's good to have you on board."

He nodded, his forearm extending towards me. As he grabbed my open palm, a fully tattooed sleeve moved up and down with every shake of his wrist. Right at the top, between his bicep and the base of his shoulder, a Japanese temple inked his skin. *Temple guy.*

"What do you plan on doing with these?" I squatted until I reached the ingredients in the plastic container by his feet. Dried herbs, gravy powders, cans of soups, spice mixes, and every other kitchen cheat gathered in one place. *He's amassed himself a whole kitchen graveyard.*

"Me? Nothing." He pushed the container closer to me. "But they're not staying in this kitchen."

My mouth formed a wide 'O' before I jumped to my feet. "Are you planning on throwing all of these out?" *Is this guy for real?*

"Yep." Another can landed in the bin with a loud thud. He didn't even look as he tossed it out.

My lips twitched. Someone needed a serious attitude adjustment. I raised my voice slightly and placed both hands on my hips. "Did you plan on asking me before emptying half my kitchen?"

"Nope."

When the next rejected item began to drop, I kicked the container with my toes right on time for the can to crash by his foot instead. Mr Bossy avoided the impact before it landed on his Vans. Our eyes met. Mine narrowed to slits. His, a mixture of surprise and curiosity. *Yes, buddy. MY kitchen. My house. My rules.*

Slowly, and without ever breaking eye contact, Avery lowered himself, his calf muscles flexing in delayed motion. I looked down at the man squatting below my waist, ambivalence poking at me. The temperature in the room soared, and I jumped back, a strange feeling stirring in the pit of my stomach. *Is it me, or did the air-con just die?*

Strong hands brought the container back to where it was originally positioned, and within one second, a soup sachet sat on top of the rest of the ingredients that hadn't made the cut. My new chef rose to his feet, another smirk building between two unmistakable dimples.

God... Why does he have to have dimples? I shook the thought out of my head, cursing at the inner teenage girl with no grit. Where the hell had my bravado gone?

"I'm guessing there's a memo here I'm supposed to get?" He pivoted to the pantry and tossed a packet of two-minute noodles by our feet. Just to add insult to injury, he turned to his phone and pressed *next* on his playlist. "Africa" by Toto crackled in the background.

God, somebody crank up the air-con! "These are things

we..." I stammered, pointing towards the kids jogging by. "Stuff the kids might eat." My throat could barely get the words out. Partly because this guy had some crazy voodoo impact on my brain, and partly because I had no idea we'd allowed that much crap to make its way into the kitchen. When had *that* happened? Bloody noodles, chips of every kind, and so much processed food. It was a disgrace, especially given Nutrify's mission statement. I released the breath I'd been holding in, but it didn't help dissipate the shame and embarrassment.

"These are things your kids snack on behind your back, *Mum*." Avery grabbed a couple of corn chips packets and stared at them like he was considering his options. "These, we could still use with sweet mince, guacamole, and salads." He tossed them on the counter, the lines around his eyes lifting. "After all, I'm not completely heartless."

Don't fall for his act. Dig your spine out of the clouds. You're in charge, remember? I inhaled sharply, in a bid to regain my composure. I'd be damned if *Temple Guy* was going to kick me out of my own kitchen. "Avery, now might be a good time to establish some roles and boundaries." I leaned against the countertop and crossed my arms.

He glanced twice in my direction, his lips twitching. I'd hit a nerve.

Spine back in business, baby! "I love ideas and suggestions, but I'd appreciate if you ran things by me first." I pushed the chock-a-block container towards him again with my foot.

The hard look I received in return said it all, as did the artery jumping in his neck and the sudden darkness clouding his pupils. He froze, then plastered his best saccharin smile on his face. No dimples this time. "No worries, Grace. You're the boss." He glared at the box between us, his eyebrows furrowed until a line appeared between his eyes the size of the M1. After tossing the last item from his hand, he grabbed his phone and keys from the counter and saluted me on his way out. "Best I catch you tomorrow for a proper start, I think."

A mix of disappointment and justification filled my brain. Who did he think he was? Throwing stuff away without asking was just plain rude.

As soon as the kitchen door shut, I sat crossed-legged on the floor and lifted each item one by one, reading the labels like my honour depended on it. Sugars. Colorants. Preservatives. A wave of hopelessness hit me like a freight train. First in my chest, then in my head, and finally through all ten fingers. Nutrify planned to revolutionise the way we thought about food. It promised to be life-changing. But not until I faced the amount of work we'd have to do to get there.

I grabbed a rubbish bag from under the sink and flung each item into the black plastic. They bounced quietly, like they shared my shame. I puffed my cheeks, a lame attempt at self-soothing. It couldn't be that bad, right? After all, I was justified in being a little mad. Who in their right mind would discard perfectly good supplies without checking, anyway?

Someone who truly understood what the project was actually about.

Chapter 4
Avery

The door of my Navara slammed hard, but not as hard as my hand against the steering wheel. Like a concrete wave, the pain shot through my palm before crashing into my wrists.

"Fuck!" The taste of iron filled my mouth almost as quickly as aggravation drilled into my gut. I threw my phone on the seat next to me, on top of the chef jacket I'd forgotten. Under it sat the paperwork highlighting all the bitch jobs I'd have to agree to, just to get Sienna off Hal Cooper's hook. I flicked through each page, ripping them from the staple holding them together.

Get a fucking grip. Air whizzed in and out of my lungs, until eventually my heart stopped jack-hammering against my chest and the fury fogging my brain died down. If I didn't get a hold of myself, it'd be my mind I couldn't keep together. And that wasn't an option. Not when this was my last job. The last stride before Sienna and I were off to Rome.

I took a closer look at the KPIs I allegedly promised to deliver. I had to give it to Cooper and his gang. The guy knew how to speak the lingo. The application shone as much as if I'd actually written it.

Meal planning, community education, and commercial epiphanies.

I raked my fingertips through my beard, closing my eyes while working on the tension buzzing through the rest of me.

This is just the beginning. The beginning of working under some chick who couldn't even keep a decent inventory. I'm sure she was a nice woman and all, but good looks and a professional title didn't mean jack shit when it came to culinary art.

This is a job. For Hal Cooper. Not an Australian Food Guide Awards ceremony. If she wanted to swap ketchup for fresh tomatoes or salt sticks for snacks, then so be it. The tender didn't say we had to achieve whatever cute dream she'd concocted. Only that I had to deliver tasty, dietetics-approved dishes. *Her* dietetics-approved menu.

My fingers trailed the embroidered AFGA logo on the front of my jacket, the memory of my last award fresh in my mind. Back when life was simpler.

Suck it up, princess, and let her be the boss of whatever farce this is. My knuckles grew white against the steering wheel as the realisation hit me.

"Argh." I had to go back. I had to let her be in charge. Let her think I cared and valued her input. At least until I got the info on the child shrink. And then, all bets were off.

The chick's reflection through the glass was tragic. Kneeling down with a trash bag in one hand, she threw the contents of my container in the bin, one at a time, a glare of utter disgust on her face. Maybe there was hope for the woman after all.

The door squeaked slightly when I pushed it in, but she didn't look up. Either she was deaf, or she was as pissed as she appeared. *Awesome. My new boss. The sulking girl without tastebuds.*

My teeth nibbled on my bottom lip, sucking it in and out until I crossed the five metres between us. *She's the boss. She's in charge. Pretend you fucking love noodles.*

"We may have started on the wrong foot." I bit the corner of my cheek, hard, then bent down until my knees touched the ground. A packet of chips landed in the bag as she glared up at me. She nodded and grabbed the next item from her pile.

"Just to be clear, I don't condone half this stuff," Grace spat. She snatched the next wrapper before tossing it in.

"Okay."

She narrowed her eyes at me, the subsequent packet hitting the bin with more force. I pulled the opening of the bag with both hands, while she emptied the whole container into the trash in one fell swoop. "No. Don't *okay* me," she snarled. "They're kids. You turn your back for one second, and this is what happens."

"Yep. I get it." My eyes trailed the woman in front of me. Blonde hair, piercing blue eyes that threw daggers my way, and a nice set of tits that swelled up and down in tune with her erratic breathing.

She straightened herself and dropped the container on the counter. It echoed in the room, and she flinched, her pupils widening for a microsecond. When I ignored the smack, she crossed her arms and eyed the rubbish bag swinging between my hands.

Not gonna let it go, are you? A tinge of amusement filled

me. She was Sienna 2.0, but in a grown-up package. Clearly, she wasn't going to be the first one to bury the hatchet, and I needed her (and her project) in order to get on with my life, so now was as good a time as ever to lure *Sulky Girl* out of her mood. Chin pointing towards the pile of crap, I asked, "Bin, tin, or sin?" She fixed her gaze, curiosity etched on her face. A quick head tilt, a slight smirk, and I had the woman melting in my hand. "Come on? Don't tell me you've never sinned before?"

I grabbed a stray muesli bar from the bag and ripped its wrapping off with my teeth. Her eyes widened and her top lip twitched, like she fought a grin. Right before I tore into the chocolate, and with the speed of lightning, she snatched a piece and shoved it in her mouth. As she chewed, her lips dancing the salsa, she closed her eyes. The epitome of Eve binging on Hell's apple. *That's it, Sulky Girl. You're almost there.*

The shit they kept in there was good quality. I had to give them that. The chocolate chips were the perfect blend of dark chocolate, and the honey just ripe. I licked the residue off my fingers and studied the woman in front of me, before tossing the wrapper in the can by her side. The pink of her lips spread from her cheeks to her neck, right as her eyes snapped themselves away from my face. *Was she just checking me out?*

She knew that I knew, but being the bastard I was, I stared at her—a Dolmio grin on my face—until she cleared her throat and pulled us chairs. She settled in one and pointed at me to do the same. "So, I don't need a PhD to work out what the sin part is." She laughed. "Bin, I can gather, but that leaves tin. I'm baffled by that one."

Fingers laced behind my neck, I stretched on the legs of my chair until my feet balanced me back and forth. "Ahhh, the unforgiving kitchen trio," I crooned. Her face relaxed. The ice queen was finally melting, and the room didn't feel like Antarctica anymore. Maybe more like Hobart during an autumn cookout. But still a step up, considering I had to be on my best behaviour for the next month or two. I went on to explain, "In major kitchens, when we screw up our orders, or food's about to go off, we either bin them, eat them, or give them up."

She tilted her head, her lips scrunched. "I don't get it."

The chair stopped rocking. When the next five seconds dripped in silence, I lost hope when it came to her working it out by herself. "Come on! Aren't you going to try to guess?"

She smiled, her eyes twinkling as if not figuring it out would kill her. "I *am* trying to guess. Did you make this up?" Her tone was laced with hilarious doubt.

"No way. Nope. This is fair dinkum."

At first, she froze, then a small giggle took over. "Stop laughing," she coughed. Her hand covered her mouth.

I liked it. We'd moved from Hobart to New Castle. "Okay. Okay. I'll stop when you finally get it." My finger moved from side to side. "I swear it's easy, Grace." Her name had a different ring when she laughed. Maybe the job wouldn't be so bad if I just gave her a chance.

"God, shoot me now." She placed her palm up in warning. "That's it, put me out of my misery. What is the *tin* bit?"

I pointed towards the group of kids playing handball outside the window. "Tin, as in cans. As in donations."

She pursed her lips. "Ahhh, of course." She turned back until she faced the bag of food items we were ditching. "Sin, bin, or tin. I like it."

"I like it too." Memories of last year's Christmas appeal

came to mind. Ole, the restaurant I was working at then, had tinned almost half a ton of food to the Salvos and a local DV shelter. The look on those families' faces still haunted me, and I'd made a promise to never just throw food out for the sake of it. "There's always a cause, or someone who could use the stuff. Especially people in crappy situations."

"Wow," Grace said, her eyes now the size of kiwi fruits.

"What?"

"Nothing. It's just…" She bit the nail of her thumb. "You just didn't strike me as…"

"The type?" I teased. No one ever took me as *the type*. Must have been the beard, the tatts, and piercings. My thumb and index finger moved to my eyebrow and twisted the small black ring on its axis.

"I definitely vote for tinning these, then." Grace stood up, breaking the awkward silence, and invited me to follow her. When we reached the counter, she plonked the big bag of junk in my arms. We'd moved from New Castle to the Gold Coast in record time. "Let's take these outside," she said. "I want to introduce you to a few people." She pointed to a bunch of kids hovering close by. "They're all pretty much in care, or from terrible backgrounds. I can't wait till you get to know them." She sighed. "They could do with some more honest, genuine role models."

Kids with hand-me-downs, hair way too long, and the energy equivalence of a colony of fire ants stared back our way. My throat seized, and the guilt of why I was really here showered me like I'd fallen through an icy river.

And just like that, Antarctica was back on the map.

Chapter 5
Grace

The waitress smiled awkwardly, before making googly eyes at the broad chest sitting across from me. In a white and grey buttoned-up shirt, the sleeves folded to his elbows, Avery looked so smooth that I almost forgave the blonde cutting into my business meeting by batting her eyelashes at my chef like a schoolgirl. Avery winked back at her as he reached for the menu she was holding. She slowly poured the water into his glass.

Business meeting, people! I cleared my throat while rearranging the notebook at my side, my fingers tapping the hard cover featuring a bunch of creamy cupcakes. The waitress turned around, her lips pursed. Her head swung from Avery to me, then back to Avery again. "Oh, I'm sorry," she crooned to my partner. "I'm making your date uncomfortable."

Uncomfortable? Who does she think she is?

From the other side of our table, Avery choked on his water. "Not a date," he sputtered, his hands waving in the air. "Definitely not a date."

My eyes grew as big as his, and I snapped at the pain-in-the-ass still gawking at him. "But we are on a business brunch, so, if you wouldn't mind?"

Her mouth opened. She nodded curtly and took off, leaving Avery smirking at me as if I'd been caught acting like a jealous girlfriend. "She was rude," I mumbled.

"Uh-huh?"

"Tell me she wasn't?"

"She was being friendly." Avery laughed. "You know, relaxed, fun, light-hearted." His finger twirled in front of me, zooming in on my navy-blue suit, perfectly aligned documents, and blow-dried hair.

I scoffed, twirling my finger back at him. "Hey, don't diss the uniform. I wore compulsory navy-blue dresses at the H.I.P. for a decade, so it's comforting." I took a breath.

Avery leaned back in his chair. "I'm teasing. You'd look great for a date."

Don't blush. Don't freaking blush! Too late. Heat crawled up my cheeks. I couldn't tell if it was the giant dimples or the very unwanted vision of us on a date that flashed before my eyes. *Very unwanted.* He was an ass. A cocky one at that.

Right after our meals arrived, Avery asked, "Tell me about the H.I.P.? I always get the Hope Island General and the Hope Island Private confused."

Memories of the last few years came to mind. My time with April at The Private. Jarryd joining the team. The court debacle that sent all of us in a spin, and Jarryd almost losing his medical licence. Shivers brought me back to the present. Six years on, and so much had happened. Riley had escaped from his father's claws, April and Jarryd were married with kids, and I was about to launch the state's biggest dietetics project.

"The Hope Island Private is where April and I worked

together for over five years. It's an amazing facility. They actually funded a good chunk of Legacy."

"Youth Legacy? April's gig?"

I nodded as I finished swallowing a forkful of my vegie stack. "Yeah, that's the one."

Avery slowly cut into a piece of chicken breast, his eyes cast to the meat drowning in mustard sauce. "Why? Seems very..." He cocked an eyebrow. "Generous?"

I rolled my eyes. It wasn't quite the time (or the place) to explain to our new chef how Jarryd pleaded guilty to drug possession to get Riley away from his drug lord father, all while entering into a very unethical relationship with his court-appointed future wife. Instead, I just sighed. "Long story."

"How long?"

I shook my head. "Very. Anyway, April and I worked in the same allied health department. Later, Jarryd joined us in mental health as a registrar." Another spoonful reached my lips, and I continued. "But he didn't stay super long. He went back to the Hope Island General, where his step-dad was the clinical director." I left out that it had been to save April from disciplinary action.

Avery wiped his mouth with one of the napkins between us. "Do you miss working in a hospital?"

Did I? Not really. Going into my own business was pretty *lit*, as the kids from Legacy would say. "Sometimes. But overall, what we have going on is cool. I've been doing heaps of work at the centre, but now that I get to own my own part in it, it's even better."

"What does this part mean for you, Grace?" Avery laced his fingers behind his head and leaned back on the cushion.

A deep breath loaded in my lungs, and I began my usual spiel. "Well, we are going to create a national, revolutionary way of look—"

"No. That's not what I mean." Avery narrowed his eyes at me and moved forward. "I want to know what it really means to you. What difference does it make in your life, whether you succeed with it or you don't?"

A cold wave travelled through my bones. I wrapped my arms around my middle and exhaled. Avery's bright brown eyes stared back at me. Underneath the toughness, the guy threw a deep question at me. One I'd be too afraid to face. If I didn't make it, I'd just go back to being the sidekick next door, the friend who helped everyone achieve their dreams but never her own. The little girl who made up recipes with her dolls and taught them to eat healthy, in order to forget jam toast was on the dinner menu for the fourth night in a row.

I poured myself some water. Then, in silence, my finger circled the rim of the glass. After a few seconds, I cleared my throat. "Well, I suppose it would be nice to have something to my name?"

Avery shrugged. "You don't strike me as the shallow type."

"I'm not shallow," I snapped. I should have known better than to go down that rabbit hole with him. "And does it matter what it means to me?"

Avery whistled, his chair no longer swinging. "I think we just discovered it does."

"You wouldn't understand," I said through clenched teeth, my blood pressure rising slightly.

"Try me."

I crossed my arms in defiance. He could go to hell. As

good looking as he was, as deep as he came across, he wasn't my friend. He was my chef. That's all he'd ever be.

He relaxed his brow before swinging his chair again. "Grace, it was just a question."

You're being an idiot, girl. I took a deep breath and the fog cleared from my head. "A lot. It would mean a lot. I..." I jabbed my spoon into the apple pie that had been placed on our table a few minutes earlier. The spoon stabbed into it like a psycho woman on a bad dissociative trip.

A hand snatched the plate away from me. "This is mine." Avery chuckled as his spoon explored the damage.

"Oh my god," I said, horrified. "I'm so sorry! I thought that was my apple pie." At second glance, my brain recognised the bright-red berries bleeding onto the crust. That was no apple pie.

Avery tipped his chin towards the other plate. There, a perfectly unscathed apple pie waited for me. As if he didn't care, he salvaged what was left of his dessert and scarfed it down. "I'm guessing I shouldn't ask questions from now on?" He winked at me while pointing at my food.

My heart warmed at his calm composure. There was something about him. Somewhat of a mystery. I chuckled. "Do you want me to order you another pie?"

He pulled the spoon out of his mouth and gestured towards himself. "You know I'm a chef, right?"

We both laughed. My guess was he could have ten of those whipped up by dinnertime tonight. "And based on your CV, a bloody good one at that."

Avery lifted his spoon in a mock salute. "That would be me."

While an awkward minute of silence passed between us, I realised he couldn't have known why Nutrify was so important to me, and in all fairness, not many people knew about my toast-related trauma. Instead, like a good clinician, I deflected. My brightest smile in tow, I asked, "What about you? What does this work mean to you?"

Chapter 6
Avery

F*uck*. Grace was waiting for me to answer, her blue eyes wide and inquisitive. In my misery, I didn't even have a freaking pie to destroy to shut her up.

If she starts questioning me, it's going to get real tense real quick. What did the work mean to me? Jack shit. A one-way ticket away from Hal Cooper's fucked-up world. Safety for Sienna. An asshole move from me, but I'd done worse, so the odds were I'd still sleep well when it was over with. I really wished I had more than a pie to stab. When Grace asked to meet outside the office, to get to know each other a bit more and to talk about some important meeting coming up, I didn't expect all of this to feel so real.

"Sorry, did you need me to clarify the question?" Grace teased, her smile screaming *payback*. She was on the uptight side, but it didn't distract from her looks. Her navy suit matched her eyes. I'd guess it was a little dressier than that uniform from the H.I.P. she talked about. But it worked. Her lilac shirt was cozied against a pair of good-sized tits and tucked into a skirt, which gave enough of her waist and legs to assume she ate what she preached. Minus the pie. Rest its soul.

"No, smart-ass, I got the question."

"Just checkin'." She chuckled. "I mean, one wouldn't think it's that hard of a question, right?" The corner of her mouth lifted.

If it wasn't for the light in her eyes, I'd have thought she was serious. "Right?" I said. "It's a good gig. Money's not bad…"

The colour on her face drained until she was paler than the napkin she picked up. Her fingers played with it until the paper was as thin as lettuce shreds. I'd touched a nerve.

You dickhead. You're supposed to be mega inspiring. My jaw clenched slightly. I was no angel, and the job for Hal seemed simple enough, but I hadn't banked on feeling bad for the woman. Clearly being here for the money wasn't the answer she'd hoped for. Though I'd bet it was far better in her book than admitting the actual truth.

"Sorry, I mean, it sounded like a great project," I said, fake enthusiasm oozing from my pours.

Her fingers stopped threading the napkin, and she tossed it on her plate, the pink of her cheeks spreading. "It sure is."

"What made you think of it?" To give her credit, it *was* a pretty good idea. If she could pull it off. If *we* could pull it off.

She shuffled on her chair and leaned in. As she moved closer, the scent of jasmine filled the air. I wasn't sure what it was, but it smelled good. Peaceful. "People often have nutritional issues for a few reasons. They might have comorbid health conditions. They might have learnt habits they can't quite shake…" She paused, a darkness taking over her usually sparkly eyes. "Or they're just too poor to buy food, especially nutritious food."

I wondered if the pie-stabbing incident was related to the sudden doom that befell her when she mentioned money. Maybe underneath the upper-class demeanour hid something else. "That's true. People are quick to judge."

Grace took a breath, like she was about to say something but changed her mind. Instead, her eyes scanned the sleeves on my forearms. Quietly, she asked, "Do people judge you?"

"What? The tattoos?"

"Yeah." Then she pointed to the earrings and the beard.

I shrugged. "Probably." I rolled my shirt up so she could see more of the ink. "But they all mean something, and to be honest, they make me look tough." I laughed.

"That, they do." Her eyes locked on the Japanese design. "I don't actually know much about you. Where do you stay?"

"I'm in Coomera at the moment. With my sister."

She paused, like I'd told her I ran a brothel. "Your sister?"

"Yes?" I said, the syllable stretched out in exaggeration.

She shook her head, trying hard to contain her smile. "Sorry, it's just that you look more like the eternal bachelor rather than a *little bro* to anyone."

I tossed a bread crumb in her direction. She threw it back at me with more force. I grabbed it and put it in my mouth. "I *am* an eternal bachelor, and I'm definitely no one's *little bro*."

She cocked an eyebrow. "Didn't you just say..."

"Ha. No. I said I'm no *little bro* to anyone. Last I checked, no one's washing my clothes." I picked at another bread crumb. "*But* I have a little sister. She's been with me for a couple of years now."

Her eyes widened, as if she'd just found out I was St Peter at the gates of Heaven.

"What?" I waited for the surprise on her face to die down. "A guy with tattoos can't have a little sister in his care?"

"It's the nurturing part I didn't see coming." She stumbled over the last part.

A snort built in my throat. Laughing, I tapped my more recent tatt. "It's the kraken, isn't it? He has that effect on people."

She shook her head, her bottom lip hiding between her teeth. "No, I didn't—"

"I mean, I can have a chat with him and tell him to lay low for a while." I pretended to look at the sea monster on my forearm, my brow frowning as if I'd told off a naughty kid.

"Will you stop it?" She giggled, then eyed the mythical creature in question. "It does look a bit scary."

I lowered my sleeve again, before motioning to the waitress in the distance for the check. "Nah, be reassured, he's harmless. Unlike my sister."

Grace smiled. "Tell me more about her."

I sighed. God, Sienna wasn't part of the act. But since she was probably the only real thing I could share, I figured I owed my new boss some semblance of truth. I continued. "She's sixteen. Been with me for about seven years. Her dad, she's not known much of the guy, and our mum, she just took off one day, so Sienna came to live with me."

Grace frowned. "Aw, that's sad."

"There're days where Sienna hates me because she misses our mother, and days where she knows I'm never gonna leave her." Visions of seeing my sister lost in Hal Cooper's shitty gang made my blood boil. I ran a hand over my scalp, the regrowth tickling my palm. *Time for another shave.*

"You're a good brother. I bet she knows that."

I raised my eyebrows, my head going in a circle. "Yeah, unless she's after more money, asking to go out, or ruining my peaceful night one way or another."

Grace narrowed her eyes at me, the dark humour tinkling in them. "You know, Avery, it's okay to show you care."

I did care about my sister. I'd do anything to protect her.

As if on cue, Grace tapped the notebook in front of her. "You remember about tomorrow's meeting?" Some important appointment with members of Parliament. It would finalise a few vital things she needed for the big reveal. Stocktakes, lists of suppliers, quotes. That's about all I remembered. Between Hal Cooper's fucking reminders, Sienna's dramas, and the actual work I had to pull through to make this charade believable, I'd overlooked the fine print.

"Yep, I'll be there." *How hard could a meeting be?*

"Before I forget, here's the prep work for it." She handed me a bunch of documents. Creases lined her forehead as she waited for a commitment from me.

"You got it, Grace."

The lines smoothed themselves out. I dropped a fifty on the table, and together, we moved towards our respective cars. Right as she clicked her door open, Grace turned around, a grin on her face when she pointed to my forearm and added, "Maybe you should have a chat with him before tomorrow."

I nodded, a twinge of guilt coursing through my veins. The kraken was the least of her worries.

Chapter 7
Grace

A very had about 2.4 seconds to magic his ass into the meeting room before I officially lost my crap. The heavy glass doors pulled open for the umpteenth time, but it still wasn't my chef walking through them. *Where the hell is he?*

My fingers curled around the manilla folder in front of me, straightening the spine, then the sides, and finally pushing pieces of paper back into the cream-coloured cardboard, until the pile itself could have been used as a builder's perfect benchmark of measurements. Across the table, our local member of Parliament, grey-haired and balding, stared at my fingers restarting their repetitive ritual.

"Shall we begin?" Member Allan's nostrils flared in an attempt to stifle a yawn. When he failed, he covered his mouth with his hand and mumbled, "Or reschedule?"

Behind me, the door slammed, and heavy footsteps hurried in. The chair next to me scraped the floor, and I exhaled the breath I'd been holding. Finally. *There is a God after all.*

"My apologies to everyone." Avery settled in his seat,

like having two government officials and their minute-takers waiting for twenty-one minutes was no biggie. "Parking in the CBD is a bit—"

I cleared my throat and jabbed him with my shoe.

"Business. Parking in the city is hard business." Avery groaned as he finished, his smile ineffectually hiding the shock on his face. Black pants, a maroon shirt, and his trademark Vans shuffled in place. He glared at me sideways before crossing his wrists on the table.

"Thank you so much for the meeting today, Member Allan, Member Jones," I said, ignoring the chair to my left distancing itself.

He arrives late, almost swears in public, and he's the one acting annoyed now? Jesus. We'd have another conversation on expectations after this, but for now, all that mattered was getting through this meeting. If our local Parliament didn't approve Nutrify going live, it would be the end of the road, and I'd be damned if I was going to let that happen.

"Firstly, thank you for arranging the initial step of the tender to be finalised so quickly. The funds have been agreed upon. Many thanks." I nodded towards the middle-aged executives at the table. Next to me, Avery perked up. *What is it, Linguini? The word 'funds'?*

My shoulders squared and legs crossed, I contained the smirk on my face. I threw a quick glance towards him, and based on the raised eyebrow, he'd got the memo. There'd be no money until we'd actually worked for it.

I continued. "The next step in the project is the redesign phase." I pulled some brightly coloured graphs out of my folder and passed a copy to everyone. "As you can see, we're aiming to replace all high carbohydrate and fat items with low ones, while making a point to source the ingredients locally."

Avery uncrossed his hands to push the paper back. "I think what we'd like to stress as well is that it's not just about focusing on calories."

The two executives nodded at each other, and Member Jones added, "Good. The community tends to prefer nonclinical goals and outcomes, and that's what this tender is about."

"Of course, but we just need... we just need to..." I stammered. What the hell did we need? This wasn't a *let's trick everyone* proposal. This was a clinical and professional endeavour that one would assume senior members of our local government could get without me babying down the lingo.

Between their lack of seeing the bigger picture and his arriving late, the meeting was as helpful as an ice cube in Hell. April and Jarryd's words materialised in my vision: *You've got this. You've got this. You've got this.*

A deep breath settled my skittering heart rate. I forced my shoulders down, my hands unclenching. Then I leaned back on my chair, the three men eyeing me like I'd grown a second nose. When everyone had gone quiet, I addressed the room, my tone as stern as my grade-six teacher. "Gentlemen, while I appreciate the need to present our project with the appropriate language and definitely do not want to focus *just* on calories, we need to consider the latest research and academic links between mental health and obesity, trauma, and eating disorders, and the cause and effect when it comes to people's lifestyle choices." The folder in front of me whooshed when I opened it and removed the next handout. This time, Avery accepted the document, studying it almost as readily as the two men across from us.

You've got this. You've got this. You've got this.

"Very nice," Avery whispered.

"So, yes, once we've chosen the right ingredients, and translated them into tasty, healthy, and local options, we will rebrand them into everyday alternatives for the community until they forget these are dietetics-approved meals. Instead, it will, indeed, be about the life-long relearning of healthy eating habits."

Avery cleared his throat and tucked in his elbows, his demeanour relaxing. "What I love about this is the opportunity to blend good, everyday ingredients into new dishes. Because the reality, as my colleague already stated, is that for the majority of people, obesity isn't medical. It's poor lifestyle choices, and it's financial, and it's—"

"Single mothers with no income, no time, and no energy," I finished. Avery's smile matched mine. Warmth replaced frustration, and hope sat where twenty seconds ago, despair had drilled into my gut.

Member Allan nodded. "We've loved Nutrify since the beginning, Ms Lawson. This has only strengthened the council's excitement to support it."

"Tell us more about phase three. This is the one we're looking forward to." Member Jones chuckled, most likely referring to the feast we'd promised to deliver his whole department as the project's final trial. Another handout made its way around the table, the three men observably engrossed in the information. I watched them with a satisfied smile, the tension easing in my belly.

Seven weeks. Six entrees, eight meals, and six desserts. All calorie-controlled and divine-tasting. *Not that hard, right?* My heart fluttered in my chest. Truth be told, it could be as easy as Avery and me finishing each other's sentences. Or it could be just that hard, considering it could very well be the project that landed me in jail for: grievous bodily harm inflicted on another person.

The road to a great kitchen is paved with stormy recipes.

The second the two men were out of sight, Avery pushed his seat back, laced his fingers behind his head, and leaned against his chair. "I think it went pretty well."

"For sure. We're lucky it went at all, seeing as you were half an hour late to begin with."

Palms up, he grimaced an apology. "Yes. About that. Didn't think it would be that busy…"

"Really? 10 a.m. on a Wednesday, in the middle of Brisbane? You didn't think it would be busy?" I deadpanned.

"It's all subjective, isn't it?" He winked before he continued. "Seriously though, lesson learnt, boss."

I rolled my eyes, fighting a smile. I was yet to meet someone as irritating and intriguing as our friend, here. *Who are you really, Avery Curtis?* "Thank you for truly understanding Nutrify," I said.

Dimples appeared on his cheeks, as perfect front teeth shone when he smiled. His light-brown eyes sparkled, and for the first time, I saw beyond the rough edges. My mouth dried up, something in my belly stirring. He ran one hand over his beard, while the other moved close to me. Instead of making contact though, Avery pulled one more sheet out of my folder. "We never got to discuss this one?"

The man had eyes everywhere. I'd left that last document out on purpose. One that I hadn't quite gotten approval or funding for. Yet.

My finger traced the headings, lingering on each word like they fuelled hopes and goals as they connected. My breath hitched as the words willed themselves out of my throat, despite my better judgement. What stopped the man from running away with my life-long ideas? Nothing, and yet, the prospect of sharing them with someone who cared about food as much as I did was too strong. I exhaled a breath, excitement building. "This is phase four."

"Phase four?"

I nodded. "If all goes well, I've made some enquiries to turn our meals commercial." Avery whistled, the question sitting between us. "I know." I sighed. "Early days. And clearly, if there ever is a phase four, I would credit you as the chef in the project—"

"How long would it take for this stage four to be good to go?" Avery's forehead creased, the vein in his neck pulsing harder.

I leaned on my forearms, studying the expression darkening his face. Like I'd thrown a curve ball at the man, rather than a lifetime opportunity to make a name (and money) for himself. "Does it matter? I know your initial contract was for two months, but I have no doubt we could extend it." Avery passed the document back to me, and I placed it in the folder. We pushed the chairs in and made our way towards the foyer. When he kept silent, and the niggling thought in my mind grew too loud, I finally caved. "Is that what you're worried about? That we won't be able to extend your contract? Because I'm prett—"

"No," Avery said without making eye contact. "I have an offer overseas after we're done here."

Disappointment crept in, and I ignored the tightening in my throat. If the chef designing the meals left before we commercialised the patent, it would throw a major spanner in the works. I'd need legal advice. Any advice. I'd have to ask Jarryd quickly. Since his trial, he'd learnt a few legal shortcuts.

I blew a breath and passed Avery through the threshold of the building. He held the door for both of us. "I understand. Listen, why don't we meet with a friend of mine tomorrow and discuss practicalities? It might be best to work out your involvement in all phases?"

Avery checked his phone, the dimples long gone. "Sorry, I have something on tomorrow. Won't work for me, Grace."

My keys clinked at the bottom of my bag as I rummaged through it. I found them and unlocked my car. "Too bad. I'll have to check what other days Jarryd is free." I opened the door and tossed my bag on the passenger seat.

Avery followed me to the driver's side. "Who's Jarryd?" His head rested across the top of the doorframe.

"Jarryd Williams. He's lots of things. Do you know him?"

He pushed the door closed and waited for me to wind down the window. He leaned in. "Nope. I'll see if I can change my plans and let you know." He tapped my roof with one hand as I slowly pulled out. "Look forward to meeting you both in the morning."

His reflection shrank with every metre of separation, but even as a tiny man in my rear-view mirror, there was something oddly attractive about the guy. Mysterious. Aloof. Assured. Everything I *should* stay away from, and everything I'd avoided for the last three decades. Mentally, I prayed that common sense would have the better of me for once. Then, I reached for my mirror, twisting it until Avery's silhouette was gone.

Chapter 8
Avery

S ienna didn't pipe up the whole drive to work. She clenched her fists, her face locked as far away from me as she could. Her chestnut hair lay tucked to the side, the three metal studs in her ears shining in the sunlight.

I turned the music down and cleared my throat. For fuck's sake, she was acting like it was my fault she'd been sent home from school. Again. "Probably time to end the silent treatment, Shorty." My eyes zoomed in on the empty road ahead. Dry bush passed us, dust and bugs collecting on my windscreen. "I know you miss Mum. I do too. But I'm it for now. So bloody talk to me."

"Got nothing to say." My sister huffed, before readjusting her earbuds and cranking her music to full blast.

Keep it together, dude. It's the adjustment disease, or whatever her shrink called it. My chest tensed, pent-up anger and frustration threatening to erupt. First, Mum taking off with her boyfriend to God knows where. Then, Cooper roping Sienna into shady drug muling. And now, this whole fucking spy act to protect my spoilt brat of a sister, who clearly didn't give a shit about our lives being turned upside down. "I suggest you open your mouth, because I've had it with you."

"I didn't ask you to come and get me!"

"No, you didn't. Your principal did," I answered through clenched teeth.

"I told him I could walk home. I'm almost seventeen. Not a baby."

I rolled my eyes. Sometimes it felt like I'd been dumped with one, though. "An adult has to look after you. It's me or welfare. If you'd rather the latter, pretty sure they're on speed dial in my phone." I grabbed my mobile from the console and tossed it on her lap.

She unlocked the screen, but instead of scrolling down the contacts, she swiped through the photos one by one, sniffing louder and louder as the memories of the last few years passed before our eyes. The weekend away after Mum fucked off with Joe, her trying on the black dress I bought her for her sweet sixteen, and a couple of the incredible mains we'd put together as a team. A sob ripped from her throat.

I glanced up, and as soon as I registered the fat tears running down her cheeks, my *big jerk* ego mellowed. *It's not her fault. Love her or hand her over to welfare, jackass.* "Come on, Sienna. It's not that bad." My hand cupped her knee briefly.

The bawling continued. "It *is* that bad. Mum doesn't care. Dad never has. You're stuck with me, and I'm always in trouble." She yanked her sleeve over her hand and wiped her nose with it.

"If I didn't want to be stuck with you, I wouldn't be. I *want* to be your big bro."

"You'd be in Europe already if it wasn't for me."

My blood iced. Did she know about the new job? If Cooper had approached her again, that fuckwit was as good as dead. A deep breath tempered my rage, enough for me to be able to form my next sentence. "What makes you say that?"

"You've got to be sick of me, Av." She lowered her voice. "I'm sorry about last year. I never thought one trip could mess everything up like that."

My vision now blurred, I focused my eyes on the white lines of the asphalt. How was I supposed to find out what she knew without asking straight up? "Sienna, did you get involved with Hal Cooper's crew again?"

"What? No! Never!" More nose wiping. "I know you had to pay Cooper almost a grand to let me off the hook."

More like twenty, one drug run (her failed drug run), and this trade concerning the child shrink. My lips pressed against my bottom teeth to avoid correcting the lie. Maybe I should have told her the truth, to finally sever her from the less-than-stellar company she liked to keep. "I'm serious, Sienna. This is non-negotiable. You stay away from them. They're dangerous."

She snuffled and turned towards me, her eyes wet with unshed tears. "I swear." Then, she added, her voice breaking, "Will you leave me behind when you go to Europe?"

Youth Legacy's front gate came into view, and I pulled into a visitor's car park. The seat squeaked when my whole body shifted in her direction. "Shorty, let me make myself clear. I'm never leaving you behind. You and me, we're a package deal. Wherever I go, you go." My throat closed up, but I continued. "It would help if you could behave until we're ready to leave, though."

She chuckled, tear tracks drying on her face. "I want to go now. Just to start fresh, you know?"

That, I did know. I couldn't fucking wait either. "I have one more job I have to finish. Seven weeks, and we're sipping Campari on an Italian porch."

"Am I wearing Sergio Rossi's?"

A genuine laugh rambled from the pit of my stomach. God, that kid never ceased to surprise me. "Yeah, but for me to be able to afford any of that stuff, I need the money from this job. Got it?"

She nodded. "Got it."

"You'll have to wait in the car. I can't very well bring my baby sister in, my first week on the job." Guilt pinched a nerve, like a little too much salt in a bad dish. "You have your phone and your never-ending playlist. Just entertain yourself until I get back."

"No worries, big bro. I won't embarrass you in front of your lady boss." Instead of the watery eyes, she sported a grin, the one she wore when she had cornered me into a spot.

"How do you know my boss isn't a dude or a three-legged pirate?" I took my seat belt off, my other hand on the lever of the door.

She pointed past the windscreen, her lips pursed. "'Cause of her."

My eyes followed Sienna's index finger all the way to Grace waving at us on the front deck of the commercial kitchen. "Fuck!"

"Already? Wow, bro. I thought you were stopping with the one-night stands." She exploded into laughter, her head nodding in fun mockery.

"No! That's not what I meant..."

"Hey, it's not my fault you're always swearing." She

waved back at Grace. "She doesn't look bad. Maybe you *should* fuck her."

"Enough," I said, my brain begging for a way out. Considering Grace was marching to us, I had less than thirty seconds to find one. "I'll stop swearing, if you don't put your foot in it with her." Less than fifteen metres separated my sister from my boss now. "I'm serious, Sienna. This is a complicated job." Sweat pooled around the base of my skull, my tongue as dried up as a package of bay leaves on a hot day.

"Why? What's so complicated about it?"

It's complicated because this nice, hot, bossy woman is being used for our benefit. She's being used so that you and I can disappear for good. "Stop with the questions, Sienna. Shut it, okay?"

Grace was four metres from me now, her kind demeanour making me feel like a complete asshole.

"Well, looks like I ain't staying in the car after all." Sienna unbuckled her seat belt and winked at me. From there, all I registered was her door shutting and Grace welcoming her to Legacy. As they embraced—my extrovert, pain-in-the-ass sister talking to her like they'd bred pigs together—my heart sunk. Because at that moment, as Grace introduced her to a couple of teenagers who had gathered around, Sienna looked pretty cosy. One arm around my sister's shoulder, Grace steered her towards a smaller group of youths. A girl showed her something on her phone, and they laughed.

Don't get comfortable, Sienna. They're just the key to our passports. Eyes closed, I forced a deep breath in. Despair clawed at my gut. It was easier to be a bastard to them all *for* Sienna, without Sienna being thrown in the mix.

My door opened, the clicking of the metal dragging me

out of my mental blank. Grace stood by me, a soft smile on her face. Deep-blue eyes beamed in my direction. Eyes that I'd never really looked into before. They were kind, nurturing, and *sexy*. Why hadn't I noticed them till now? *Because you're on a job, jackass. She's supposed to be the enemy.*

"I'm so glad you brought Sienna. Look at her," Grace crooned.

I stepped closer to her. "Sorry, it wasn't plan—"

Grace's hand settled on my forearm. She nodded towards the new group forming ahead. "I disagree. I think she fits just fine."

My head turned from Sienna to Grace, and back to Sienna again. "She doesn't have the best track record when it comes to choosing friends," I murmured, more to myself than anyone else.

"Kids speak their own universal language. And these kids here, they'll get her."

I cleared my throat, chasing away the weird emotion tearing through my soul. A mix of hope, angst, and shame. "She can't get attached. We're leaving in less than seven weeks. She's gone through too much shit for me to put her at risk now."

"At risk?" Grace's eyes met mine, the question asked with the furrowing of her brows. "This is what we do here, Avery. This is what this place is all about. The kids quickly become family." She nodded her head, warmth oozing out of her. "She'll be safe here, I promise you."

I studied the woman in front of me, from head to toe. Her bright-blue eyes, her warm smile, her blonde bob that never stayed in place, and the hot body underneath the professional dress. Her self-confidence, passion, and dedication whacked me in the face like a boxer who'd just taken a punch.

My agreement with Cooper was life or death, and it was fixed, but I'd be damned if I did a shit job for Grace in the meantime. I extended my hand towards the building, and smiling, Grace headed for the kitchen. "Then, we better plan these meals."

Chapter 9
Grace

My chef bounced with a different gait today. I couldn't quite put my finger on it. Like he carried one less drama around, and yet all I'd done was introduce his sister to a bunch of new friends.

"Sienna seems like a lovely young lady."

He nodded. "She is."

"When's the last time she heard from her mum?"

Avery's lip twitched, but he remained silent, as if he was deciding whether to answer or not. He continued setting up our meal-planning templates, hard lines materializing on his forehead.

"I'm sorry. I didn't mean to pry." It seemed I'd touched a nerve. Upon reflection, I didn't know much of the man, other than our quick chats here and there. He was all mystery, forbidden and ambiguous. However, when it came to his sister, there was an element of protection and major nurturing that didn't quite match the rest of the exterior.

"Almost four years." Avery spread a piece of A3 paper, grabbed a couple of markers, and pushed the lot between us. "It's just me and Shorty these days."

A purple pen in my hand, I traced eight lines, one for each of the meals we planned to deliver. "Well, you know she's welcome here anytime. It's not like she'll stand out or stop us from working."

Avery lifted his head, the creases around his eyes fading, and paused his list-making to stare into my pupils. With less than half a metre between us, I caught a whiff of him. Musky, strong, and intoxicating.

Move back...You're way too close for comfort. Tingles spread through my fingers as I gawked at the dimples and the beard. In my mind, I pictured what it would be like to rake my tips through it.

What is wrong with me? Being attracted to him was insane. As insane as flying over the jungle on a dingy plane with no parachute. Like being drawn to fire.

His dimples deepened to crescent moons. "Thanks. Tell me, Grace, what does this place *actually* do?"

The question snapped me out of my swoon-induced coma. Avery had written such a touching memo on why he was the right person to work within the centre. Had he forgotten it already? Disappointment niggled at me. Something didn't quite add up. Every man and his dog knew about this place. It was number one in the southeast. "Should I assume you didn't write your application yourself?"

"Beg yours?" The eyebrow cock, the tilted head, and the hand freeze confirmed this wasn't a stupid question.

"You heard me."

"Of course, I did. But it was so long ago, I don't rememb—"

I scoffed. "Come on, Chef. It's only been three weeks. And it wasn't something anyone could forget."

Avery blew out a big breath, a hand running over his

head. The pain and fatigue burdening his features at this moment, made him look much older than his thirty-odd years. "Grace, there's a lot going on. Don't take my over-loaded-brain personally."

Something in my heart broke for him. Though he was an emotional fortress, this shone a crack in his usual cool-as-a-cucumber demeanour. Maybe Sienna's appearance today had something to do with it. "I just hope you know I can take the truth." I removed the lid from my pen and added boxes on our planner where needed.

Avery matched my boxes on his side of the document. "Nobody can take the whole truth." His eyes followed the tracing of his hand; they'd retreated behind the guarded wall of his mind.

What dark secrets were buried under the strong shoulders, olive skin, and confident persona? Probably the same ones that were buried in the sister out there. A professional calling pulled at my heartstrings. *Treat them like you would treat any other damaged person coming to the centre. With care, authenticity, and hope.*

"Legacy is April Williams's baby. Not her actual baby." I chuckled and pointed to the little girl playing outside with the big kids. "Her *actual* baby is Liz, over there by Sienna, but you know what I mean."

Avery narrowed his eyes at the toddler being carried by his sister, both girls tickling each other. "I think so."

"I told you we all used to work together at the Hope Island Private? Well, after that, April opened this place, and we all followed at some point."

"In what way?"

I laughed. God, the memories. The poor guy thought he was the only one with a shady background. If only he knew. "April opened Legacy three years ago. A year later, I followed. Jarryd still works as a consultant at the Hope Island General, but he spends most of his time here." I waved back at the little girl from a distance. "Everyone has a story, and everyone really wants to make a difference."

"I never had good experiences in schools or in these types of places. The way I look at it, everyone wants to help, but when it comes down to crunch time, they bail."

Was he speaking for himself, or for Sienna? His hand felt cold to the touch. As if surprised by the contact, Avery's eyes widened, but he didn't flinch. Instead, something shifted in the way he looked at me. I sighed. "This is why this place and these projects are so important. They're for kids like Riley, Oliver, and Sienna."

"She just wants to fit in. Belong somewhere." His thumb stroked mine, something in him calling for reassurance from the depths of my soul. Then, as if he realised what he was doing, he cleared his throat, straightened his back, and my hand lost its grip on his.

"We all do. It's human nature," I said softly. "And given that she's already got these kids wrapped around her finger, I'd say she's in the right place." I slapped my palms on the table, snapping both of us from this weird twilight zone we were dangerously diving into, and called us back to work. "All right, enough wasting time, Chef. We have meals to plan."

In slow motion, Avery dragged his eyes from the kids outside and met mine. The wrinkles that had been there thirty seconds before vanished, and instead, something of a creative genius took over. Before I knew it, a list of basic ingredients, all fresh and Heart Foundation approved, appeared on our paper, and lines ran from one to another.

"We could start with listing herbs, then spices, and a mix of meats or protein supplements with vegetables until we form combinations." His hand kept moving like it was possessed. "It's a good way to make sure that our eight meals don't repeat themselves. Know what I mean?"

I nodded and grabbed a different colour marker to join him. "I love it. Different bases have to produce completely different meals, right?"

Avery winked at me, his freaking dimples blowing oxytocin straight to my ovaries. *Stop this immediately. Not happening. He is completely and utterly out of bounds.*

"I tell you what," he added. "We already have a combination of eleven herb bases. Why don't we pick one each and start with our first two dishes?"

Excitement buzzed through me. Despite the rough start between us, something was just coming together today. The brightness on his face, the lightness in his tone, and the knack he showed for mixing flavours and aromas. The whole damn thing was contagious. And I wanted more.

"Yes! Let's do it." Using a variety of colours, I linked rosemary, mustard, and chicken with broccoli and yellow beans on the paper. My fingers drummed on the small calculator in front of us, the overall caloric number perfectly acceptable. "Less than six hundred calories, and everyone loves mustard and chicken."

Across from me, Avery's palm waited. As soon as I slapped it, a 'yeah baby' came out of his mouth, and he grabbed his own marker for a turn. "God, this is perfect." He linked sage with pumpkin, and then added pork to ricotta and spinach. "Sage doesn't go with everything, but it goes great with pumpkin. We gotta have it." His eyes pleaded with mine.

"Hey, don't ask me." My finger moved between us. "We're partners now. Equal partners."

Avery whistled before he burst into a deep laugh.

"Grace, you gotta be careful here, 'cause too much of that, and I'll have to kiss you."

My skin prickled from the base of my neck, heat spreading from my lower belly to my cheeks. Though he meant nothing by it, the thought of being kissed by that mouth turned me on more than I cared to admit. The bottle of water in front of me had *rescue* written all over it. I chugged it down, the cold liquid giving my beating heart a stern talking to. "God, you have a way with women." I chuckled, avoiding eye contact. "That sounds really good." I keyed in the numbers, and when they passed our caloric goal, I lifted the screen and showed him. "Another winner."

Thirty minutes later, we had our eight mains. From a mix of cultures and dietary requirements, all were brilliantly designed with a touch of the *A* magic. Right as we were about to do the same with the entrees, the kitchen door busted open, and a shriek had us turning around.

"Inside voice, Lizzy," I said to the little girl. In tow, April ambled, her belly bigger than it was last week. "Geez, lady, are you sure there's only one in there?" I stood up and hugged my best friend.

April waved at Avery, teasing me back. "I hope you learn to ignore her too." She extended her palm. "I'm April."

Avery rose to his feet and shook both her *and* Lizzy's hand. "I'm Avery. Nutrify's new executive chef."

April settled on a chair, huffing and puffing with every move. She grabbed one of the bottles on the table and sipped on it. Then she made Lizzy take her own sip of the liquid. "God, one would think that all women would stop after the first kid. Why go for more? This is bloody exhausting." April sighed as she rubbed her belly.

"Cute kid." Avery pointed at the little girl. "Maybe that's why."

April's smile screamed *maternal love* more than I'd ever understand. "Yep. You're right."

Her hard bump vibrated against my hand. "Yep. But now that's three. Two boys and a girl. She's done." I blew her a kiss, and she poked her tongue back at me.

"All right, we just came in to say hello and get a drink." April crawled up from her chair and motioned to Lizzy. "Sienna is a cute kid too. Riley hasn't left her side. I think they'll get along."

"God, help us." I laughed, both because of the comment and the look of fear on Avery's face. When the girls had left, Avery stood by the porch with me, taking in the outdoor area of the centre. The five o'clock breeze had settled. "Who's Riley?" he asked. "Her kid too?"

"Sort of. Though, he came along before April and Jarryd got together."

In the distance, Riley and Sienna rocked on swings in what seemed like a deep conversation. Fond memories of this kid's progress flooded my mind. If he wanted to tell Sienna where he came from, that would be up to him, but until then, it wasn't my place to shed light on the details of how Riley became a Williams.

"Ah. I see. I thought she looked too young to be the bio-mum. But I have lots of respect for stepparents. Good on her for taking on the challenge."

"Yeah, he's a good kid." Avery rolled his eyes at my assessment, a fine line deepening between his eyebrows. I narrowed mine at the chef. "Don't go all papa bear on him. Sienna has found a good friend here."

Avery smiled, a cross between relief and complete terror. God, between him and April, if this was parenthood,

I didn't want a bar of it. "Thanks," he said. "I better get her home."

"I'm sorry Jarryd had a last-minute medical review." I pressed my palms together in a light apology. "But it's definitely happening tomorrow."

He nodded, his fingers lifting in a mock salute. "Looking forward to meeting Riley and his dad then."

I saluted back, with a growing hope that Avery was just what Nutrify had needed all along.

Chapter 10
Avery

One whole week of prancing around the paperwork and meal plans, and finally the fun part peaked. I tied the denim apron around my waist and placed the wooden chopping board over the damp tea towel on the counter. Next to me, juicy capsicums, fresh peas and corn, onions, and a mix of pork and beef mince awaited the slice of death from my newest blade. I sharpened it, the scraping sound soothing to my ears.

"Shorty, if you insist on coming to work with me, could you at least make yourself useful and put on some music?"

Sienna lifted her head from the laptop long enough to say, "Nope. Your music sucks."

"For fuck's sake, Sienna, put on some music." I emptied and sliced the capsicums, then started on the stuffing. The aromas kicked off. If they tasted as fresh as they smelled, I'd be a happy chef. "Or I'll stuff you with these." I tossed a piece of onion in her hair.

She squealed and giggled before throwing it back at me. "You promised you'd stop swearing, old man. Something else you suck at."

Hands deep in mince, I tilted my chin at the phone next to her. "You put on some music, and I swear I'll turn into a choir boy, just for you, my favourite sister in the world."

Her laughter resonated in the room, almost as loudly as the hand she slammed on my back as she walked to the other side of the counter.

"Ouch. That was uncalled for," I teased, but winked at her when a random playlist finally vibrated through the speakers.

Her body leaned over mine so she could take a better look at the creation unfolding in front of her. She took a big whiff of the fresh herbs. "Do you think this is how our home will smell in Italy?"

You bet, Shorty. You bet.

When the sound of tyres registered and a black Ute pulled up, she tossed the spices back on the counter and squealed again, then kissed me on the cheek and bolted. "Riley's here. I'll see you around, old man."

Before I had time to give her a big bro lecture, she'd met the kid and his baby sister by the side of the car. The three of them, as relaxed as one another, gravitated to the main building. Within seconds, I'd lost sight of the trio. Maybe it wasn't such a good idea for her to spend so much time here. Especially when my job was to fuck over her buddy's dad. Though, for all intents and purposes, no one would ever have to know what my part in this was.

Get the info. Feed it back to Hal. Sip cocktails on the terrace.

For all I knew, they were having a tiff over gold cufflinks or something. Nothing to lose sleep over. Not my fucking business.

I trailed Sienna through the window, the knot in my gut

twisting as I watched her punch the boy softly, right before he chased her around the swing set. *I should have never brought her here.*

Cooper was bad news, which meant Williams was bad news too, and she wouldn't be safe playing googly eyes with his son. *You threw her right back to where she came from.*

"Damn it." The blade sliced faster in front of my knuckles until the red onions were pureed. My fingers clawed against the knife as it carved into the wooden board.

Fix this. It was one thing for me to walk that tight rope, another one to think Sienna would make the distinction between reality and fantasy. The fake and the genuine. The safe and the destructive. My mind grew blurry with visions of Grace's nurturing bright-blue eyes and Sienna's progress in a week. All buried under the false pretense that this was a good place.

My heart pumped against my rib cage, thrumming between my ears like a rusty chainsaw on Friday the 13th. Anyone doing business with Hal Cooper, anyone stupid enough to steal from the man, deserved what was coming to them. The odds were this was either a test from the bastard, or I'd just thrown my sister to a pack of wolves far worse than those I was hoping to save her from. Because at least Cooper never pretended he cared.

Deep breath. Focus. You can still manage this.

The door swung open, and some pretty boy strolled in. Black hair, long shorts, a Gant polo shirt, and Adidas runners. Clearly, whoever he was, he didn't do much running. The white material shone as brightly as an ad for dental veneers.

"You must be Avery." He placed a prescription pad on the kitchen counter and extended his hand. "I'm sorry I missed you the other day." A quick glance at the name scrolled across the top told me everything I needed to know. *Dr Jarryd Williams – Consultant child psychiatrist.*

"Sorry, I imagine you'd prefer to stay clean." My hands shook in the air, chunks of mince and onions dribbling off my fingers.

"Probably." He laughed before pulling up a stool and settling on it. It had to be about fraud. The guy clearly had money. That, or he was dealing big for Hal. Maybe pills on the black market?

A spray of soapy water had my hands clean in seconds. I dried them on my apron, turned the other way, and leaned against the bench.

He spoke first, a wide smile on his face. "It's great to have you on board. Grace had amazing things to say about you."

"Did she? Nice to know."

He tilted his head towards the pile of recipes farther on the bench. "Looks like you got busy?"

"She has good ideas. She's ambitious."

Jarryd nodded. "For sure. She's gung-ho about this project. She'll die trying to promote it if that's the last thing she does."

"That bad?" As much as I wasn't ready for the answer, the question still floated in my head. *What part did Grace play in Jarryd Williams's shady dealings?*

His kids were cute. His wife seemed normal. Grace, definitely sincere. How much did the guy in front of me share with his precious family? I bet they didn't know he'd double-crossed one of the nastiest pieces of shit in history. Without the blood money from Cooper, maybe his white shoes would shine a little less.

"Yeah, that bad. She's a passionate woman, and she

cares about people. She really thinks that, with your help, she can impact this community a great deal." Legs crossed in front of him, Jarryd leaned against the back of his stool, his forehead smooth and the lines around his eyes flat. He didn't strike me as someone on edge.

Anyone dumb enough to get involved with Cooper and get away with it is bound to come across as confident. Doesn't mean much. Get your job done. "So, Grace tells me you're a doctor?"

He moved, a weird mix between a nod and a shake of his head. "Yeah, but everyone here plays a vital role. I'm just another part of a fine-tuned machine. I was a youth worker for some years before I fully finished medicine."

"Fair enough." *Get the fucking job done.* "I bet you've seen your share of dicey backgrounds. A lot of drugs?" It might have helped if I knew what I was looking for. Tension crawled up my legs. I shuffled on my feet before hoisting myself on the bench.

"These look nice. Can't wait to try the meals." Jarryd pointed at the half-stuffed capsicums.

"That's the idea." Had he ignored my question on purpose? I persisted. "Do kids get prescribed much these days?" I motioned towards the script pad. "Or do they still prefer *the good stuff?*"

Jarryd cocked an eyebrow. "I prescribe when I have to. Try not to, though."

What the hell am I looking for? As much as I despised the idea, I'd have to call Cooper and find out. Until then, this was a lost cause.

"Grace said the meal planning went great and the trial phase looks promising." Jarryd pushed to his feet, grabbed his pad from the counter, and made his way to the door. "Another reason for us to catch up properly."

As soon as he'd disappeared and the door had closed behind him, leaving me alone within a fifty-metre radius, I surrendered to my next move. Fighting the urge to punch a wall, I dialled the number and immediately regretted it. Hearing Cooper's grating tone was as exciting as a tooth extraction. "Avery, my man," said his voice on the other line. "I was getting worried you'd try to bolt."

"What is it I'm looking for?" I grunted.

"You don't need to know. *Yet*," Cooper warned, before he continued. "Have you met my friend?"

"Yes. I met the shrink and his family." The thought of the kids and the wife getting caught in the crossfire didn't sit well with me. "Your beef's with the shrink or the whole family?"

Cooper *tsked* on the line. "Now, now. Don't go all noble on me, Chef. If it helps, I want nothing to do with the woman and her brood."

Slight relief eased the tension building at the back of my shoulders. "I don't know what info you want. I met him, now what?"

"Great. Now, why don't you start by getting yourself acquainted with his schedule. When he's at The General, and when he's playing God in his centre."

I grumbled, "Fine. Anything else?"

Instead of an answer, the line went dead, the long beeps ringing in my ear until the dread of what I had to do next sucked out all the emotions left in me for the day. With my head cradled in the palm of my hands, I rehearsed what I was going to tell Sienna. My throat tightened at the thought that she'd probably pull the blinds from the world again, hating me every second of it for ruining her life.

My chest rose up and down, my brain growing dizzy from too much oxygen. I'd done this to her. I'd brought her right back into Cooper's line of fire. All I could do now was take her out. Whether she liked it or not, that was the only way. Because tomorrow, I'd start digging into where the Williams ate, slept, worked, and played. And I'd feed it right back to the devil himself.

Chapter 11
Grace

Avery and I glared at each other, the competitive vibe buzzing in the commercial kitchen. Riley chuckled at both our attempts to throw the other off as he checked our list of ingredients.

Avery rolled his eyes. "The woman thinks she has a chance."

"Bloody oath, I do. I'm not scared of a little challenge." I narrowed my gaze, my grin wide. *So not going down without a fight, Chef.*

A couple of metres away, Avery's dimples flashed. He winked at me. Clearly, he didn't plan on it either. In front of us, ingredients, pots and pans, as well as kitchen bits were ready, and all we were waiting on was for Riley to blow his whistle.

"Just so we're clear, here are the rules again." He paced between us, pointing to the items as he went on. "You have ninety minutes from start to finish. Now that you've chosen your ingredients, you can't change or add to them."

"Won't need to." Avery smirked. He spread his palms

over the counter and caressed the metal like he would a lover.

Riley cocked an eyebrow. "God, I don't want to know what else happens in this kitchen."

Heat spread over my cheeks. It wasn't like I hadn't entertained the fantasies before. The more time I spent with my chef, no matter how aloof he came across, the more every part of me was drawn to his peculiarities: how he carried himself and made me feel like everything was possible.

"Anyone caught trying to sabotage the other is instantly eliminated," Riley warned.

Avery chuckled and pointed at me. "Hey, it's her you should tell."

"It *was* her I was referring to," Riley teased.

When he lifted his palm for Avery to slap it, I crossed my arms and poked my tongue out at him. "I'll get back at you for this, young man." The room resonated with laughter.

"All right, so unless there's anything else, your time starts..." Riley placed the silver whistle in his mouth and blew it once. "Now." He waved at us as he hummed towards the exit. "So, kids, when I come back, I expect two awesome dessert options and a clean kitchen."

Once he'd left, Avery faced me, his signature grin pasted along his mouth. "As the awesome partner that you are, you don't object to my music playing in the background, do you?"

Lips curled, I turned towards my lot, grabbed a large metal bowl, and spooned a dollop of butter. "Assuming we'll be blessed with the usual '80s music you seem to like?" I said, my voice silvery.

"Nothing but the best." He fiddled with his phone until a tune played through a small speaker between us. "I will take requests today though," he rasped, "if you're a good girl."

Is he flirting with me? His pupils had darkened as he leaned on the counter, his legs crossed and his biceps tensed. The bastard probably was. I chuckled to myself, a fight raging between my head and my ovaries. "I know what you're doing, Chef. If you think you can distract me from winning our dessert trial competition, you have another thing coming."

He winked. "It's cute that you think you have a chance." His bowl banged as he poured fresh mascarpone into it and tossed vanilla beans in another.

Of course I didn't have a chance, but it was fun to pretend I did. "Since we can't change or add ingredients, your paranoia should be eased." I laughed as I pitched cut strawberries and a dash of sugar in a saucepan. "Tell me what you're making."

"Only after you tell me first." He chuckled as he added his beans to egg whites.

I threw a strawberry his way. He grabbed it mid-flight and lifted it in a mock toast before he shoved it into his mouth. "One less for your magic recipe, *babe.* Think about that before you throw the whole kitchen at me."

A snort escaped at his accurate assessment. He probably knew me well enough to tell the competition would drive me wild. "Don't worry about my magic recipe, *muffin.* I've got it under control." I tossed another strawberry at him. This time he caught it with his mouth.

"Juicy," he purred, his voice muffled by the chewing. "Fine. I'll start. I'm making original tiramisu." He pointed to the Italian savoiardy biscuits and the mascarpone. "These are imported from Europe... *directly*." Then, he bent over and rummaged through his bag until a glass flask made its way out. "Marsala." He unfastened the lid and took a swig. "It burns in all the right places." He studied me from head to toe as he pronounced the words one by one.

Warmth spread to my lower region, my arms fighting the urge to cross over my breasts. It wasn't just the alcohol *burning* at the moment. "Mister Curtis! Drinking on the job, are we?" I ran my tongue over my bottom lip and sashayed the couple of metres separating us.

He blinked, his lips slightly parted.

Once in front of him, my hand slowly crept up his chest until I reached the flask still clutched in his grip. My fingers laced over his, and I lowered our arms until the opening of the bottle kissed my lips. "What would happen to *your* magic recipe if I drank it all?" I murmured, in my sexiest voice.

His pupils darkened to a stormy brown, and he swallowed hard. "I'd say we'd have to make sure we split it evenly." He poured a swig through my lips, but before I could swallow, his mouth brushed mine, and he sucked the bulk of the liquid back.

God Almighty.

He stood tall, eyes closed, his tongue licking the wetness we'd shared on his glistening lips. A cyclone raged in my belly, and my panties dampened at the contact. I gripped the edge of the counter and worked on settling the beating my heart was taking.

For a second, neither of us spoke. Frozen in our dangerous game. His chest heaved up and down, and I waited until my legs no longer felt numb to step back. Like he was as surprised as I was, Avery cracked a smile, the flask now sitting on top of the shelf above him. "As much as I love my grog, let's leave that one till the end, I think."

The awkwardness broken, I nodded—a light giggle dancing in my throat—and settled myself in front of my recipe. *Yes, any more of this, and I'm no longer accountable for my actions, muffin.*

I cleared my throat. "Mine is a strawberry mousse, with strawberry glaze and a biscuit base." I beat the berries and the caster sugar until a soft gel formed. Then I added gelatine and blended it together. *That's it. Beat your hormones back into shape, you crazy woman.*

"Nice. It will be a great dessert. Worthy of second place." The tone in his voice left no room for doubt.

If I didn't want this to be a humiliating loss, I really had to focus. He'd already turned back to the counter. The scent of coffee travelled through the room as he poured it slowly. He paid attention to every single step in his recipe, like a mother watching over her newborn child. There was a touch here that went beyond his professionalism. To him, this was an art, and it showed in the way he knew how to perfectly blend each ingredient. He smiled, his bottom lip caught between his teeth, as he meticulously dunked each biscuit in the coffee mix.

Dimples. Bloody dimples. Stop staring at his dimples. My eyes rolled for my own benefit, and I smacked myself into gear. I had a cooking competition to win in the next hour. The blender screamed, a welcomed distraction from the thoughts racing in my head, and for a moment, all that mattered was the perfect ration of mousse versus glaze.

The timer startled me. My eyes lifted to the clock above us. "Crap. Can't believe it's time already." My strawberry mousse looked decent, but from the way it bobbed, it would need to set before anyone could dig into it.

Avery trailed my eyes and nodded. "Mine's pretty wobbly. Ideally, we should both let them set overnight." His tiramisu looked perfect. Shop-quality. It smelled like we'd taken a stroll in Milan or something. "What do you say we rest them until tomorrow, partner?" he asked, pointing towards the commercial fridge ahead.

"You got it. As long as you don't mind waiting to hear mine is out of this world," I joked.

He waggled his eyebrow as he opened the fridge door for our pans. My tray sat perfectly against his. A contrast of colour. Mine, bright pink. His, a sober combination of light brown and white. The strawberry mousse was cute. Something to be enjoyed with girlfriends alongside a serving of tea. But it was nothing compared to what he'd presented. In all honesty, I couldn't wait to try it.

He pulled me by the hand and led me to the small table by the porch. "There's something I wanna do."

I settled on the chair, my head tilting at the secretive mission. Within seconds, Avery was back with a couple of saucers. Two spoons clunked on the table between our left-over bowls.

"Close your eyes," Avery directed. In the darkness, I recognised the sound of a spoon scraping the sides of metal. "Now, open."

A cold mixture made its way past my lips. It was smooth. Delicate. Tasty. I allowed the flavours to settle on my tongue and rocked the cream and biscuit pieces in my mouth. "Hmmmm. God, Avery. It's amazing."

Using my spoon, he dolloped some for himself and pushed it into his. "Not bad. Not bad at all," he said. "You know what's next?"

I nodded and grabbed a new spoon from the table. The pink mélange sailed to his lips, and he opened his mouth until it all disappeared. Before he had time to finish tasting it, I dunked my finger in the bowl and dashed it to my own lips. "That's the way my grandma used to do it." I laughed while sucking on the digit.

The vein in his neck pulsed faster. "I bet it tastes better like that," he said, his voice growing huskier. His eyes followed my hand, and he stilled like he was waiting for my permission. When no words came out, he grabbed my finger covered in pink and brought it to his mouth, his eyes never leaving mine. Heat travelled through me. My face burned, and my toes curled. My finger entered his mouth, his tongue stroking the cream off it. Then his lips caressed the digit as he pulled it out. Softly. Carefully. I crossed my legs, a moan sounding in my throat before I realized it.

"Avery..." I whispered, my own voice a stranger to me.

In one stride, he was on the other side of the table. His hands cradled my face. Right as he lowered his mouth to mine, his lips brushing over my neck, the door creaked open and Riley barged in. Avery jerked back, his head shaking like he'd woken up from a daze. "Damn." He pointed to the Marsala on the counter. "No more of that from now on." In one swift move, Avery was standing by the kitchen bench, a fake focus in progress.

"Do I need to remind you that the cleaning is part of your job here, children?" Riley mocked, his eyes going from the sink full of dishes to the leftovers on our table.

Frozen in my seat, ambivalence coursing through me, I studied the boys and the mess ahead. As they laughed and

Avery began clearing it, one question remained. It slapped me in the face, over and over again. Like a confused teenager, hormones seemed to cloud my sense of reality.

Had I imagined the connection between my chef and me?

Chapter 12
Avery

The phone sunk into my quilt as it landed next to me on the bed. An arm over my eyes, I ignored the second beep coming from the device. Instead, I rolled over onto my side, the blanket covering my shoulders, and hoped to God that the barrage of questions from Hal Cooper would soon fucking stop. But who was I kidding? Either I replied or he would be turning up, in his usual signature dick move. With Sienna still home before school, I couldn't risk it. I grabbed the phone and unlocked the screen. Two new messages from Hal. Unread.

> HAL
>
> There's a small parcel on your front porch.
> It goes under the good doctor's car. Got it?
> Hal: I suggest you get out of bed. Young
> Sienna is all by her lonesome making
> breakfast. Since you're not answering, you
> won't mind if Alessandro gives the parcel
> to her, will you?

My heart jumped out of my chest, and before my feet registered the cold tiles beneath them, I'd barged in the kitchen to Sienna pouring eggs on a plate. "Cover yourself, dude!" My sister rolled her eyes and turned her back to me. "You realise you're half-naked, right?"

I marched past her towards the front door, my heart pounding harder than a train hitting a wall at full speed. "Sorry," I mumbled, before yanking the door open. I narrowed my eyes at the black car across the road, ignoring the hand waving in my direction. Cold sweat dripped off me at the sight of the small black box on the welcome mat. *It couldn't be a car bomb, right?*

My fingers dug into the cardboard as I swallowed hard. How far deep had I gone with this? I'd agreed to get some info on Jarryd Williams, so Cooper could settle whatever his issue was, but it sure as hell never included blowing up a car. I grabbed the box and went back into the house.

"What is it?" Sienna piped up in the background. Sounds of metal clunking on plates, drinks being poured, and a chair being dragged covered whatever she said next.

"What?" I asked, my hands shaking over the cardboard. I avoided her gaze. She'd be part of none of this.

"Breakfast. It's served. Put your toy away and come and eat. My bus will be here in five."

Though all I wanted to do was tear into the damn fucking box, I couldn't risk Sienna's questions if I opened it right then and there. Instead, I hid it behind a cushion on the couch. Out of sight, out of mind. For now.

As soon as Sienna's bus had turned the corner, my hands tore into the cardboard. A small grey device (no bigger than my palm) sat at the bottom of the box. Other than the device and a folded note, there was nothing else included. *That is no bomb.* As pissed and freaked out as I was, this was only a GPS. I flicked it over, my fingers tracing the hard casing. Then, I opened the note.

GPS, zip ties, shrink's car. Easy as pie.

Pie. Guilt flooded me with memories of Grace's furious stabbing of the apple pie, crust flying on the table, and her face as she realised it was my dessert she'd murdered. A couple of weeks had gone by since I started on this project, and her vision had grown on me. I actually *liked* her. More than I thought I would.

Like her? What project? What is wrong with you? As cold as a shower at four a.m., I quickly got my brain back into gear. There was no real project. There was a job to do, Hal's job, just to get Sienna off the hook. There was no partnership, no vision, and definitely no Grace.

My car barely fit in the bay next to Jarryd's. Door closed, I marched around the area, doing my best to avoid anyone who'd ask questions as to how that fucking GPS found a spot under the chassis of the shrink's Ute. The air of my front tyre hissed as it was let out. Carefully, I lowered myself to the ground between the two cars, making sure the spare tyre kit was in the way.

Thank God Jarryd drove a monster of a truck. My head fitted well under it, and there was plenty of space to tie the GPS. Hand extended, I reached for the front axle above my forehead.

"Flat tyre?" a voice called out.

Startled, I flinched, my head banging on the metal underbelly. I grabbed the first thing I found. "Yeah. Damn wrench rolled under the car."

The kid looked at me like I was the dumbest grown-ass

adult he'd ever seen. "I might get you some help here?" And just like that, he was gone.

Damn. My fist connected with the bonnet of my car, a red mark quickly spreading. I didn't need any fucking help. All I needed was five minutes of peace so I could get on with my job. This kid was about to make my life even harder. When footsteps grew louder, I put on my dimwit face, holding the jack in one hand and the wrench in the other.

Shoot me dead.

"Looks like you've got a flat tyre," a familiar voice said. As soon as he kneeled down, I recognised Jarryd Williams. Out of every man and his dog on this campus, that kid had to fetch my target. Of course.

My jaw clenched at the irony. A fake smile pasted on my face, I sat upright and continued with the charade. "Yeah, looks like it."

Jarryd extended his hand towards me. I grabbed it, his grip strong. Once on my feet, I pointed towards the deflated front tyre. "Probably just a nail." I chuckled. "I'll be fine. Don't let me stop you from important business." *Fuck off already, mate.*

Jarryd kneeled down, his lips pursed. "Might be." He ran his hand over the rubber, inspecting it for obvious holes. "Can't see anything outstanding, though."

The jack creaked with the weight of my car. Without waiting for me, Jarryd had the bolts removed in less time than it'd taken me to get up. Then, he turned the wheel back and forth until it came loose. "Do you know how to get the spare tyre?"

If it wasn't for the smooth forehead and the lack of a mouth curl, I would have thought he was pulling my leg.

That he was being a sarcastic ass. But based on his genuine tone, the dude was seriously trying to be helpful.

Don't try to make sense of anything, man. Even sharks sleep from time to time. "Yep. Sure. I'll get it." This wasn't going according to plan. But there was always room to adjust. "Nice ride," I said, tapping the roof of his Ute with my palm.

He nodded. "Yeah, it is." He pointed towards the dark-grey coating with his spare hand, the other one holding my flat tyre. "It's my first real car, so to speak." My ears pricked. That didn't quite fit the profile I had in mind. "I drove my mum's car for years while I studied," he continued. "God, the memories of that tiny Mazda." He shook his head, a light laugh adding to the weird new info. "But with a third child to drive around, we really needed a larger option."

"I can imagine." I passed him the spare tyre, then stepped to the other side of his car. My hand felt the hard case through the pocket of my cargo pants. Still there.

"Sounds like you have the perfect 2.5 kids, gorgeous wife, and picket fence. Lucky guy." My breath grew heavier. Why had he jeopardised all of *that* for Hal Cooper? I'd never been the envious type, but with a life like his, I'd have protected it with all I had.

Clanking noises grew louder, Jarryd's voice sounding farther away as he swapped the spare. "It wasn't easy. I'm not perfect."

An awkward silence filled the air. I leaned back against the cold sheet, happy I couldn't see his face. The pain etched in his tone was bad enough. My heart rate peaked as I lowered myself, hiding behind a ton of metal.

"There was a time a few years ago, when I thought I'd lose it all," his voice was but a whisper. "But it was worth it, and I'd do it all again to protect those I love."

My throat tightened. My gut ached. My fingers burned as I pulled the GPS out of my pocket. I hated how much I related to that last sentence. Because I'd do anything to protect the ones I loved too.

The GPS clicked as it lodged under the rim. The silent light, barely visible to the outsider, began flashing. I lowered my head on the concrete and closed my eyes, swallowing hard. "I get it, pal."

I just wish I didn't.

Chapter 13
Grace

Although it was only a rehearsal to test the meals, hosting this night for all the staff and their families from Youth Legacy and Nutrify was incredible. My eyes scanned the room. Eight round tables—decorated with cream tablecloths, small bunches of flowers, and crafty menu cards—really made the night a distinct shade of formal, especially against my midnight-blue cocktail dress and Avery's black tux. I took in the smiles, the warmth, and the food being served. When everyone's face relaxed within the first few mouthfuls, my shoulders dropped, relief spreading through me.

A special launch for our big family.

"Thanks, guys, for coming. We are super-duper excited to have you all be the first to try the meals Avery designed this mont—"

A hand on the small of my back interrupted me, followed by warm breath near my neck. "Don't give me all the credit. This was both of us," Avery murmured in my ear, before clearing his throat and addressing our little committee. "I don't need to tell you how humble this woman is—"

"Woohoo, that's my girl," April yelled out, her stomach bigger than the toddler swinging on her stepson's lap beside her.

"Oh god." The room got hotter, if that was at all possible.

As if Avery felt my embarrassment, he leaned into me, his mouth reaching my ear. "Relax, I'm right here, and they love you anyway."

I glanced at him, something intimate twinkling in his eyes. He'd warmed up to me in the last couple of weeks, and it was getting harder and harder to ignore his charms. I almost placed a hand on top of his, but stopped myself.

"Go, Miss," a bunch of teens screamed in the background. Jarryd turned and gave them a thumbs up. Then, as if they understood a secret signal, they stopped.

"So, as I was saying," Avery continued. "Miss Grace is being way too shy. Not only was this whole project her idea, but she also designed the meals with me." Whistling from all sides of the room infiltrated the dining area.

God, you're out of your depth, girl.

Avery cleared his throat for a second time. "Riley, did you want to tell everyone what's on the cards for dessert?"

The kid lowered his sister from his knee. She happily ambled to her father. In front of me, the picture-perfect family stared back. April, Jarryd, their kids, and the new bundle of joy in progress. I blinked, pushing the happy emotions away, and refocused on Riley. The young adult bowed at the crowd and sing-sang, "Aunty Grace here is the ultimate designer of the biggest and bestest dessert competition of Youth Legacy." He pointed towards the man by my side. "Killing our master chef's tiramisu." He winked at Avery.

Bold, kid. A grin grew on my lips, my facial muscles

aching from not being able to participate in the open teasing. A priceless opportunity for him to score a point against Avery on the down low. *Yep. Brilliant.* It seemed everyone at the centre played games, and my chef had been dragged into the fun too. Giggles escaped my throat. "Jesus, he went there, didn't he?"

Avery leaned into me, our bodies touching. "Oh, he sure did. I'll get back at him."

My head dropping towards him, I said, "You know there's no way I won against you, right?"

He kept his glare focused on the white fairy lights at the back of the room. "Winning is subjective, isn't it?"

Visions of my finger dipped in pink goo entering his mouth floated above us. I shuffled on my feet as I remembered the intimate gesture and our almost kiss.

God, shake that thought before you find yourself kissing him already. It was a matter of time. Resisting the pull grew harder with each day I spent around Avery. There was an appeal I'd never experienced before. My hand crawled closer to the menu he was holding, our pinkies now touching, and I whispered, "Having you as my honest partner is the real win here."

Avery flinched, like the words jabbed him in the wrong parts. He did a double take, glancing towards me long enough to see the colour drain from his face, but not long enough to read his mind.

"Thanks."

Thanks? That was a pretty anticlimactic response, if I ever heard one. Avery had made it clear that he couldn't stay permanently, but since things had gone so well between us and with Nutrify, I'd hoped he'd change his mind. I ignored the doom filling my chest. We still had a month to go. Plenty of time for the variables to shift, and realistically, I always got what I wanted in the end. Why would this time be any different?

I pasted the brightest smile on my face, grabbed the champagne flute he was holding, and brought it to my mouth. He cocked a brow as his eye locked on the liquid wetting my lips. The vein by his neck pulsed a little faster. One hand on his chest, I brought the glass to his mouth, and he opened, letting me pour the alcohol between his lips. In the background, the crowd grew silent. All I registered was my best friend shouting the words, "About bloody time."

Based on the feedback and the hundred hugs coming our way, it was clear everyone had loved the meals. In addition to the surveys left on the table, little notes, pictures, and various types of love hearts had been added to the vital information we'd gathered from tonight. I looked over the empty dining area, the deserted tables looking forlorn, like a child's lounge room the day after Christmas.

"How do you think it went?" I asked my chef.

He lifted his head, unusual dark circles showing under his eyes. "Good. Great, I'm sure."

Avery returned to sorting out the surveys based on which meal they'd been served, each of the eight tables having sampled one of our eight newly designed options. Lines creased his forehead. His lips were pinched. Now that he'd taken off his jacket and rolled up his sleeves, it wasn't hard to see his tensed muscles. This wasn't a man who'd had a successful business night. Something was bothering him. I just couldn't put my finger on it.

"Avery, is there something the matter?" I asked, my tone cautious.

His lack of eye contact added to my suspicions. "Nope."

"Everyone has left. We can talk fre—"

"There's nothing to talk about," he clipped.

I snatched the surveys from his hands. "Yeah? So why do you look like you've just buried your dog, instead of pulling off a pretty amazing professional gathering."

Slowly, his head turned towards me, a cold glare meeting mine. For a second, I froze, his kraken looking scarier than it ever had before. Maybe there truly was something to watch out for with this man. As much as I was attracted to him and as vital as he had been to Nutrify, I didn't know a lot about him. Silence filled the air, enough for my brain to check in with my gut.

"Avery, if it's about Sienna, I'm here to listen." I moved so I faced him. "She hasn't been at the centre for almost ten days and—"

He jumped to his feet, the chair dragging behind him. "For fuck's sake, Sienna's fine. She's busy and..." He ran a hand over his head. "Busy. She's just busy."

Jesus. Someone needs a good sleep. Was he hiding more of Sienna's tantrums? Something seemed a little extreme in his reaction. Riley, too, had been mega disappointed that she hadn't shown up tonight. Hopefully she wasn't up to anything sinister, because based on how cosy those kids had become, I'd expected her to be here. Nothing quite added up. When he started pacing like a mad lion, I followed his steps, matching his gait. "Will you just stop? I just want to talk."

He grumbled, passing me. "You always want to talk. That's your problem."

His body stopped when I plonked myself in front of him. Hands on my hips, I narrowed my eyes at the guy. "Enough."

His shoulders moved up and down with each breath. "You just need to back off a bit," he barked.

I shook my head. "Yeah, nah. With all due respect, you're carrying on like a pork chop."

The table shook with the weight of his palm slamming the glass. "You just need to mind your own business. I'm fine. Everything's fine. The night was great. Let's call it a day."

"I said no," I yelled, my hand hitting his chest. "You're not the only one who can act all mean and scary." My attitude died down, unlike the shame filling me. *Maybe he's just not into you.* Rejection stung like a thousand wasps. "Avery, I'm sorry if I misread the cues." I ignored the emotions a grown woman shouldn't feel for a complete stranger and moved out of his way. "I didn't mean to make you angry."

The frown on his face melted, and in its place, lifeless eyes stared out in the distance. His voice low, almost like he talked to himself, he whispered, "I didn't think it would be this hard."

I inched closer, hesitantly, my heart rate pounding in my chest. "What would, Avery?"

When he didn't answer, I stepped forward and placed a hand over his chest. His heart beat as fast as mine. Spell broken, he looked up, pain haunting his features. "Sometimes I wish I could just do what I wanted without anyone getting hurt."

"What is it you'd like to do right now?" My fingers stroked his shoulder in slow motion. Whatever it was, if I could help him, I wanted to try. Our eyes met. The tension in the room shifted. He took a step forward, his breath teasing me. He grabbed a hold of my wrist, pressing it firmer onto his chest. His grip was strong. Powerful. My other hand traced his shoulder, a tingle rocking me from the tips of my fingers to my belly.

He let go of my wrist, cupping my chin. "Grace." He'd lost the anger in his tone. Instead, there was a need I recognised. The same need cycloned in the pit of my stomach. "I don't want to be the bad guy." He spoke every word slowly, each syllable caressing my cheek. The crook of my neck opened for him, and as if on cue, he lowered his mouth to it, nibbling at the flesh.

"You're not." My right hand pressed down on his head. His muscles tensed under my fingers. I kneaded the flesh, both our breathing accelerating.

"Grace," he said again, this time more forceful, his mouth migrating to the corner of my lips. "Do you want this?"

I gasped and pressed my lips against his. He opened for me, our tongues touching so slightly. A moan sounded in the back of my throat, and just like a sudden permission, Avery's touch became more urgent. More intense. Like he needed it for his salvation. He moved closer, our chests touching. I wrapped my arms around his neck, and in one swift move, he lifted me on top of the table. My dress bunched up as I leaned back against the glass top. Palms on my knees, he parted my legs and nestled between them. Then, he locked one hand on the table by my head and allowed the other to explore my thigh.

A thousand electrical currents zapped every part of my being, my core now on fire. Through my knickers, wetness spread as his hand travelled to the seam of the lacey underwear. He stopped to feel the barrier, slowly running his thumb up and down the material. I gasped, my legs lifting around his waist.

"Don't stop," I begged, my pelvis pushing against his.

The throbbing pinned me in place. He pressed himself into me, then leaned forward for a kiss, letting his fingertip find my wet lips. He glided it slowly until the moisture spread, nibbling at my neck while pushing his finger inside me. I shivered, a guttural moan growing louder in the empty room. The need for him had taken over my senses. It didn't matter what he had to say. I just wanted more of him.

"Let's not talk anymore, okay?" A slight frown crowded his features as he asked the question, but as soon as my hand worked at the buttons of his shirt, the creases disappeared. The buttons now unfastened, Avery let me go and lowered his shirt from his broad shoulders. I pushed on my elbows, the detailed artwork on his chest turning the man from eye candy into a god. He smirked, a twinkle in his eyes and the bulge in his pants swelling.

In one move, he lifted my thighs to his shoulders, and with hurried fingers, took my underwear off and tossed them on the table. The front of his pants thickened, and I opened my legs wider, begging for more. He stiffened when I whimpered, then relaxed, a slight chuckle vibrating against my neck as his hands slid under my dress to explore my breasts. My nipples hardened at his touch.

He drew a breath, his pants dropping to his knees. Then he pulled my ass closer to the edge of the table and pressed the tip of his dick against my entrance. "Tell me you still want this," he breathed out, his voice shaking with each word.

"I thought we weren't talking anymore," I said, half-joking, half-desperate. If he made me wait any longer, I'd lose my mind.

"We aren't." He rested his head on my shoulder and pushed himself in. The relief was instant, and I moaned loudly, my fingers digging into his shoulders. His lips skimmed my collarbone and with every thrust, he exhaled louder and faster. I shook at the ongoing pleasure, fighting my own explosion as he kept thrusting, each time deeper. More intense.

As if he sensed it, he murmured between breaths, "Don't fight it, Grace."

I pressed my lips against his mouth, gently sucking on it while my hands held on to his face, like a reminder it was really happening. I'd never experienced this level of intensity. It was both exhilarating and frightening. "You're gonna make me come." I dug into his shoulders.

"I would hope so, baby." He chuckled, right before his thrusts increased in speed and force. Resistance was futile. I stared into his brown eyes one last time, then closed them hard. "Do it. Do it now." His forehead rested on mine, his fingers pressing harder against the top of my thigh. The pinch built my orgasm even higher, and almost instantly, pleasure overwhelmed me. A current travelled through my core, and I allowed myself the release I'd been lacking for weeks. Like my explosion triggered his, Avery's breaths grew shallow and his grunts more pressing. He came, both of us consumed by the passion and exhausted from the high.

As we caught our breaths, my fingers caressed along Avery's spine. I didn't know what I was expecting, but this strong man nestled in my arms wasn't quite it. I held him for what seemed like ages. When his heart rate had slowed, he kissed my forehead and gently lowered my legs before tucking a lock of hair behind my ear. Then, he grabbed my fingers and pulled me up.

"Are you okay?" he asked, as he handed me back my underwear.

"I sure am." I winked. "Are you?"

The cloud over my chef's face was back. There was a

darkness that made me want to hold him a little longer, but instead, he shook his head and pulled himself away from me. Then he motioned for my hand, turned the lights off, and led me to the car park in complete silence.

Just as I was about to say something, he brought his index finger to his lips, his brown eyes nearly black. "Sometimes, not saying things out loud stops them from becoming real."

And sometimes, it just eats at you until there's nothing left.

He kissed me again, closed my car door, and walked away into the night.

Chapter 14
Avery

The massive white columns by the door did nothing to alleviate my discomfort over being here. Neither did the security gate, the bouncer, or the three cameras that zoomed in every time I shifted. Being Cooper's bitch didn't get easier with time.

A Latina woman in a maid's uniform opened the door and motioned me forward. I strolled past her, taking in the gold-framed art and the crystal chandeliers hanging from the twelve-foot ceilings. I passed a wide glass table, a leather corner lounge, and a library that covered two whole walls before being offered a chair in front of a mahogany desk. For a thug, Cooper had taste.

Within minutes, Hal ambled in, his dress shirt opened lower than my eyes and my stomach would have liked. Black hair stuck out, sweat glistening on his neck. *God, I hate this guy.*

"What a lovely surprise, Avery." He took a seat behind the desk. Hands spread on his fat stomach, he leaned back as far as the chair would allow.

"You summoned me, Hal. Not quite a surprise," I

hissed. I didn't want to be here any more than I had any of the other times. Tension built across my shoulders.

"Semantics." He brushed the space between us with his hand. "I knew you were keen to share the update on your work for me."

Keen, my ass.

"Tell me about your cooking fun, first." An exaggerated smile stretched his lips. "After all, I did give you a great opportunity, did I not?"

I sighed, trying hard to keep Grace out of my thoughts and not sneer at what he called a fucking *opportunity*. Arguing with a gang leader was a waste of time. For him, for me, and for the dude who'd be forced to bury me in a shallow grave in his backyard. "Yep. Great opportunity."

"Have you been paid your fifty yet?"

I jerked my head up. I'd forgotten there was genuine money at stake. I'd been so focused on planning my way out of this mess. "I assumed I'd get paid at the end."

Cooper pursed his lips. "You should learn to read *your* tenders." He emphasised *your,* like I was a moron drowning in my own spit. "Fifty grand when the meal plans are finalised. Another fifty after the big party."

"Right. I knew that." That would mean the money was scheduled to hit my account this week, if it wasn't already there now. Images of airfares, airports, and Italian gelatos flashed in my mind. If I played my cards right, this charade would be over soon.

Cooper glared at me. "How's Dr Williams these days?"

"Fine. Seems healthy to me." I couldn't say that the shrink and I got into anything. Good or bad. The few times we'd run into each other, he seemed pretty all right. But underneath the pretty boy facade, there clearly was more to Williams.

It was his wife and kids I felt sorry for. Riley had grown on me, and on Sienna, and the little one was cute enough. But the thought of the shrink being such a fraud made me want to out him to the hundreds of youths and the staff believing in 'the Williams' charisma with all their hearts. Staff like Grace. My jaw tightened.

"Glad to hear. Jarryd and I go way back." He smirked. "How's his family? Wife still pregnant?"

I nodded. "Pretty fat now, so I'd say due soon." My fingers drummed on the table. I didn't like where this was going.

"Cute. Boy or girl, this time?"

"How the fuck am I supposed to know, Hal? Do I look like a fucking midwife?"

Cooper's whole body moved up to the edge of his desk. His hands left his stomach until his palms had crawled halfway between us. He leaned forward, his tone like ice. "Do you want to try that again?" His right hook punched me in the gut, knocking the wind out of me. My chest burnt with every attempt at taking a breath. Yet, I could do nothing but bite my tongue. Like a boxer taking a beating with his hands tied behind his back.

"I don't know. I haven't asked," I wheezed out, my hand running over my face. "They have one of each already, so I don't think they care."

Hal perked up. "One of each?"

I sighed. "Yep. A toddler girl and the older boy. He's not hers from what I can gather."

He hummed, his eyes darkening. "Right. Did you work out his whereabouts?"

I tossed copies of Williams's diary on the table. "He works at The General three days a week. And at the centre... two. But that's what the GPS is for, right?"

He skimmed through the copies, tossing them away like they clearly weren't good enough. "No, actually. It's to track the boy."

My breath hitched. Riley was never part of the plan. Why the hell did he want to know about the kid. "You said you wouldn't touch the family," I growled.

Hal threaded his fingers behind his head as he rocked his chair. "And I gave you my word. Now spill."

Stop stalling, Curtis. It's not like there's an alternate ending hidden somewhere. "Looks like there're plans for the kid to take on some more responsibility when he graduates as a youth mentor after this whole project is over," I added. "Or close enough."

"Close enough?" The loud pitch echoed through the whole room, the chandelier vibrating as he slammed his hands on the desk. Black Tulip marched in and settled against the door. He grinned at me, his palm gripping the handgun resting on his waistband. Something about Williams, his son, or the diary had triggered Cooper. As much as I wanted to ask, I shut my mouth and didn't. Hal and his enforcer locked eyes, then Cooper called him up through gritted teeth. "Our friend, here, might need a reminder on how to do his job properly."

In an instant, Black Tulip's waist was by my head. Before I could jump to my feet, he'd elbowed me in the mouth. It stung like a bitch. The taste of metal drowned my gums, and his shoes turned crimson as I spat blood on Cooper's pristine tiles. "Fighting back will only make it more fun for me." Black Tulip smirked.

Even without my current circumstances in mind (no gun in my hand, pain dulling my senses, and locked in Cooper's fortress), there was only one way out. I'd take the pounding and thank them for it at the end, or Sienna would be next.

"Get on with it, then," I snapped at the goon, the adrenaline pumping in my veins. The only thing worse than getting beaten up was getting beaten up without being able to fight back. I braced for the next blow.

Black Tulip threw another punch. Right before his fist connected with my jaw, I dodged it. His lips formed a flat line before he mumbled, "Get that fucking grin off your face." When I didn't, he raised his Glock from its holster and brought it down on the back of my skull as hard as his six-foot-four frame could muster. Blackness overtook me, the world spinning as my head crunched on the desk in front of me.

Just breathe. Stop being a warrior. Stay alive.

"I think Avery has his bearings now." Cooper's voice floated in the background, every word sounding like I'd downed a couple of whiskey bottles. Footsteps clunked away, and when I managed to straighten up, that prick was no longer in sight. Cooper hurled a dirty rag at me. "Clean yourself up."

Hands shaking and nausea pounding me like a drunk sailor, I pressed the cloth to my head. I could only open one eye and my top lip was busted. From the amount of blood seeping, I'd need a good clean up before Sienna got home, though I sported a headache that probably should get looked at. But it wouldn't. The last thing I wanted was to attract attention.

"So, here's what's going to happen," Cooper said, like I didn't just get the shit whipped out of me in his house. "You're going to work a little bit harder. I want everything, from his calendar to his phone data. Hell, I even want to know what bedtime stories the wife reads to those kids."

My head throbbed even more. If that was possible. April and the kids flashed in my mind. Sienna. Riley... *Grace*. "Hal, you said the kids were never goin—"

Cooper stood so fast the back of his chair thumped against the wall behind him. He towered over me, his words spoken carefully. "You know what else I said? Huh?" My eyes squeezed shut, the pain piercing through my lip. Like it would stop me from hearing the rest. "That I wouldn't touch Sienna. But unless I have what I want in the next forty-eight hours, I'll change my mind." He marched from the room, but right before he disappeared, he shouted, "And get the fuck out of my house."

Despair clawed through my gut almost as much as pain sliced through my every nerve ending. Sitting on that chair, unable to move, blood inking my body, the decision came to me easily. I liked Grace. I really cared about her. And I cared about Riley and the rest of the kids too. But I had forty-eight hours to get Cooper everything he asked for, and the same amount of time to organise getting Sienna out of the country.

Chapter 15
Grace

The last of the launch plan was done. Finally. From the menu to the seating arrangement, Avery and I had sorted all the fine details for the big day. Since our hot 'after party' last week, he'd been a little more guarded. We'd been strictly business from then. Considering how time-pressed we were, I was okay with that.

Only ten days to go and Nutrify would be recognised state-wide. The pile of paperwork now filed in the locked cabinet, I crumpled on the high-back chair of Jarryd's office, my shoulders dropping like a body chained to a thousand bricks.

If I died now, I'd die a happy woman. Almost one hundred patrons would be attending the fundraiser. We'd listed Legacy as the charity (proceeds would serve to get resilience programs into the schools in the state), and if all went well, the meal plans would also receive approval for commercial manufacturing. All in all, I was pretty chuffed.

"How many times have I offered to get you your own office?" Jarryd teased as he pushed past the door and beelined to his desk. "I feel like I'm losing it." He rummaged through his belongings, rifling amidst pieces of papers, and opening and closing the drawers. When he couldn't find whatever the hell he was looking for, he settled on a chair across from me. Between the shirt untucked and the flushed cheeks, he looked beat.

"What have you lost?"

He rolled his eyes, his head shaking just slightly. "I swear, you'll have me on an Involuntary Treatment Authority at this rate."

I reached for the jug and cups between us. The glass condensed as soon as the cold water hit it. I pushed the liquid towards him. "If you're worried about anyone putting you on a TA, it must be pretty bad."

"It started a couple of weeks ago. I'd left my diary in here, but when I came back to get it, it was gone. I told April about it, and when she looked for it, she couldn't find it either." His tone raised by a few decibels as he pointed to the middle of the desk.

"It happens to me all the time, Jarryd. It's nothing."

"Yep. That's what I thought, initially. Then, the next day, it was the filing cabinet I found opened, and the day after, Lizzy's day care bag had been moved."

"You do realise you sound like the patients, right?"

"Laugh all you want," he warned with a smirk. "I'm serious. Something's going on."

Despite my best attempts at compassion, hysterics rambled inside me. "You're growing all paranoid because a two-year-old's bag moved?" My grin grew bigger, and when Jarryd himself cracked a smile, I gave into the cackling. It had to be a joke. "Maybe it was Casper the friendly ghost. Maybe he didn't like the bag in the middle of the way, and did you a favour and moved it to the side."

"Oh, shut up, will ya?" He snorted. "I'll give you Casper in a minute."

"Risperidone, two milligrams for the good doctor." I winked at him.

He raised his palms, his head shaking in defeat. "God, I can see why my wife keeps you around as her best friend. She spilt the same lame joke." The glimmer in his eyes and the slight lip curl told me he still enjoyed my company. Lame jokes included.

Once we'd both got it out of our systems, I found some sympathy in the pit of my stomach. Though no part of me took a toddler's bag moving seriously, Jarryd seemed concerned. "Have you asked the staff? Maybe it was the cleaner, or the admin?" The reality is everyone came and went out of Jarryd's office. Me being in here today was just further proof. "I mean, realistically, it could be anyone." I pointed to the door. "Do you think it's time to put locks on things?"

Jarryd tilted his head, his chin pointing at me. "And tell people to get their own offices?"

I poked my tongue out before adding, "Most people."

He shuffled to the window, his elbows leaning on the sill. "Maybe. We never wanted the centre to get to that. You know, like we have things to hide."

"I know." I sighed. In a bid to lift the mood, I continued. "I guess with great power, comes great respons—"

"Jesus." Jarryd raised his eyebrows. He laughed as he picked up his keys from the desk. "That would be my cue. I'll talk to you tomorrow."

I waved him off. "I'll make sure to scare Casper away." *Poor guy. He must be overworked.* I made a mental note to check in with April. Between the pregnancy, the kids, the centre, and Jarryd's work, a good friend ought to have offered more support. A pang of guilt twisted in my gut. I reached out for my phone and dialled my best friend's number. As her voice crooned to leave her a message, my eyes scanned the room for anything worth stealing. A kid's bag and a doctor's diary didn't quite make the cut. From the chair I sat in, my hands laced over my lap, none of it made sense.

Maybe it's time to get my own office. Pink lace curtains and soft pastel paintings. After the launch, all going well.

My ringtone jerked me out of my reverie. She didn't take long to call back. My apology flooded the receiver. "I'm so sorry I've been a terrible friend, sweetie."

"Hello?" A small voice answered. *This isn't April.* My eyes narrowed at the private listing showing on the screen.

"Hi, who is this?"

Some sniffles resonated on the other line. Whoever it was, she wasn't happy. "It's Sienna. Sienna Curtis."

"Hey," was the only word that escaped my mouth. *Why is she ringing me at this time?* Sienna had been MIA for the last two weeks, and according to Avery, she was too busy with school and friends. As far as I knew, even Riley hadn't heard from her.

"Sorry, this was a mistake," Sienna's broken voice hiccupped.

She was definitely upset. I sat up straight. "Sienna, no. Not at all, darling. What's wrong?"

There was a pause on the other end, and right as I thought she had hung up, she said, "Avery and I had a fight. I ran away..."

An invisible hand squeezed my heart. I caught my breath while something in my brain pressed the panic button. It screamed red and loud. The type that warned to stay out of it, but as she started sobbing again, I asked, "Where are you right now?"

In the background, I could hear a train line and some traffic. Maybe a highway? A couple of voices grew louder and left again. "At a petrol station in Eagleby."

Eagleby? Out of all the places on Earth, she had to land in Logan, and one of the worst towns in Logan at that. The clock on the wall showed shy of six. It would be dark in thirty minutes.

Ring her brother and let him sort this out. "Are you safe?"

Her voice shook. "I think so. Some guys drove me, but now they've dumped me here and left to go to some party."

"I'm going to ring Avery, okay?"

"No, you can't. He's really mad at me, and he'll be even madder that I rang you."

With one hand on the phone and the other feeling for my keys in my purse, I dashed to the car and loaded the GPS on the console. "Sweetie, I want you to text me the exact address, and I'll be there in about..." I waited for the GPS to vaguely calculate my directions. "In about twenty minutes. Go inside the petrol station and wait there. Do you understand me?"

Why would he be pissed that she rang me? By the time Sienna texted me the street number, I was only ten minutes away. If Avery was still waiting for her at home, we had at least a thirty-minute head start before he got to us.

Within minutes, the station appeared and the car was parked in a lit area. Through the window, Sienna's shadow emerged, leaning against the Slurpee machine—above her head, a flashing sign that did nothing for the colour of her skin. The kid's eyes were red and swollen, and her normally pink complexion had turned grey. When she saw me, she yanked her fingernail out of her mouth and ran out, almost toppling both of us in the process. "Thank you so much for coming," she cried.

I pushed a lock of her messed-up hair behind her ear, my eyes searching hers. "Of course, I came. That's what friends do." I motioned towards the car. "Let's talk inside, hey?"

She nodded, and as I opened the passenger door, I added, "Don't be mad, but I told your brother where we were. We have thirty minutes before he turns up. That's *if* he doesn't speed like a maniac."

Sienna slumped down on the seat. "So, basically, we have twenty."

I kept the grin off my face. She sure bounced back quickly.

Once we'd settled and she'd calmed down, three things came out of her monologue. First, Avery was more protective of his sister than a mama bear. Second, she'd got caught sneaking out at night and copped a consequence she didn't like. And third, she hadn't gone MIA. She just wasn't allowed back at the centre.

Wow. Let's not take it personally. Why would she not be allowed? She had to have misunderstood. With my lips pursed and gaze lost in the darkness outside, I cradled Sienna's head against my chest until the smell of tyres burning overwhelmed my senses. In my rear-view mirror, Avery's grey sedan dived into a bay a couple of spaces away. His door slammed, and he was at my side in record time, checking his sister from head to toe through the window.

I took a double take at the black eyes and busted lip, before moving a finger to my mouth and settling Sienna on the headrest. She stirred but then snuggled against her jacket, her soft snoring in the background. I got out of the car and met Avery on the other side of the door.

"Is she okay?" The artery in his neck pumped hard.

"Yes, she seems fine. What happened to your face?" I tilted my head, my eyes studying the mix of blue and purple bruising. He looked like he had jumped into a pretty bad boxing match.

A long breath left him, like a deflated balloon, and he finally stopped staring at her. "Don't worry about it." He turned and leaned on the door, his eyes closed and his hands behind his neck. "She'll be the death of me."

The metal felt cool against my back. In the sky above us, a thousand stars mocked our shared ignorance as parents. "I think you're doing a fine job."

He scoffed. "Clearly."

"It's not easy." My body pivoted until we faced each other. "Especially if you insist on doing it alone."

His head lifted until our eyes met. "I take it she told you?"

"Yep. I don't get it."

His chest rose a couple of times in tune with his Adam's apple. There was a sadness seeping through his pores, and when he covered his face with his palms, I moved in front of him and grabbed his wrists.

"Hey, I don't know why, and I don't need to know why," I pleaded. When his hands lowered from his face, I moved mine until my fingers held his. He grabbed them, like a swimmer hanging on to life moments before their first gulp of sea water. I continued. "Right now, she's safe. You're safe. Just don't shut a friend out."

"I don't want to hurt you." His voice broke. His pain screamed in the way he forced his eyes shut, in the way his breaths grew shallow, and in the way he let his forehead dip to mine. Emotions filled my throat, like a beach front on a stormy night. I cleared it, and when no words came out, I raised one of my hands to the back of his neck and kneaded it softly. A gentle nudge pulled my chin, his breath blowing on my mouth. A mix of mint and cinnamon. "You should stay away from me."

The lines around his eyes wrinkled, and the frown on his forehead deepened almost instantly. I blinked at the man in front of me. This wasn't the cocky chef I'd worked with for the last couple of weeks. This was a shell of something else. A man trying to survive. Survive what? I didn't know.

I snaked my arms around his waist, and he wrapped his tight around me, his head tucked in the crook of my neck. "I wish we could be more..."

The vibration of his voice against my skin sent goosebumps through my core. "We could—"

He moved his hands to my hips and pushed me back a little. His stare studied me, and our eyes met, his glistening. "No, we can't. Not if I want to protect you both."

I sucked in my breath, the pain of his words stinging deep. My pain. His pain. Sienna's pain. "From what?" Tears welled in my eyes.

"Fuck," he groaned. His hands cupped my cheeks, the softness in his move surprising me. Our lips touched. Slowly first, then with more pressure. Avery's thumb stroked my face as my mouth opened to him. Our tongues danced, our bodies and minds synching like long-time lovers. His hand lowered and pressed against the top of my thigh. A quiet moan escaped my throat, a buzzing coursing through me and my mind growing blank.

Memories of how he'd made love to me just a week ago hit me like a freight train. How he'd held me for what seemed like forever. How, for a minute, he allowed himself to feel. Right as I fisted Avery's shirt, the slamming of a door jolted me.

"Wow. Priceless," Sienna yelled from the other side of the car. She crossed her arms.

Avery jerked his head towards his sister, his hand still holding on to mine. "Get in my car, Sienna."

She narrowed her eyes. "So, she's not good enough for me, but she's good enough for you?"

He slapped the roof of the vehicle, letting me go. "Sienna, get in the fucking car!"

My whole body shook, my nails digging into my palms. The taste of his tongue faded out of my memory as my brain tried to make sense of their silent conversation. What she said hurt, but not as much as what he wasn't saying. *Not good enough...*

She stormed off to his car, the door vibrating when she slammed it with full force. He faced me, his eyes empty. "I'm sorry," he said, then pressed his lips on my forehead. The kiss was soft. Slow. Like an apology I couldn't quite make out.

"It's okay," I meant to say. But before I could finish my sentence, his car had disappeared into the darkness.

Chapter 16
Avery

My doorbell rang, stirring the neighbour's dog. I never liked it, but right now I needed the extra five minutes of diversion. The Pug barked, but not enough to send Cooper's fuckwits running for too long. A fist thumped the front door a couple of times while my name got yelled across town.

Hurry up. I flung our new passports, credit cards, and cash back into the small box—our boarding passes and hotel reservations in their plastic sleeves—and slid the whole lot under the bed, right next to the USB stick filled with all I'd dug out on Cooper and Williams.

The banging grew louder. The last thing I wanted was one of them breaking down my door four hours prior to our flights. One palm on the handle, I glanced at the time before yanking the door open. Ninety minutes until Sienna got home.

"Can't you knock like a normal person?" I snapped towards Fish, one of Cooper's recruits of the last few months.

"Always a pleasure, Curtis." He shouldered me past the threshold. Cooper hadn't mucked around when he picked that deadbeat. He was massive. With a good head taller than me and an easy forty kilos, the stickler could probably break my neck with one hand. "Do you have what Hal asked for?" He paused in front of the large print hanging in the hallway. "Tuscany, right?"

The picture of Chianti's olive groves could have been anything. For most people, it was just some sunny landscape and a bit of olive oil. I cocked an eyebrow. "Might be?"

With a quick tilt of the chin, he pointed to my chef jacket hanging off a chair in the kitchen. "My bro migrated to Florence. He owns a café. Nice gelatos too."

Fuck me dead. Like the planet wasn't big enough to have none of these dimwits living on my new continent.

The carton (filled with Jarryd Williams's schedules, phone data, and even family photos) went from the table to Fish's arms. Why Cooper had needed a passport-size photo of Riley was beyond me.

"That's everything. Tell Hal there wasn't anything of value. They lock nothing. It wasn't hard to go through the joint." I tossed some gold cufflinks in the box. "That's probably about it. If Williams poached big, he's not keeping it at the centre."

"I'll pass it on."

My fists tensed, a current in my body zapping me like a dog being pulled back on its chain. "Tell him I'm done. I've kept my word. Now we're settled."

Fish grinned. "You're done when Hal says you're done."

I'm done in four hours, you fuckwit. Gone and forgotten. My throat dried up as I marched towards the front door.

"Whatever. He's chasing rainbows at that centre. There's nothing there. It's legit."

"As legit as what he took from the boss," Fish said. A grin lit his face. "And we both know that ain't going down. He'll get it back."

A fight was brewing in me. On one hand, what I had seen from Williams and his family, the way Sienna had gelled with the son, and Grace's dedication to their work, none of it struck me as gang mentality. On the other, Hal Cooper would never give up. He'd hunt them down until he got his drugs, his money, or whatever the fuck Williams had lifted from him, and I wanted my sister as far away from it as possible before the shit really hit the fan.

"No longer my problem." I opened the front door and motioned out. "Good day to you."

Fish's lips curled up, and right as he was about to drive into me as he walked out, I moved sideways, avoiding the blow. The door closed. I checked the time again. Sixty-five minutes left to pack for both of us.

The key turned in the door, then it slammed. "I'm home!" Sienna yelled in the hallway. Then a thump, I assumed her school bag hitting the wooden floors, followed by water running in the kitchen.

"In your room," I yelled back.

Her footsteps grew louder. "Get out of my roo—". Her face appeared in the doorway, and she froze. Her eyes trailed the suitcase opened on her bed and the empty drawers by her bedside table. "What are you doing?" The words didn't quite hide the panic in her tone.

The mattress sunk with my weight. I patted the space next to me. "Sit with me."

Her lip wobbled, tears welling in her eyes. "I'm sorry. Avery, please." She took a step towards the bed. "I'll be better. I want to stay here with you."

A storm shoved me in the gut. First Grace, then Sienna. Even when I tried to do right by everybody, they ended up getting hurt. I really sucked at this. "You *are* staying with me." I pulled her hand until she reached me.

Legs crossed on the mattress, she played with the foot sticking out from underneath her thigh. "I don't understand. If this is about yesterday, I won't call Grace anymore, I swear."

I glanced towards the clock. Our flights were in less than three hours. If I wanted to skip the country without Hal Cooper making me pay for it, we had to have this heart-to-heart another time. "Shorty, you've done nothing wrong. Remember our big plan? Rome?" I tapped her temple. "It's time. We're leaving for good."

Her head tilted, her eyes widened, and her mouth opened. Her brain was ticking. "Now?"

"Yes."

"Right now?"

I nodded.

She shook her head. "What about your big gig? Isn't it like next week?"

My jaw clenched. Memories of Grace's laugh as we worked out the meals for the first time, her confidence and trust in my delivery, and the promise I'd made to her, all bulldozed what was left of my integrity. I was an asshole. I'd ended up using her. *But what other choice did I have?*

Last night's kiss felt old now. Cold. Like waking up the

next morning knowing none of it was real. "They'll just have to manage without me," I clipped.

"What about my friends?" Her pitch grew by a dozen decibels. More tears ran down her face.

Another glance towards the time. Two hours and twenty minutes. My shit still to pack, I snapped, "Sienna, I don't have time for this." I jumped to my feet, straightened, and pointed to her bags on the floor. "You have ten minutes to fit whatever you want in these bags. What doesn't fit, doesn't come."

Her body blocked the doorway before I got to it. "No! This isn't the way we were meant to leave. This isn't happy." Her hands hit my chest as she cried. "You're lying to me. Why?"

Anger boiled up through every part of me. My back stiffened, all my muscles screaming to punch every wall in that room. My body ached. My mind fogged. I'd had enough. "You want the fucking truth, Sienna?" The last four years of fixing her shit erupted. "How many of your so-called friends got away from Hal Cooper like you did? Huh? Do you think you're special?"

Her eyebrows lowered until a frown darkened her face. A gleam of fear flashed in her eyes. First, she blanched, then she sat back down on the bed behind her. "Oh god," she murmured, "What did you do?"

"What did I do?" I yelled through the room, my finger stabbing at my chest over and over again. "I did what I had to do to keep you away from that club. Whatever Cooper asked for, I did. Just so you could keep going to school and not be the one waking up with a new fucking job over your head every month."

She no longer looked at me. Instead, she hugged her legs, her crying muffled by her head hiding between her knees. "Is that why you took on the job with Grace? Is that a Cooper thing too?"

Pain sliced through me. The despair in her voice... The disappointment in her words... Knowing she was right... It all came crashing down. I grabbed a cushion that had been tossed on her desk and hurled it through the room. It plonked against the back wall and died quietly on the ground. "Yes! It was a Cooper thing. I got him the stuff he needed, and now we're leaving." I shuffled closer to her. Once I was crouched by her legs, I continued. "We're not safe here anymore, Shorty."

She looked up and wiped her nose with the sleeve of something on her bed. "Why would that son of a bitch want anything to do with the centre?"

Something I'm still trying to figure out. "Jarryd Williams has links to Cooper. There's bad blood."

"Riley's dad? He's a doctor. Why would he let a drug lord near his family?"

My hands rose in defeat as I straightened. "Don't know. Don't care. It's between them."

She jumped to her feet and grabbed my hands, squeezing hard. "No! We can't leave them to *him*. Riley could get hurt. Grace too. What about Lizzy? They're innocent!"

An hour and twenty-five minutes till our flights. Unless we left in the next five minutes, we weren't making the trip out of the country. My voice rose until there was no mistake in the plan. "Listen, there's only one priority, and that's getting you out." I pointed to her bags. "Get them in the car right now. No more fucking arguing." I turned back. When I heard the suitcase zipping, I released a breath and rushed to my own bags.

Today, we were starting over. No more Cooper, no more jobs, and no more threats over our heads.

As I waited for Sienna in the hallway, I paused in front of the large frame that had started my Italian dream. Then, I glanced at it again before closing the door on our home for the last time. I'd give Grace a ring as soon as we'd landed. Maybe the warm Mediterranean air of Tuscany would be enough to make me forget how I'd destroyed her dream.

Chapter 17
Grace

The list of menus, name tags, and yet another to-do form sat on one side of the kitchen counter. The papers lay in neat piles, ready for our final seal of approval. *There's still so much to do.* I wiped my hands on my purple apron, the excitement of the upcoming day buzzing through me.

On the opposite end of the bench, ingredients' inventories, meal prep details and a printout of Avery's staff for the big moment also waited. I glanced at the list of kitchen staff, from dishies to cooks to actual chefs. None of the names rang a bell, but he'd vouched for them on multiple occasions, his confidence unmistakable. That, and knowing what I knew about my chef, he wouldn't associate with second-grade professionals. My shoulders relaxed as I filled my chest with clean, fresh air. Almost as fresh as the herbs growing on the windowsill. I inhaled the thyme and rosemary, my fingers lingering on the plants. Once we'd polished these bits and pieces today, we'd be ready to get into full swing.

Three-day countdown starts now.

I glanced towards Avery's wireless speaker, the usual vibrating dock looking as abandoned as a lost puppy. With a snap of the wrist, my Fitbit flashed close to ten.

I bet if I touch his precious music, he'll speed up his arrival. Pumped like a provocative teenager, I plugged my phone into the device and scrolled various songs on my playlist. Nothing triggered my fancy and I paused, the thought of what Avery would choose floating in my head. A smirk tickled my face, followed by the crazy realisation that I'd grown to love my chef's quirky music taste as he created masterpieces in my kitchen.

Best of the '80s flashed on my screen, and I pressed play. Within seconds, "Livin' on a Prayer" rocked the walls, and my pen scribbled frantic notes at the bottom of the summaries for each workstation designated for the night. Overall, everything seemed ready to go. The only thing I didn't have was the signed contracts for the staff and their personal numbers to confirm details. Avery hand-picking *the best* was great, but right now, all I had were first names and a lame rating on how they scored at Fortnite. *He has so many quirks!*

Another flick of my wrist, this time a little more forceful, triggered the clock to display on my Fitbit again. Almost half an hour had passed, at least an hour since Avery's usual start time. *Where the hell are you?*

A dash of unease dried up my throat until it felt like powdery sand. Not that I didn't trust in my own abilities, but with most of the staff being *his* contacts and the meals being executed *his* way, I really needed him to seal the approval today, so I could focus on Nutrify's marketing and the promotional aspects.

My phone pinged. An email. I loaded the document, my shoulders relaxing at the memo from the council

RSVPing for the function. When it was followed by another three, all major stakeholders and their teams confirming their attendance at what they called the 'most promising public health initiative for Queensland,' I finally allowed my pent-up excitement to bubble to the surface. My jaw hurt from smiling, almost as much as my rib cage hurt from the pounding in my chest. I'd done it! It was happening. In less than three days, we'd show the world that Nutrify was worthy of state and national endorsements.

That's it. I'm ringing him. The room grew silent as I unplugged my phone from the jack and pressed his name on the screen. When it went straight to voicemail, heaviness filled my stomach, but I kept my tone light. "Hi, Avery. Where is my chef?" I sighed before continuing. "Come on, partner, we only have two and a half days to go before the big reveal." The door slammed behind me. Startled, my back hit the side wall, but when I recognised Riley barging in the kitchen, his cheeks flushed, I turned towards the phone and finished. "Please call me."

Without waiting for an invitation, Riley beelined to the fridge and grabbed a can of Sprite. His eyes shone with a different light today, one I couldn't quite place, and his chest heaved up and down as he hoisted himself on the bench. With one swipe of the hand, he tossed all my papers out of the way and popped the soda open.

I frowned, palms on my hips. "Riley, I don't know what's got into you, but you don't get to barge in and throw my stuff out of the way. Whatever it is —"

"She's gone." His tone didn't leave any room for a fight. He lifted his chin up until his eyes zoomed in on whatever was painted on the ceiling. Riley's usual tough demeanour showed some cracks. I hadn't seen him upset in a long time, and for a moment, I was willing to forget my own deadlines. My elbows leaning on the back counter, I settled by his side, avoiding eye contact.

Child Psychiatry 101: Make them feel safe before you enter their space. Advice, compliments of Jarryd Williams. "Who's gone, Riley?" I lowered my voice.

He took a sip of his can (I suspected to hide the emotions) before he answered, "Sienna. She's gone."

That's why Avery is late. Sienna's done another runner. Frustration drilled through me. I took a deep breath, working on containing my personal thoughts on Sienna's latest transgression. I got that the kid was going through a few issues, but surely, she had to know how important this week was for her brother. I shook my head before lifting my eyes to meet Riley's. "What happened?"

Riley ran a hand over his face and wiped the sweat bead forming by his hairline. "We sort of had an argument yesterday."

"Okay?"

"She went to kiss me." He sighed, then narrowed his eyes at me. "I already know what you're gonna say. She's underage. I'm a staff member. Ethics 101."

My mouth dropped open. This was a repeat of April and Jarryd's story, but worse. Sienna was a minor. "I'm so sorry. I know you like her."

"I do." He stared through the window, his eyes locking on some invisible target. "But I can't get involved. It would be wrong."

My heart cracked. "You're an incredible role model, Riley. I hope you know that."

"Sometimes, I just wish karma would cut me a break," he said, his gaze back in the room. I smiled and nodded, my hand tapping on his knee briefly for encouragement. "I really care about her." His fingers crushed the can. When the liquid threatened to spill, he slid it across the counter. "I took her out for breakfast before school yesterday. She'd had a fight with Avery the night prior, so I thought it'd make her feel better."

I remembered everything about that night. *Everything*. Avery's smell. His strength. His pain. The way his fingers lingered on my cheek as he kissed me. Sienna was making a habit out of running away, except this time, she hadn't tried to ring me. I glanced towards my phone, and when no missed call from either of them flashed, I turned back to the teen sitting on my bench. "Okay."

"When I drove her to school, she asked me if I liked her." He cleared his throat, avoiding eye contact with me. "I told her I did, and my plan was to explain to her why nothing could ever happen, but as soon as I'd said yes, she'd moved forward to kiss me. Grace, the look on her face when I pushed her back..."

A small nurturing smile lifted my lips. It took every bone in my body not to hug this kid. As nonmaternal as I ever was, in that moment, I wanted to take the pain away from him. This kid had barely survived his share of emotional childhood trauma. "Riley, you did the right thing. We've been there, done that. April was lucky." *Right?*

He shrugged. A move that screamed 'not helping.' After a few seconds, Riley reached down for his Sprite and took another gulp. "She cried. She said she'd never felt loved before, and that she didn't know how to deal with it."

"This must have been so sad. For you both."

His jaw clenched. "I was gutted," he said. "How can wanting to make someone feel safe end up making them feel like shit?"

I shrugged and shook my head, wishing I had the right

answer. "I don't know, Riley. I think Sienna has pain that you were able to help alleviate, but it is what it is. She's sixteen. You're almost twenty-one and her youth worker. It's a problem. Plain and simple. I'm sure once she hears what you have to say, and why you did what you did, she'll be glad to have you."

"But she hasn't given me a chance, has she?" Riley's tone blew up. "Now, she'll forever think she wasn't good enough."

I crossed my arms and parked myself in front of him. These teenagers did my head in right now. Another flick of the wrist and almost lunchtime flashed on my watch. Still no news from Avery, and now only two days to go. I exhaled. I didn't have time for all their drama. I still had so much to do to make sure our event was ready for the state's big head-honchos. "Riley, I'm sure she'll come around. Avery will bring her back, and we can all sit down together and clear the misunderstanding, okay?" With determination, I snatched the can out of his hand and motioned for him to climb off the bench.

Time to let me get on with my day, kid.

"No, he won't." Instead of grabbing his drink from me, Riley stared at me with wide eyes. Something pulsed at the base of his neck, like he realised the issue was bigger than him.

"He won't what, Riley?" I extended my hand, hoping he'd grab his half-crushed can anytime now and let me sort out my own crap. The longer this went on, the less time I had to hunt down the staff's details.

"He won't bring her back."

A dull buzzing settled in my skull, the pride I'd felt five minutes ago turning into an overwhelming need to beg April to take over her adopted son's emotional issues. A headache was definitely on its way. I took a deep breath and exhaled before articulating the words, "Riley, Avery will sort this out. He always brings her back. It's just what she does when she's upset."

Riley shook his head as he climbed off the bench and dragged himself towards the exit. However, right as he opened the door, he froze, a sad smile on his face. "Their house is empty. He's left with her."

A sharp pain pierced through my chest, and I clutched it with one fist. The air coming in and out of my lungs burnt with every breath, and I braced myself against the wall.

What does he mean 'he left'? Inside my head, Riley's words played in a loop, over and over, until they were nothing but a screaming match between my ears. But before his declaration made any sense, all I could process was the Sprite dripping down my clothes.

Chapter 18
Avery

I jammed the shifter into fourth, dumped the clutch, and mashed the gas pedal to the floor. The car swerved left and hit the next street. "Slow down!" Sienna screamed, her hands pressed against the dashboard.

I ignored her. A quick glance in my rear-view mirror confirmed a white sedan was catching up. Shifting into fifth, I pushed the engine as far as it would go. My eyes focused on the traffic light turning red just in time to avoid crashing into a minivan through the intersection.

Fuck, Fuck, Fuck. The car veered sharply right, skidding off the main road and into a side street. My seat belt caught before slamming me back. Next to me, Sienna's hard breathing matched mine. "Avery. Please," she cried, "tell me what's going on? Is Hal following us?"

Jaw clenched, I barked, "I don't know. Just hang tight."

The distance between the white sedan and ours grew, but I managed to fly past the incoming truck. They didn't. Their car flipped off the road, the shattering of glass and metal screeching in the background. Checking the rear-view mirror, I watched as their sedan smoked, swallowed by the sound of sirens and pedestrians rushing to the scene. Unfortunately, both Black Tulip and some other guy stumbled out of the car in one piece. In the distance, one of them gave me the finger.

My foot lifted off the pedal, my breath hitching while my mind counted backwards.

Ten... nine... eight... seven...

My shoulders loosened up as the pounding in my chest eased off.

In and out... six... five... four...

My hands massaged the leather cover of my steering wheel as my knuckles regained colour.

Three... two... one...

"Are you okay?" A quick skim towards my sister, and I knew the answer. Instead of the usual Madonna look, Sienna's hair was plastered all over her forehead, her eyes drowned by smudged mascara, and her mouth gaped like her jaw was permanently fused open.

"Are you fucking kidding me?" she screeched, her hysteria growing by the second. In her defence, she'd have been completely nuts if she'd replied she was fine.

"Okay, let's take a deep breath, Shorty."

"You can just fuck off."

"Will you fucking stop swearing?" I snapped. I got that she was scared and angry, and I wasn't feeling crash hot either, but unless we worked together, we'd never get out of the country.

She scoffed between clenched teeth. "Yeah, it's not like I learnt from the best."

She had a point. "All right, relax. We have a flight to Singapore in an hour, then an overnight stay before a direct flight to Rome the following day."

"I don't want to go."

I rolled my eyes. "Yeah, I gathered that. You'd rather stay here and wait for Hal Cooper to track you down?"

"Can I at least ring Riley to explain?"

"Explain?" I shot daggers her way. "Explain what? That your brother has been feeding information about his dad to one of the biggest thugs in the state? Yeah, I don't think so, Sienna."

"I could just say goodbye. I wouldn't have to say anythi—"

"No."

"Can I at least send a text?"

"No. I've disconnected your phone anyway."

Sienna's breath caught in her throat, and she wiped a mix of tears and snot on her sleeve. "I hate you."

Gloom swirled in the pit of my stomach. My back stuck to my shirt while it bonded to my leather seat. I was drenched with sweat. I stunk. God, it was a good thing Grace didn't get to see me like this. *Grace...* A wave of guilt swamped me. I'd planned on leaving her a note, but Fish's impromptu visit this morning had thrown a spanner in my works. I'd never meant to leave Grace in the lurch, especially three days before the event. Her face filled my vision. Blue eyes and blonde bob shaking as she laughed at my stupid jokes, the trembling in her body every time mine brushed hers. Her mouth, as our tongues tasted each other last night. My chest tightened, my gut suddenly weighing a hundred pounds. *Maybe I could call her quickly at the airport?*

"You feel guilty too, don't you?" Sienna asked, her tone a mix of concern and teen manipulation.

"It's not ideal," I answered through clenched teeth. Ideal? That was an understatement. The menus were done, food ready to be delivered, and staff on standby. But honestly, life in a kitchen—especially during an event the size of this one—got pretty rough. I'd give Scott (my 2IC) a ring as soon as I could to make sure he kept the others in line for her, but even so, I'd have been lying if I said I was comfortable.

"If you let me call Riley, you could talk to Grace too." Her puppy-dog eyes matched her whiney tone. Neither helped.

"What's the go with you and the kid, anyway?" I watched as her lips pressed into a thin line, her cheeks growing pink. She opened her mouth to talk, but no words came out. "Is he your boyfriend or something?"

Tears filled her eyes, and her lip wobbled as she answered, "Nope."

I raised an eyebrow. "Your choice or his?"

"I like him. A lot." Her chest expanded with a huge gulp of air. "But he doesn't like me like that."

"That sounds like a lot of ifs, buts, and maybes, Shorty. Just sayin'."

She narrowed her eyes. "If you're gonna ask questions, the least you can do is shut up and listen."

God, as much as my sister was a pain in my ass a lot of the time, she was growing into a strong woman. I breathed better knowing she'd be able to hold her own one day. No matter what happened from here. "Message received. Shutting up now. Please continue." I extended my palm into a mock salute and her lips curled, a tiny smile morphing her face. *That's my girl.*

"He never said anything, but we've been hanging out, and yesterday, I thought we'd be more."

"More?"

She ignored my question. Instead, she continued. "Riley

gets me. I don't really know what happened to him. He says he'll tell me one day, but he makes me feel like I'm not a complete lost cause. That, maybe, I am loveable."

As we turned into Airport Drive, I shook my head towards her, before focusing my eyes to the road again. "Sienna, you are the most loveable girl I know. Don't let our dead-beat parents or the likes of Hal Cooper convince you otherwise."

More tears filled her eyes, but this time, she didn't stop them. "I can't believe I won't see him again." Her voice broke, and she sunk her shoulders back into her seat. She suddenly looked small.

Maybe I should have let her go to juvie for six months. That's probably all she would have got for smuggling a bit of pot, and instead of being blackmailed by Satan and his spawns for the last four years, we'd be living a normal life.

When my brain couldn't filter the right and wrong things to say to her anymore, I sighed and tightened my grip on the steering wheel. If Grace was here, she'd tell me what to say to make my sister feel better. The thought pierced through me. But Grace wasn't here, and like Riley, I'd probably never see her again.

Neither Sienna nor I spoke. Instead, we stared at the International Airport sign flashing in front of us, the ambiance in the car dropping to icy levels. In contrast to the grief and adrenaline running through our bodies, the massive building screamed happy families, holiday-goers, and warm memories. The fucking irony goaded me, and I shoved it back down to the pits of my soul.

We parked the car and loaded our suitcases onto the trolley, the duffel bag holding the fifty grand and our passports right by my side. "Will we ever come back home?" Sienna murmured in a small voice.

As I watched the streaks of black makeup running down her cheeks, her defeated shoulders, and beaten gait, I was tempted to lie. But lying to her felt wrong. No matter how much the truth would hurt. So, I pushed the trolley forward. "No, Sienna. Probably not."

Chapter 19
Grace

The clicking of April's fingers snapped me out of my daze. Any closer to my face, and she might as well be smacking me. I wish she had, just for my brain to accept this was really happening. Avery had dumped me forty hours before the launch, and with him gone, so drowned the rest of my dream. There was no way I could pull this off alone.

"Riley could have got it wrong, you know?" A grimace distorted April's mouth as she pronounced the words very carefully.

Who are you lying to, sister? Me or you? I rolled my eyes, a big sigh shaking my shoulders. "He's not wrong. They're really gone. I can feel it."

Silence filled the room. April opened her mouth to speak, but no sound came out. Instead, she grabbed my hand and squeezed it twice. In the background, basketballs bounced against walls, the teenagers' voices floating like white noise into my ears. "So, I'm gonna let you wallow in your misery for about another thirty seconds, and then we're going to talk about plan B."

The bubbling of steamy water followed by the clinking

of metal against porcelain startled me. I turned my head, her warning sinking in. Green eyes stared back at me, the black wrap she wore accentuating her pregnant body. Her hand cupped the top of her belly, the loving gesture contrasting with the deep frown on her face.

She tilted her head as she narrowed her eyes at me. "I'm serious. Drink your tea."

"Okay." I sighed. If anyone had a miracle in store, I'd happily have accepted it. Arms out. No questions asked. The thumping against the wall resumed. I glanced towards the window, the shadow of a few kids flashing before the glass like ants running from fire. *Do I look that bad?* Above April, the small hand on the clock ticked. Second by second, the soft clicking grew louder. Ears buzzing with the imaginary noise, I tilted my head towards my friend and tapped my fingers on the table for added emphasis. When her mouth gaped open, I shrugged. "So, now would be a good time to share your amazing plan."

She pursed her lips and ran a hand through her hair. "Argh, I don't have one," she blurted out, then blew a big breath. The chair creaked with her weight as she leaned back.

I rolled my eyes. "I rest my case. I am screwed."

"Oh god. Stop with the drama." She narrowed her eyes, her thumbs typing on her phone at the speed of lightning. "I give up. I'm texting Jarryd."

"Why is that giving up?" I cocked an eyebrow. "Though I do resent how much we're relying on these men," I mumbled under my breath.

Phone back on the table, hands laced over her belly, April sighed, a slight line or two appearing on her forehead. "I was trying to avoid overloading him. He's a bit preoccupied lately."

"Hope Island General being its usual slave machine?" I asked, trying hard to show sympathy in the midst of my own crisis.

She shook her head. "A bit more than that. We just didn't want to say anything until the launch was out of the way, but Hal Cooper reappeared on the scene a few days ago." A nail went to her mouth. She continued. "It might be nothing, but Jarryd's just laying low while he investigates what these scumbags are after this time."

My mouth dropped. Jarryd had indeed made himself a little scarce lately. So had Riley, for that matter. Today was the first time I'd seen him in a week, and I guessed it was to hunt Sienna down. It all made sense. A slight pang of guilt pinched me. "I'm sorry. I've been so consumed with the launch that I didn't really pay attention."

April leaned forward, her hand covering mine. "Don't be silly, and it's probably nothing anyway. He's just being his usual hypervigilant, hotshot self." A smile curled her lips, but it didn't quite reach her eyes.

"Tell me what you know." Fear paralysed me. For my friends. For their children. For the disasters that kept on coming. "Then, we'll sort out my plan B."

A large breath lifted her breasts, her shoulders dropping as she exhaled. "Jarryd thought someone had followed him from The General a couple of weeks ago. I mean, initially, he assumed it might have been a patient he'd admitted involuntarily last year."

"Definitely not impossible."

"Right? But just as he pulled up and took a good look at the driver, he recognised Trey."

"What?" My eyes grew wide. Riley's brother was out of jail again.

She pursed her lips. "Bigger and bolder. Tattooed from head to toe, and I'll let you guess it..."

"The Cooper crest on his forearm?" My tone lowered, the answer already confirmed in my mind.

"Yep." She took a sip of her tea. "Then, the next week, a note was left in Jarryd's office, addressed to Riley." Her back straightened. "Now, before you ask, yes, Jarryd opened it. And no, Riley never found out." Her green eyes grew moist.

"They're wanting him back, right?" A lump settled in my throat. Five years of watching my best friends fight to protect this kid from his fate had just come full circle. That, and Avery's betrayal suddenly hit me like a ton of bricks. *Nothing's ever fair. You should never have expected more.* A chill ran through my core, my voice breaking as I fought the tears spilling. Shame filled me. These guys were going through so much, and yet the will to make Nutrify a state success continued to be a massive priority in my heart. "I'm sorry." I dabbed a couple of tears with a napkin lying on the table.

April passed me a bunch of them before checking the beep coming from her phone. "He just said to stop panicking, and that he'll touch base once he's finished his clinic."

I nodded in silence, tears flowing on my face. It wasn't like I had much to add to this disaster.

Her bottom lip wobbled between her teeth. For a second, it looked like she was going to cry too. But she didn't. Instead, she dragged her chair closer to me and leaned forward. Her voice was soft. Caring. Professional. "I know we promised never to psychoanalyse each other, but I have to ask. What's really going on between you and your chef?"

My eyes avoided her gaze as I turned my head towards the front of the kitchen, where everything promised to happen just a couple of days ago. Memories of our cooking challenges, our first stolen kiss, even our first argument drilled through me. Avery was rough on the edges and hadn't been mega forthcoming with what was going on in his personal life, but never in a million years would I have expected him to ghost me days before my launch.

Days after he'd made love to me like there'd been more. I sighed, and fat shameful tears ran down my face. "All these years of wondering how you'd fallen for a patient." I instantly regretted the low blow. "Sorry, I mean a colleague." When April's face failed to harden, I continued. "And I just ended up doing the same thing anyway."

April ignored a ball hitting the window behind us and nodded, encouraging me to go on.

"He's cold. Quite distant," I said, staring at an invisible spot on the ceiling, "but he's also so warm. He's so protective of those he loves." *You're just not one of them.* My stomach tightened, and I took a deep breath to loosen it. "We started with a bit of a love-hate relationship." I chuckled. "But as soon as I saw him with his sister, I saw the real him. I knew there was something special behind the tatts and the piercings."

Nurturing lines deepened around April's eyes, followed by a professional nod. "I get the feeling you shared something more than a work relationship?"

Jaw clenched, I stared ahead, avoiding my friend's gaze. "Nothing worth mentioning. All I'll miss really is the extra hands to deliver this launch." *Not the dimples when he smiled. Not the protective heart. And definitely not the way his hands crawled over my body.* I swallowed the emotion choking me. "But what is worth talking about... is plan B."

Chapter 20
Avery

The scratchy voice over the loudspeaker did nothing for my restless legs. My ankle bounced over my knee faster than a jackhammer on steroids. Finally, I jumped to my feet and marched to the departure counter as the Qantas hostess waved us closer.

"Do you have our passports?" Sienna asked, aggravation still evident in her tone.

I rolled my eyes and rested my forearms on the desk. "Hi." I slid our boarding passes and passports to the brunette in front of me.

"Good afternoon, Mister..." She opened the first page of the passport, scrutinizing my face. "Curtis."

Yeah, that's me. Now get on with it. Sienna's irritation was rubbing off on me. I wouldn't be able to relax until we were on that goddamn plane. Until then, all I could think about was whether Hal Cooper would stick to his word, final job and all, or send another crew our way. The doubts felt like shit, but that was nothing in comparison to how it felt listening to Grace's voicemails.

You didn't have a choice.

"One-way to Rome with a stop in Hong Kong," Tania, according to her name tag, crooned as my passport swapped from one of her hands to another. When the typing, stamping, and fussing ended, a bunch of stickers printed out of a small machine. The hostess handed me my boarding pass and tags for my suitcase. I passed them to Sienna, my eyes zooming in on the hostess's sudden frown.

"Put these on, will ya?"

My sister's grumble registered behind me, followed by huffing and puffing as my suitcase rammed me in the calf. The woman in front of me snapped her head up and glanced towards Sienna's commotion. Her lip twitched.

Right, okay, lady. The girl is pissed. Not worth having a stroke over.

The conveyor belt shifted with the weight of Sienna's luggage. Despite rushing like maniacs, that kid had managed to pack everything but the freaking kitchen sink. The woman puckered her lips, her eyes darting between the weight displaying on the screen and me. Thick lines appeared around her mouth.

"I'll pay for the excess weight." I pulled my wallet out of my back pocket, pushing the Mastercard towards her. Frantic typing resumed across the counter, in silence, while the ice queen tossed pages of Sienna's passport back and forth like a teacher marking a shit paper. "Or we can empty the excess weight," I snapped, "whatever suits so we don't miss our plane, Tania."

Slowly, she met my eyes, and we exchanged a glance. "How old is the child?"

"Who is she calling a child?" Sienna mumbled, her body warmth growing closer to my back now.

"She's seventeen in six weeks. Why?" A cold wave hit me in the gut. I instantly regretted my passive-aggressive dig at her five seconds ago. A fake smile curled my lips, my hand moving closer to the hostess until our fingers almost touched. Feeling like a cheap whore, I continued. "Teenagers, hey? But she's a good kid. Just didn't sleep enough last night."

Tania nodded and moved her hand back to the keyboard, and a different screen appeared. "I'm sorry, Mr Curtis, but her passport is damaged."

Sienna's fingers gripped my wrist. *How can her passport be damaged and not mine?* "With all due respect, it's a mistake. Both these passports are in the exact same condition. Fair. Done together seven years ago." Memories of our last holiday with Mum, visiting her Texas hobo of the time, jumped at me. Sienna as a kid, smearing Tex-Mex all over her face. The Riverwalk in San Antonio. And the Houston Space Centre. No, these passports were fine. It wasn't like Sienna's had pages dangling off it.

"You're not her parent, clearly?" the hostess asked, right before she paged someone from a small contraption pinned to her uniform.

"He's my brother," Sienna said, her voice shaking. "He didn't kidnap me or anything."

As Sienna's panic spread, Tania smiled at my sister, her head tilting. "I wasn't thinking he kidnapped you, sweetie. I'm just trying to see how to get you a new passport quicker." Her words didn't register in my brain. How could Sienna's passport be invalid? My eyes darted to a tiny mark over the serial number that the woman wiped at over and over.

It's barely a mark. Nothing's ripped and nothing's missing. "It can't be right." I grabbed the passports (now sitting on the counter), found tiny marks at the front of mine, and tapped them back and forth with my index finger. "See, they were both granted seven years ago. At the same time, and they're in the same condition."

"Don't leave me behind," Sienna murmured, her voice now choking.

A large, older male with a bright-orange sticker on his right shoulder (most likely Tania's supervisor) met us by the counter. "Damaged passport?" he asked Tania, before nodding a curt hello in our direction.

She nodded back, then handed him my sister's passport. "By not much, unfortunately. But enough that the system won't register it."

My fingers raked the back of my neck, beads of sweat now pooling at the base as reality sunk in. "How can a microscopic mark cause all this drama? Surely, you have to see how ridiculous it is from here."

"Passports are very sensitive documents. They have to scan across multiple systems, and across any country." An awkward grimace took over Tania's face. "Even if we let you through, you wouldn't make it out of Rome's airport."

The clock above the desk showed nineteen minutes till take off. Sienna grabbed me, her fingers digging into my bicep. "Please, don't leave me behind."

Eyes closed and throat tight, I pressed a kiss on her forehead. "Never." The sounds of my baby sister's sniffles, compounded by the sympathetic looks of the two airport staff in front of me, gave me renewed energy. I had to fix this. A deep breath filled my lungs. "Okay. What do I need to do?"

As if he'd read my mind, the supervisor grabbed papers freshly printed from behind him. He straightened the pile on the counter and handed it to me, our passports tucked safely between. "Here's what we can do for you. We can delay your flights by seventy-two hours, free of charge, if you're willing to get her an express passport renewal online."

Seventy-two hours. My knuckles cracked with the clenching of my fists, and I ignored the void growing in the pit of my stomach. *Three whole days.*

"Can we just go home until my new passport arrives?" Sienna murmured, her tone suddenly much younger than a soon-to-be seventeen-year-old.

There was no way we could go back home. Too many people would be knocking on the door. Hal. Riley. *Grace.* Fighting the need to see her again, I shut off the internal plea and allowed my brain to take over. *Think. Don't feel.* There was no time for lust when it came to protecting Sienna. *It wasn't lust.* "Fuck." I leaned across the counter, an elbow cradling my head. The weight of the universe making me pay for my betrayal.

"Sir?" Tania asked, her eyes going from me to her supervisor. "That's the best we can do."

Feet squared, I straightened my rib cage until my breathing eased off. "I'm sorry. I appreciate it."

"Your new boarding details are on these forms." The supervisor pointed to the papers I now held. "Just come back two hours before take-off and we'll have the rest sorted." He winked at Sienna. "Just bring your brand-spanking-new passport, young lady."

She smiled back with something closer to a grimace and followed my lead, her footsteps shuffling as fast as they could go until she was ahead of me. "Stop, Avery."

I could barely answer my own mental monologue, so dealing with her would have to wait until we regrouped somewhere. Long enough to process our next move. A coffee shop sign flashed in front of me like a water fountain on a deserted island. "Come on, Shorty. Milkshake time."

Our suitcases tucked by a table, Sienna and I settled in a booth, its red vinyl having seen better days. While Sienna ordered at the counter, I skimmed through the forms. Ordering a passport express was fairly easy. If I sent the application today, we could definitely be on that plane in a couple of days. Slight relief buzzed through my veins. As long as we remained on the down-low, the plan was only delayed. Not cancelled. *We've dealt with worse.*

A Google search and a couple of clicks later, and we'd anonymously checked in to a fancy hotel by the airport for the next few days. Milkshakes appeared in front of me. Sienna's smile was a bit more genuine as she sipped on a strawberry beverage, the pink topping zigzagging against the clear glass. My iced coffee seemed bland in comparison. I took a sip, the cold brew soothing me.

"So, here's the plan." I pointed to the image of the hotel on my phone. "We're going to relax for the next few days while we wait for your passport to come back."

"Is there a pool in that hotel?" A smirk lifted the corner of her lips.

I ignored her, relief growing with my sister's comeback. "And, in three days, we're on a porch sipping cocktails." A ping shook my phone, the notification icon taking over the hotel logo. We both cast our eyes down. *Grace.* Her face danced on the screen as the phone vibrated against the table. It stopped, and a one-liner appeared as a text.

GRACE

How could you do this to me?

With one finger, I swiped the message away and wished the motion could swipe the guilt just as easily. Sienna shook her head, her eyes rolling slightly before she finished her drink. The slurping stopped. "I'm done."

"Good. Let's check in." I jumped to my feet and grabbed our suitcases. The sooner we got to the hotel, the sooner I sorted that passport, and the sooner we were on our way again. But until then, there was something I had to do.

Chapter 21
Grace

Guilt filled me as both April and I gawked at Jarryd like he would suddenly start waving a magic wand. The usually energetic thirty-three-year-old carried somewhat of an older vibe with the loose tie dangling from his neck, dark circles under his eyes, and hair much longer than usual. As he caught me staring, he sighed, fingers running through the front of his black locks. "Haven't had time to get it cut with everything happening."

I nodded. "I heard. Hal Cooper sent his eldest to get Riley back into the fold?"

"Yep. And when Riley didn't quite get the memo, the bastards left notes for him throughout my goddamn clinic." Next to him, April squeezed his hand. He continued. "The last couple of weeks, I've had this growing ball in the pit of my stomach. Like Riley's father is watching our every move."

"You're more of a father to Riley than Hal ever was, Jar." April's tone was pained. For the last six years, Riley had become her son too. Yet, if Cooper had decided to claim his boy back, Riley would either meet his birthright and become a proud gangster, or he'd be dead by his twenty-fifth birthday.

Sympathetic grief sliced through my heart. This was an ache I'd never want to experience. "You could be wrong. Riley is strong. He's following in your footsteps, and there're a bunch of wannabe gangsters downtown Hal Cooper might decide to devote his mentorship to instead."

"I hope you're right." Jarryd sighed. "I can't tell anymore if it's my paranoia talking, or if there really is more happening behind the scenes. Something feels off."

April leaned over, warmth spreading between them, and she kissed him. "I love you, hotshot." April's forehead touched her husband's. "You are amazing, and I am in awe of how you are managing all this stuff at the moment."

He pecked her and then lowered his lips to her belly. She settled on his lap, his arm around her middle. Both turned towards me, their incredible intimacy still lingering in the room like the smell of rain on fresh grass. "Okay, so back to business. Fill me in," Jarryd prompted.

Envy choked the base of my throat, followed by a feeling of betrayal. On the table in front of us, Avery's paperwork, plans, and final touches cackled. They mocked me like the kids at school laughed at my second-hand clothes and dry bread for lunch all through primary school. I swallowed hard, my chest tightening while shame over how stupid and gullible I'd been spread through my every nerve ending.

You and Avery were never going to be like them. You'll always be the poor, pathetic loser no one wanted on their sports team. A tear escaped my eye, and I swiped it before they noticed. A deep breath quietened the gloomy thoughts in my mind, and instead, I did what I did best. Gathering all the anger, outrage, and revenge I could muster, I allowed the familiar volcano to build up from the pit of my stomach. It raged, punched, and erupted into a thousand screams until Avery was nothing but a lying, hypocritical, selfish bastard.

In one swift move, my fingers tapped the screen of my phone at a hundred keys a minute. I tossed the Galaxy on the table as soon as I sent my one-liner. The odds were Avery would ignore this message like he'd ignored the last ten, but I didn't care. Feeling a tinge better, I turned towards my friends. "My biggest issue is staffing. He had this whole crew lined up, but all I have here..." I ruffled the papers in front of me. "...are a bunch of first names and stupid personal details."

Jarryd leaned in, April's body undulating as he moved. They both scrutinised Avery's writing dancing all over a page of peculiar facts. "What the hell's a *heal*?" Jarryd asked, eyes wide.

I shrugged. "Hey, you're the doctor." I lowered my index finger to the next name. "This dude has no hope. Apparently, his credentials are that he's one hundred percent *TAC*."

April shook her head, a small chuckle following. "Check this one out. Our friend Danny, here, is hard to *crack* it seems. Sounds like a catch."

Laughter filled the room. My shoulders dropped, and for the first time today, my jaw stopped aching. I exhaled, grateful for the outlet, if nothing else.

"Oh god. Someone shoot me." Jarryd snorted, the document now close to his face. "Sean must be cheap. He doesn't have a battle pass."

As April and I giggled louder, tears of amusement welled in our eyes, the irony not lost on me. I'd trusted a grown-ass man to manage an enormous endeavour between

Fortnite tournaments. "Jesus Christ." I ran a hand over my face. "Tell me they actually know how to cook decen—"

We froze as my phone flashed with Avery's name on the screen. My heart rate increased until all I could hear was the blood rushing in my ears. "What do I do?" I whispered, more to myself than anyone else.

"Answer it." April wobbled towards the door and motioned Jarryd with her. She blew me a kiss, then she pointed towards the phone still vibrating on the table. "Answer him."

Hand shaking, I picked up the mobile and drew it to my ear. The kitchen door clicked, Avery's ringtone sounding louder than before now that it was just him and me. My throat felt like sandpaper. I cleared it, hoping my brain would stop throwing all the scenarios in different directions like a toddler building a thousand-piece puzzle. "Hello," I said, my strangled voice less assertive than I'd hoped.

"Hey." Heavy background noise covered Avery's soft breathing in the receiver. *Train station?*

A cocktail of emotions filled me. I closed my eyes and took a deep breath, swallowing the lump in my throat. *He's really gone.* "Why?"

A heavy sigh whizzed through the earpiece. "I had no choice. I just wanted to apologise." Avery paused for a second. "I wish it didn't have to end like this."

"What's *it*, Avery?" I snapped. "The launch or the pseudo..." I stumbled on the right word, because to be honest, even I didn't know what *it* was. *Relationship? Fucking?* "...friendship?"

"I really care about you."

"Do you?" I barked. "Because from where I'm standing, you've just left me two days before the biggest day of my life." *And two days after the most intimate.*

"I didn't plan on any of this." His voice grew by a decibel. "Not having to leave like this, not finishing the job. Definitely not what happened between us."

My chest hurt from the repressed memories begging to escape. I brought a lock of my hair to my nose, inhaling Avery's invisible scent. Only a couple of days ago, I felt his lips in the crook of my neck, nibbling at my flesh, his musky smell taking over my senses. My nails dug into my palms, the punishment for Avery's voice having the effect it shouldn't. My breathing increased. On the other end of the phone, he paused, silence dragging for what felt like an eternity. "I know better than to ask for marriage after a one-night stand, but this..." I scoffed. "...is something else."

The sound of another train (or bus maybe) covered up whatever smart-ass remark Avery had brewing. When the racket stopped, he continued. "And just so we're clear, if I really was after a one-night stand, there're easier ways to find them."

"You don't get to be funny right now," I yelled into the headset. "You tell me what I'm supposed to do, Avery?" Tears choked me, and despite my voice shaking, I continued. "I don't know what to do right now." I scanned the table for the menus. The staff list. The RSVPs from all the MPs of the region. "I can't pull this off alone." Shameful tears burnt the skin on my cheeks. No matter how many years had gone by, when it really came to crunch time, I was still the girl who didn't belong on either team. "Don't do this two days before the launch," I whispered, my voice breaking.

In my mind, I pictured him wiping my tears with his thumb as he promised he'd come back and finish what we started. He didn't. Instead, the loud whistling started through the phone again, muffling the sound of Avery's voice. "Grace, I'm so sorry." The whistling increased until his admission was but a whisper. "If I could come back, I would. I hope you know that."

No, I don't. I truly don't. The chair creaked with the weight of my body. One hand cradling my forehead, I nurtured the headache building in my skull. The noise through the phone escalated until I could almost feel vibrations through the device. "I'm only asking for two days, Avery. Two days."

Whatever he answered, I couldn't make sense of it, because the ruckus on his end screeched louder and louder. It screamed and whistled, until it felt like it had travelled through the phone and lodged itself into my eardrums. Then it hit me. Trains didn't make that level of noise. A pang of despair clawed at me. It chewed at my hope and spat it out like yesterday's lunch. *They're not trains. They're planes.* Cold air filled my lungs, aching with every breath. He wasn't coming back. Because at best, he'd left Queensland. At worst, he was out of the country.

Chapter 22
Avery

With one finger in my ear, I pressed the handset against my cheek, blocking the sound of a 747 taking off above our hotel window. For a second or two, Grace's voice was muffled, giving me a break from the guilt cutting into me like a hacksaw with blunt blades. "How could you do this to me? With everything at stake?"

"Until yesterday, I didn't know I'd have to leave like this." I pinched the bridge of my nose, massaging the headache coming on just over my brow. It wasn't a lie. Cooper had increased his friendly visits when whatever the fuck he was looking for hadn't popped up quickly enough, and the beating I took a couple of weeks ago wasn't something I wanted to experience again. Not for me if I could help it, but definitely not for Sienna. It'd become too dangerous. *That* was the truth. As much as I cared about Grace, the launch was ready to go. She'd be fine executing it without me. "Grace, I left everything prepped up. You can do this."

She scoffed. "Yeah, sure. I can cook it all. With my ten fingers."

"You have the menus; you have the staff. This is your baby, Grace. You'll be great." I only wished I'd been there to see it through. With her. Visions of her strawberry mousse flashed in front of my eyes. Followed by the navy bra I'd pushed down to cup her breast, the skirt I'd lifted to explore her ass, and how she moaned when she came twice in my arms. I'd even miss her bitching about my kitchen non-negotiables. The woman mattered to me more than I'd admitted to myself.

Her voice broke into the phone, quiet sobs followed by sniffles. "You just don't care, Avery. That's the bottom line."

"If things had been..." I paused when the room door slammed shut. From the corner of my eye, I watched my sister march to the bed, then sprawl out on the large mattress. Arms behind her head, she narrowed her gaze at me. "...I do care," I finished, my back turned away from Sienna.

Sienna cleared her throat. "If you cared, you'd have let me say goodbye to Riley."

"Zip it," I mouthed before turning away from her. The last thing I wanted was Grace, or Riley for that matter, dragged into our problems.

On the other end of the line, Grace stopped midsentence, then asked, "Is that Sienna?"

I sighed. Things were about to get more complicated. "Yes."

"Is she okay?"

A quick glance towards the teen flipping the bird at me confirmed she was fine. "Yes."

"Riley was pretty cut she'd left without saying goodbye."

My headache was building. I closed my eyes, ignoring

my sister now hovering around me. "It wasn't her fault. She did want to say goodbye, but—"

"Let me speak to her." Sienna waved her hand towards the phone. When I ignored her, she grabbed the headset and pulled on it like a bull fighting a matador in the middle of Spain.

I caved, knowing better than to make a scene so close to leaving the country. "For fuck's sake," I barked, then whispered, "watch what you say."

She rolled her eyes and grabbed the device with both hands, her cheeks pinkening. "Grace," she shrieked into the receiver. "I miss you. And Riley."

My jaw clenched. My palms grew clammy as I watched my sister sink into the hotel chaise, her heel under her thigh, like she was catching up with a best friend. These two had definitely grown close, and it didn't help the ton of guilt and confusion swirling in the pit of my gut.

"You have to tell him I'm really sorry." Sienna welled up at whatever Grace said to her. She nodded, wiping tears. Then she sighed. "I'll try. I just wish things were different."

Something inside me stirred, adding to the cocktail of shit feelings pounding down my throat. *Me and you both, Shorty.*

As the girls talked for the next few minutes, I pushed myself from the wall and grabbed a can of Sunkist from the mini fridge. It fizzed when I popped the top, and I sculled down the cold liquid.

"I need the phone back, Shorty." I parked myself on the coffee table across from her. Elbows resting on my knees, I leaned forward until the sunlight was blocked from my eyes. Not that it helped the drilling in my skull. Sienna sighed into the receiver, told Grace she had to go, then tossed the device at me.

"Hey." Hearing Grace's voice, no matter how pissed she was, gave me some comfort. Everything had started to pile up, and regardless of how tough I liked to think I was—between Cooper, Sienna, the passport issue, and leaving Grace in the lurch—my resolve was starting to wear thin. "That's two of us you're screwing with," Grace deadpanned.

The pressure in my head rose until the thought of slowly pushing an ice pick through my temple seemed like a good relief option. "I know that's what it looks like."

"Whatever. Can I at least get proper names and contact details for your alleged staff?"

I raised an eyebrow. I'd left all the staff info with the rest of the paperwork. "What do you mean? It's already there."

She laughed. A laugh that probably meant she'd have me by my balls if I were in the same room as her. "Yeah? The list of first names and matching Fortnite achievements?"

Fuck. My eyes scanned the room like they had X-ray vision. I definitely didn't remember packing any of that info with us. Last I checked, I'd left the details in the kitchen with everything else needed for the launch. "Fortnite what?"

"What you left is useless," she snapped. "It doesn't have last names, and there're no contact numbers. Just first names and their video game skills set."

My palm slammed the wall, a tsunami of anger and guilt taking over my brain cells. It didn't matter how much I tried to protect everyone, I always screwed everything up. *What's the point?* My throat dried, my knuckles turning white against the thin metal of the can. I crushed it. "I'm trying, Grace," I murmured, my voice thinning.

She paused. "What's really going on?"

"A lot." The soda spilt over the white porcelain as I tossed the can in the kitchenette's sink.

"Every time I've tried to reach out, you've pushed me away." Her tone softened. "Why do you have to always fight the whole world by yourself."

Because I don't want you to get hurt. I took a calming breath and let it out slowly. "It's been me against the world for some years now. I don't know how to live any other way."

"Maybe it would be different if you'd finally let someone get close to you."

Though I'd never see her again, for the next thirty seconds, I allowed myself to imagine what it would be like to have her. Her nurturing vibe, her sassy comebacks, and her sexy presence. If there ever was a reason to stay put, she'd be it.

On the bed, Sienna curled up, an elbow bent under her head. Eyes closed. Lightly snoring. Fast-asleep. Innocent. Resolve filled me as I watched my sister lie there, with me as her only protector. If there ever was a reason *to leave*, this kid was it. There was no way I was letting Hal Cooper get his claws into her. Destroy her life like he'd destroyed hundreds of others. If it meant I never got to feel Grace in my arms again, then it was the way it had to be. "I swear to God, if I could, I'd fucking be there."

"Will you just tell me what it is, Avery? I can't trust what you're not telling me."

I didn't blame her. From where she stood, it looked bad. Like an asshole making excuses. A bastard leaving her in the lurch. She didn't even know about the worst part yet: the fact that I was a fucking spy who'd used her for a job. "I'm sorry."

Silence stretched between us. On the bed, Sienna stirred.

"Can I at least get these guys' phone numbers?"

I'd have to make a call or two to collect them all, but it could be done before this damn passport was granted. "Yes. And I'll get my man Scott to ring you first thing. He'll keep these guys in check."

She scoffed. "Like you were supposed to?"

I ignored the dig. "It will be a great launch. You've got this."

"So, is that it?" Grace asked, all sarcasm now gone.

Prolonging death by a thousand cuts wasn't helping anyone. I took a deep breath and braced for the final blow. "Goodbye Grace," I murmured, my head resting against the cold wall behind me.

She sniffled. "I'm not ready to say goodbye."

A lump formed in my throat. "I know." Memories of her body underneath mine, my lips on her forehead, ripped through my brain. In my thirty-two years of life, it was the first time I'd let a woman crawl under my skin, and letting her go hurt like a bitch.

Right as I was about to hang up, she blurted, "Avery? Let Sienna say goodbye to Riley. They need closure."

"You have my word." It couldn't do that much damage hours before we took off for Rome, anyway. I didn't know what I expected next, but it certainly wasn't the click ending the phone call to make me feel as shitty as it did.

"Is she gone?" Sienna sat upright on the bed, her brow furrowed.

"Yep." I ambled next to her, then collapsed on the mattress, feet crossed and arms over my eyes.

"Are you okay?" She pronounced each word carefully.

I lay on the bed, my chest weighing more than a thousand bricks. The ceiling above me buzzed and I forced my eyes to follow the blades, swallowing the emotions threatening to spill. "Will be. Once we get that freaking passport and get on that goddamn plane."

She turned her body until she faced me, then she murmured, "You love her, don't you?"

I uncovered my eyes and cocked my eyebrow. "You can call Riley before we leave and say goodbye."

She turned back, a massive grin on her face. After a minute, she added, "That's okay. I love her too," before closing her eyes again.

My chest heaved up and down, my lungs aching with each breath. A thousand thoughts raged in my head, a battle between body and mind. Sienna was wrong. There was no way I could be in love with Grace. It was way too soon. I might have loved her smile, her smart-ass comments, her futile attempts at beating my desserts, her body, her mind, and our fights about music all equally, but surely it couldn't mean that the void in my stomach signified more than that.

Slight dizziness took over as I processed Sienna's words. I let go of the breath I was hanging on to, my shoulders dropping at the same time. *It doesn't matter now.*

With my thumb, I scrolled the apps on my phone, found the Spotify playlist I was looking for, then clicked the share icon and added Grace's name to it. I attached a message, hoping it would let her feel me on the big day in some way, shape, or form. Then I sent it, picturing her in another world, sipping wine with us in Rome.

> When you listen to my '80s playlist, think of me cheering you on while you kick their asses in the kitchen. Always.

Chapter 23
Grace

The chubby man in front of me yawned as I handed him the list of menus for tomorrow night's launch. "Scott sends his sorries, but he ain't able to help cause his missus got sick."

I refrained from rolling my eyes. Unless Scott's wife was five or crippled, I didn't want to hear it. What kind of woman needed her husband to cancel a big job just because she was *sick*? "So, just to clarify..." I ran a hand over my face. "*You're* Scott's replacement?"

With stains all over his shirt, his stomach protruding from his shorts, and thongs in a commercial kitchen, the guy was as clueless as the fresh pork lumped on my benchtop. "Yep, Miss. I've cooked brunches for my local pub, and bloody oath, let me tell ya, the folks gabbed about it all 'round the bush for yonks."

Mouth gaped, I stared at my new chef, considering the alternatives. Surely, even an apprentice on Airtasker had to be better than our friend Paul, here. "Listen, I appreciate it." I cleared my throat, my brain searching for words that didn't sound like: *I need more than an old farmer, whose experience revolves around pub food.* "I guess you might need an idea of the work before you make up your mind?"

"Sure thing, but mind's made up, Miss." He cackled, his laughter resonating through the busy kitchen. "I might even put my own little touches on some of these." He dropped a thick finger on the list of dishes. "I ain't a big fan of all that green stuff."

Oh, God Almighty. Avery would have had a stroke by now. Or stabbed the guy. Or shoved the *green* up his ass. I almost wished my pride hadn't forbidden me from calling him, because watching him deal with this would have been worth the angst choking me.

"No. We're not changing the meals twenty-four hours before the event. These are to be executed as written." *As Avery planned them.* "Why don't I give you time to look around the kitchen and go through today's deliveries while I run a couple of errands?" I needed an April break, if I was to survive the morning. I nodded curtly, and dashed towards the exit, praying my best friend would have some words of wisdom for my predicament.

April lay back in her recliner, her iPad on her belly. How she managed to type notes like that, I'd never know. She grimaced as I dropped in the chair next to her, before setting her tablet on the side table. "How is the replacement going?"

"Unless a miracle happens, this guy isn't going to manage a hundred patrons and eight different dishes." She opened her mouth as if to speak, but I stopped her. "No. I'm not calling him."

Palms raised in defeat, she shook her head. "Hey, no

harm in suggesting what you already know is common sense."

"Shut up."

"You wouldn't be here if you wanted me to shut up," she said, hands on what was left of her hips.

I sighed. She was right. "I can't call him. He's not in the country, and he's already sent me the details for the guy he recommended. It's not his fault the guy's gone MIA."

"What's the real reason, Grace?"

Mirroring my best friend's stance, I leaned back on my chair until my neck was cradled on the headrest behind me. I crossed my arms over my churning belly. "It hurts to hear his voice, so I'd rather not go through two goodbyes."

She let out a sigh. "When I thought I'd lost Jarryd before the trial... it was bad." She grabbed my fingers and squeezed them. "So, definitely not judging, sweetie."

Deep breath. Keep it together, woman. "Speaking of Jarryd. Any updates on the man?"

"Somewhat. Riley knows now. He's probably not as freaked out as we thought he would be, but he reckons he saw Cooper's enforcers both in front of the centre and home a few times."

I gasped. "No?"

She nodded. "And every time, Jarryd wasn't there. Riley thinks his father knew Jarryd's whereabouts."

"You're not saying what I think you're implying, right?"

"I wish I wasn't." She rubbed her belly, lines suddenly deepening on her forehead. "Hal's got an informant either at the centre or at The General."

"Oh god. It wouldn't be here. It'd have to be at the hospital." I racked my brain, trying to think of any newcomers with an agenda at the centre. "We know everyone. Kids and staff included. Jarryd doesn't have any enemies within these walls, and Riley even less."

April shuffled in her chair. "We're installing an upgraded security system, and Jarryd's step-dad is looking into a few leads."

Leaning forward, I reached for my friend and gave her a hug. "I'm sorry. I'm sure the dimwit will get the memo and quit soon."

Tears welled in her eyes, and she giggled, shaking them off. "Ha. Pregnancy hormones. What can I say?" She extended her hand to me and added, "Why don't we go and check on your man for tomorrow's forecast?"

The closer we got to the building, the slower April waddled. However, it had nothing to do with her pregnancy. Tango music thumped through the centre. Old, screechy beats screamed at us, not unlike the metronome of my grade-five music teacher as she threatened to whack our fingers with every wrong key. "What the hell is that?" April froze on the spot.

"I don't know?" I answered, the bones in my body shaking like a sack of dog treats.

We stepped inside the kitchen and found Paul doing some form of inventory on the stock we'd received earlier that day. In his defence, the man applied himself seriously. Lip biting, finger counting, and notebook ticking. On the bench next to him, he'd emptied the two pantries and lined up all the ingredients into piles. All he was missing was the stuff classed in alphabetical order.

"Hi, Paul. This is April, from next door." I pointed

towards the youth centre a hundred metres away from this side of the complex.

April smiled and waved at the cook. "Hello, there. Looks like a bit of a mission." She whistled. "How do you think it'll go tomorrow night?"

I cringed. Partly because, deep down, we both knew it wouldn't go the way we'd hoped. At best, we'd host somewhat of a fun networking event. At worst, I'd lose Nutrify altogether. Either way, the meals wouldn't get approval for mass production looking like this.

"What's that smell?" April beelined to the stove where a large pot was slow cooking. I followed suit. Brown stew boiled. Wide pieces of meat floated on the surface, a couple of chunky carrots and parsnip dancing around them. *What in God's name is this?*

Paul trudged towards us, a bright smile across his face. He picked up a set of spoons from the bench, excitement building through him. By the time he'd reached us, the man was glowing. He scooped up some of the casserole and passed it over. "This is a special recipe from my nonna. If it ain't making your insides warm after that." A loud chortle followed.

"It's not bad." April shrugged. "Might need a bit of salt?"

"We're not aiming for average though," I mumbled under my breath. Flashes of Avery carrying on about the importance of spices dashed in my mind: *Too much salt and you'll kill them. Not enough, you'll bore them.*

Paul pushed the second spoon to my lips. I flinched, the familiarity intrusive. Embarrassed by my reaction, I smiled and grabbed the spoon. "Thank you, Paul." *You didn't flinch when it was your chef doing it.* A heaviness assaulted my senses. It was bland. Thick. Weighty. "How much cream's in there?" My eyes grew wide when they took in the three empty plastic jars of fresh cream in the sink.

"Just enough. You ladies are beautiful as you are. No need for these silly fad diets."

My heart rate thumped in my rib cage, pain shooting through my chest. I raised a forearm to my breasts, pressing against the cardiac arrest threatening to take me down. April and I stared at each other, our mouths ajar. I must have looked ready to drop, because my best friend placed a hand on my shoulder and addressed Paul on my behalf. "I think this would be a great dish on a rainy weekend at home." He nodded, smile still pretty big. "But we're not at home on a rainy weekend." April pointed towards the blue sky outside the window. When he nodded again, this time in affirmation, she continued. "We really need to follow the plan. The plan that the head chef left for you."

A pang of guilt niggled at me. The guy was clearly a last-minute replacement, and he seemed to be trying. It really wasn't his fault that the whole launch was falling to pieces. "We appreciate your input, Paul. It must be hard to come in so late in the game. If we can stick to the plan, hopefully, it helps us all."

Paul turned down his tango and nodded towards us, his hand raised in a mock salute. We didn't follow him. Instead, we gave the man some space and grabbed ourselves chairs on the veranda at the back of the kitchen. Fresh air filled my lungs, the smell of Avery's makeshift herb garden lingering around like the warm aroma of the South of France. Behind me, a frangipani bloomed, its pink and orange flowers soothing my soul.

"What am I gonna do?" I sighed.

April picked two flowers and placed one behind her ear,

then the other behind mine. "Sometimes, we just have to have a little faith."

I tucked a strand of hair over the bud and focused on deep breathing, calling upon all the mindfulness strategies I knew of. Right when my head stopped spinning like a blender on full speed, a ping on my phone snapped me out of my trance. An email.

April shrugged, pointing at the device. "Just check it. How much worse can it get?"

I loaded the message, the official State of Queensland logo staring me in the face. I swallowed hard, my throat drowning in my own saliva.

"What does it say?"

"You've gotta be joking." I wrapped myself with my arms, fighting the shivers crawling on my skin. "The Minister for Health will be attending tomorrow to confirm the funding for the rest. I've already spent the money, even paid Avery's share already."

"Oh god." The colour drained from April's face.

A sick feeling assaulted my belly. I raised a hand to my mouth, bile threatening to follow. Tomorrow, we'd lose our tender.

Chapter 24
Avery

Presentation was vital for a chef. Whoever made up the idea that 'as long as it tasted good, the rest didn't matter' was a complete imbecile. I'd yet to see a five-star dish looking like dog shit. I prepped the yellow daffodil against the orange juice, then rearranged Sienna's breakfast until the whole tray matched better than the last three Call of Duty game covers put together.

The door creaked as my shoulder pushed into the hotel bedroom. My feet sunk into the soft carpet, each step bringing me closer to the teenager sprawled out on the queen-size bed. Four fluffy pillows. Crisp white sheets. A massive full-length mirror. I stretched my arm over my head, the pull dulling the sharp sting. Based on the aches drilling my neck and the knot in my lower back, the couch in the front room was second-grade in comparison.

Behind the curtains left ajar, the airport traffic was in full motion. Big red Qantas logos whizzed in the sky, the white noise less noticeable now. I placed the open tray on the bedside table, and in one swift move, flung the drapes open. "Good morning, sunshine!"

Sienna fussed and turned, then opened one eye before tossing a pillow at me. "Go away." She mumbled something before wrapping herself in the sheet.

"Don't make me rip the blanket off," I fake-threatened her, like I used to when she was a kid, and placed the tray next to her.

Her mouth curled. "As if. I could be naked under here."

"Oh god, don't make me lose my appetite, Shorty." I settled in the chair in the corner, a sense of ambivalence building through me with every plane that flew above us. "Look at this." My eyes switched between the palm trees, the blue skies, and the hotel pool below us, before landing back on her. "Australian lifestyle for ya."

Sienna's back pushed against the headboard, and she shuffled up until her breakfast tray fitted perfectly on her lap. She shoved a grape in the side of her cheek, her eyes going from the view outside the window to the warm croissant in front of her. She ripped a piece with her fingers. "Will you miss any of this?"

I clenched my jaw and ignored the question, mainly to save me from saying crap I'd regret later. Or making her feel bad. As much as Italy was a nice country, leaving everything and *everyone* behind left a bitter taste in my mouth. If Sienna hadn't gotten involved with Hal Cooper from day one, we'd be living the life now. *And I'd be with Grace, bracing for our big night.*

Reality slapped me in the face—more like punched me with a full fist—as I realised the word that came out of my thoughts. *Our.* I shook my head. "Your passport's good to go. We have four hours, and we're in one of those planes." I pointed to the latest take-off, the noise silencing her for the next ten seconds.

"You promised Grace I could ring Riley and say goodbye before we left."

Aggravation weighed me down. I didn't want Grace popping up in my head again. We were done. Moving on. Had found our own freaking closure. Why did she have to find a way to appear in all of my thoughts? I cracked my knuckles, my throat dry, and let a big breath escape. When Sienna narrowed her eyes at me, I leaned over, grabbed a sip of her juice, and said, "Make it quick. Don't give him details about anything. Am I clear?"

The food waltzed on the tray as Sienna jolted in bed, her eyes beaming. She clutched my phone as Riley's number loaded. The call chimed, my sister getting more and more agitated with every unanswered ring. "You plan on watching me?" she snapped, her fingers white against the device.

"Yes," I said, "in case you're... tempted to tell Riley where he might find you."

"This is worse than jail." She crossed her arms, her body turned away from me.

For you and me both, kid.

Silence spread in the room before she broke it, her voice shaking. "Riley?" When she looked like she had a handle on their conversation, I trudged to the other room, leaving the door open. Her voice resonated in the background, her tone alternating between happy, sad, and lots of things between.

Feet crossed on the coffee table, I slumped against the sofa, letting the white noise rock me to sleep like an over-tired baby. Warmth buzzed through me as I dozed just slightly, my eyes finally closing after almost twenty hours. Bits and pieces of Sienna's conversation flooded into my ears, but it was the increasing urgency in her tone that dragged me out of my slumber.

"...I have to tell him... There has to be something they can do... I'm so sorry, Riley..."

I stretched on the couch, my eyes slowly opening. In front of me, my sister marched towards me, the receiver glued to her cheek. I covered my mouth with the back of my hand as I yawned. "What's going on?"

Sienna's wide eyes stared back at me as she continued talking to her boy. "Might be quicker if I put him on the phone, and he can explain it to you."

Jesus... I swiped a hand over my face, dreading getting dragged into their affairs. Whatever Riley's issues were, truth be told, it couldn't be as bad as what we were facing if we didn't take off soon. She handed the phone to me. I dropped it on the table between us, the speaker mode bouncing Riley's greeting through the room. "How's it going, Riley?"

"Grace's going to lose her tender."

I leaned forward, my elbows resting on my knees. I wasn't getting roped into these teens' drama. The kid was almost twenty-one. There was no way he understood the business at hand here. "Mate, that's not how these things work. There's no reason she would lose her tender."

"There is, if she can't deliver your menus and whatnot."

I rolled my eyes. "Riley, I appreciate the loyalty to your mother's friend, but Grace has everything she needs. She'll be fine."

"No, she doesn—"

"Yes, she does. She has all the meal plans. The orders went in before I left, and Scott's in charge. The guy is as good as I am." Frustration sent zingers through my body. My fists opened and closed as I tried to shake the tension building.

"Your guy never turned up. Some old dude replaced him."

What the fuck? My mind reeled with Riley's information. There was no way... I grabbed my phone and scrolled to Scott's last message to me.

SCOTT

We're sweet, mate. Good to go.

"Your wires must have got crossed. Scott and I go way back. He wouldn't have just not turned up." A thought ran through my head. "Who's the old dude you're talking about?"

"I don't know. His name's Paul."

Shit. A slight sense of panic choked me. The only Paul I knew was Scott's brother-in-law. A good lad, but useless beyond a pub meal here and there. "Paul? Paul Murray?"

"No idea. Fat, old, farmer-type vibe." Things were going from bad to worse. Hand kneading the back of my neck, I prayed to the universe we were missing some important information here. I mean, after all, if things were as bad as the kid was making them out to be, Grace would have called me.

Would she? After how you've treated her? "Fuck!" I slapped the cushion to my left, dread overwhelming me. Icy blood drowned my lungs. I coughed, hoping to inhale enough air to feed my brain.

Sienna settled on the coffee table, her eyes a shade of worried. "What are you gonna do?"

The first thing I would do was have a few choice words with Scott. Then suss out how Paul was managing from there. "Give me five." At the speed of lightning, phone still on speaker, I sent Scott a barrel of *please explain*. Within a few minutes, he'd replied that his wife had pneumonia, been admitted into the hospital, and there was not much else he could do. Paul was the best he'd been able to source at such short notice.

"So?" Both Riley and Sienna called out in unison.

I shook my head. "Scott's out." I leaped to my feet and paced the room, my brain screaming a thousand things that even I couldn't quite make out. I glanced at the clock on the wall. Only a few hours before our flights.

This is fucking déjà vu.

"Help me out, Riley." I marched back towards the handset. "You're telling me that the night is going ahead, but Paul's in charge and putting spins on my meals?"

"Pretty much."

"How is she coping?" I asked, my voice deeper as my nerves took over what was left of my brain cells.

"Some big head-honchos are coming who weren't supposed to."

The thought of Grace's night being led by Paul Murray and his grandma's stew, in front of state and federal health ministers, sent me on a mental storm. Her face, her smile, her pride and excitement as we built our menu together tsunamied in my head. She didn't deserve that. She hadn't deserved any of it.

Anger flooded me. Even knowing it was all to protect Sienna didn't make me feel any better. Riley was right. If Paul was in charge of the night, and the whole event was the basis for the future funding being extended or not, Grace was done. Project zero.

"She'll lose Nutrify for good." I exhaled, my throat tight, then crumpled on the couch.

"I can't let it happen, Avery," Riley warned—an alpha side of him I'd never seen before, now kicking me in the balls. "So, you tell me how to fix it."

Sienna and I exchanged a glance. When my sister opened her mouth to talk, I pressed the mute button on the speaker. "We can't. We fly out in three hours."

She shook her head. "It's me Hal's after. It's my choice."

"Don't be fucking ridiculous," I growled. "Last I checked, the beatings had my name on them. And I'll be damned if I let you be next."

Tears welled in her eyes. "It is my fault. This whole thing is my fault, Av."

I patted the seat next to me, and she shimmied up, then snuggled against my shoulder. "It's Hal fucking Cooper's fault," I murmured into her forehead. "You were fourteen."

"I love him. Even if he doesn't love me back." She continued, her voice muffled with tears. "That's his family we've screwed over."

My head hit the back of the sofa. For a minute, I rested my eyes, ignoring Sienna's reality. Because I didn't want to admit that what she was saying was true. I'd screwed over the first woman I ever actually cared about. A woman who, despite being ditched at the last minute, rang me to ask how I was. The same woman who, instead of asking for a favour for herself, had asked me to make sure I let my sister find closure. A woman who made me feel like I mattered. Like I'd finally found my purpose. And in a couple of hours, I'd have ruined this woman and her career.

"If we skip our flight, I don't know when we'll be able to leave again."

A small nod drummed into my chest. "I know."

"Cooper could have a change of heart and come for us." I held my sister tighter.

"I know," she said again. "But I don't care. It's just wrong, and I don't want to start our new life knowing we had to screw them over to do so."

My lungs expanded as much as they could with each new breath. I inhaled the air in the room for a minute, letting the white noise of planes regulate my emotions. Once what I needed to do became clear, my tone screamed a thousand warnings. "Okay. We'll go back for a day or two, but the shrink, we stay clear of. He's in on it with Hal in some way, and until I know how deep, we say nothing to anyone."

Sienna squealed, relief pinkening her cheek. "You have my word. Thank you, big brother."

I chuckled, while she rummaged for something in my suitcase. Within seconds, my Young Chef Award jacket was placed on the table next to me, the prestigious red and blue logo kicking me in the ass. A renewed sense of conviction grew in the pit of my stomach, and a deep breath expanded my lungs, now lighter. *Go help your woman.* A smile stretched my mouth as I finally gave myself permission to stop acting like a ruthless bastard with no feelings. I unmuted the kid on the other end of the phone. "Riley?"

"Yep."

"How quickly can you put together a bunch of dishies and kitchen aids?"

Chapter 25
Grace

The cold water did nothing for my throat. No matter how much liquid I downed, it still felt like my whole body was on fire. I slammed the metal bottle on the kitchen counter of the Diamond Hotel, oblivious to the chaos going on around me. The handful of guys Paul had recruited for the launch included: Ben, a Polynesian cook, who only spoke Samoan; Jerry, who clearly had never seen the inside of an industrial kitchen; and Sam, who by the way he played on his phone, wasn't too sure what his role involved tonight.

Paul hand-signalled something to Ben. Gaging from the wide eyes, Paul was as well-versed in sign language as I was.

"Oliver," I asked one of our youths, "you reckon you can hunt down Osuelo? Pretty sure he came with the youth bus."

"The new kid from the Islands?"

I nodded. "He might be able to translate a bit faster."

Half-prepped ingredients filled the benches. Paul diced onions, taking his sweet old time, one chunk after another. Memories of Avery slicing them at the speed of lightning, his fingers dancing against the blade, filled my vision. I pushed it away, a mix of anger, despair, and frustration equally submerging my body and mind. *He abandoned you. He didn't care. Keep him out of your thoughts.*

Tonight wouldn't end well, but there was no universe where my dream would be crushed without me fighting to the death. I raised my thumb and index fingers to my forehead and massaged the flesh until the homicidal thoughts dancing to Paul's tango music quietened. A slow mental counting gave me somewhat of a grounding, and I smiled, remembering my mother's favourite saying: *When all comes crashing down, smile. At least the people around you won't hurt as much.*

A quick scan of the room brought tears to my eyes. Partly because the nightmare kept unfolding, and partly because the people driving the nightmare were somewhat trying. In front of me, Paul tangoed behind his teenage makeshift apprentice. When the kid couldn't hack the onion tears anymore, Paul chortled and tossed him a napkin.

My one-hundred-and-twenty-dollar napkins! My mouth gaped open, hyperventilation threatening to follow. First, my eyes went blurry. Then, my heartbeat jumped up and down my throat, my blood pressure promising an aneurism before the end of the night.

No, no, noooo. Around the room, the gold and burgundy napkins had found their way to every station. They served as sponges, floor mops, and hand wipes. When someone tossed a bunch on the ground to soak up some spill, I lost it. "What is wrong with you people?" The high pitch froze everyone in place. Wide eyes followed me as I dashed to every counter, piling the designer napkins in my arms until

I staggered around like a blind donkey. "These clearly aren't intended for the freaking floor!"

"I thought they looked a teeny bit fancy for us old kitchen folks." A low rumble built up from Paul's throat, but my death stare killed it instantly.

Don't you dare, old man. "I want all of these out of the kitchen." My chin motioned towards one of the guys who grabbed the napkins off me. When a few fell to the floor, blood rushing to my head and anger coursing through me, I yelled towards the back of the kitchen. "And you," I said, pointing to the guy on his phone, "get off your freaking phone and make sure that nothing a *teeny bit fancy* is left in this bloody kitchen!"

Like ants running away from a storm, the kitchen buzzed at the rhythm of my screaming. The pace increased, but we were still at least an hour behind. The onions were half-done. The tomatoes were prepped, but no one had bothered wiping away the red juice shining over everything like a tacky crime scene. Garnishes and lettuce leaves floated in semi-filled sinks, waiting to be washed and cut, and to make matters worse, no one could find the broom, so all we could do was step over the bits and pieces while praying to God no one slipped before the end of the night.

"Holy hell, what's happening in here?" Jarryd called out as he entered the kitchen. He turned, making sure the door was shut tight. "You might want to be a little quiet, 'cause some of your guests are already lining up at the front door."

"What?" I lowered my voice. "You gotta be kidding."

"I wish I was."

"I can't do this, Jar." When a tear fell, I shook my head and wiped it with the back of my hand. "This wasn't how this was supposed to pan out."

Jarryd's chest rose up and down. "I know you don't want to hear it, but you know who I blame for this, right?"

"Right now, I hate him too." I chuckled, because finding humour in the disaster was the best I could do at the moment. "Where's Riley? Did he ditch me too?"

Hands raised in the air, he answered, "I called him twice. No reply. All I got was a text that he was on his way."

"Awesome," I deadpanned.

"I'll go back and continue with the front of the house stuff. If it helps, the front looks amazing." I smiled in response, more out of politeness than anything else. As Jarryd trekked towards the exit, he called out, "Still don't want April in here?"

I shook my head. The last thing I wanted was my eight-month pregnant best friend overstepping lettuce leaves on a slippery floor, as I went psychotic on a bunch of cooks on the worst day of my life. As soon as the door closed, the kitchen commotion resumed, Paul shouting instructions right, left, and centre. Like a movie in slow motion, arms moved up and down, resuming their tasks like they were cooking a barbecue on Australia Day.

"I guess I'm the junior now," I mumbled, wrists deep in soapy water. One clean dish after another, they piled up on the sink until there was no space to load any more. A quick scan of the room and another thousand pots and pans made their way to me. "Anyone free to wipe these?" When no one answered, I called out to one of Oliver's friends by the door. "You? Can you give me a hand?" I swiped my forehead with the first tea towel I found, then passed it over to the kid.

He stared back, eyes glazed. "I don't know. I'm waiting for a lift. I was only here for the free food..." He grimaced.

"Nothing's free tonight, boy. I suggest you hang on to

this towel and start before I really get mad." I flung the flannel towards him, and this time, he grabbed it.

"Yes, Miss."

"Paul..." Behind me, Jerry called out to his boss. My ears pricked. "'Tis a bit hot in here. Any chance we can get some air-con going?"

The knot in my throat hurt like hell. As did my head, my stomach, and my back. Thousands of pins and needles trod through my muscles like an invisible shredder, and with every second, my body begged to just surrender to my mind. Especially when surrounded by a bunch like these.

You're no quitter, Grace Lawson. Get a grip. I closed my fists tight, my jaw clenching. The saccharine smile pasted on my face didn't quite fool the moron in front of me. "Jerry, how many commercial kitchens, especially in a hotel, have you seen with regular air-con?"

He stared at me in silence, as if a gust of air had blown his brains back to the village he came from.

"Why don't you ask Paul what's next?" Right as I was fantasising about punching in his off-white teeth, the door burst open and Riley and seven of the youths barged in. "Riley, you came," I said, slight relief running through me.

Riley scanned the kitchen as his friends fell into place, as if they'd been prepped with directions. "Why don't you go and change for your big speech."

I blew a breath, swallowing tears as I thanked him. "It's a lovely idea, Riley. It really is. But there'll be no speech tonight." I pointed to the clock above him. "The launch is meant to go live in ninety-five minutes—"

"A good thing I only need sixty," a familiar tone said. It was laced with authority, confidence, and warmth. I closed my eyes, my breathing growing shallow. My feet refused to turn around, and I stood there, goosebumps crawling up my arms. *It couldn't be.* My body trusted his voice more than my mind did, and a cyclone of emotions swirled in the pit of my stomach. It grew in intensity, paralysing me on the spot, until Avery's breath tickled my cheek from behind. "I'm sorry."

A wave of adrenaline took over my being. It warmed me, like a security blanket suddenly wrapping me up for comfort. Then, hysteria threatened to run me over like a freight train, and I slapped his chest with my fists until all the fear, anger, and angst of the last few days had melted against his pecs.

"Let me fix this." His arms hugged my waist while he waited for my fists to stop pounding him. "No one is killing your dream on my watch, Gracey."

My heart melted and I placed my hands over his, surrendering to how amazing it felt to be in his arms again. My head leaned back against his collarbone. "You came," I whispered, as if saying it out loud would make him vanish.

"We can do this." Avery grabbed my shoulders and turned me around until I faced him. Then, his palms gently cradled my cheeks.

As soon as my brain accepted him, relief overpowered me. A part of me was still angry at him, but the other part— the part that was staring at the crisp clean jacket, the strong arms, and the unspoken promise—*that part* fused against him. "I missed you."

The normally confident chocolate orbs shone a different light today. Avery swallowed hard, his gaze going from my eyes to my lips. I licked them, closed my lashes, and ignored the chaos around us as his head lowered to mine.

Chapter 26
Avery

Grace's lips tasted as good as I remembered. Soft. Warm. Hungry. Touching her had always felt nice, but kissing her, in my kitchen, as she held on to me as if her life depended on it, was a kick-ass feeling. Like finally admitting this woman belonged with me.

"I've missed you too." I lowered my face again until my lips reached hers. She opened her mouth, her tongue welcoming mine. Her hands settled on my chest, her fingers fisting my jacket. Her scent filled my nostrils. A mix of floral, sweetness, and sweat. She broke the kiss, our foreheads touching. I pushed a strand of hair behind her ear. "Are you ready?"

She nodded. "About time, Chef."

Behind us, the kitchen chaos had frozen in time, every station more messed up than the last. A few metres away, Paul gave me a mock salute before making his way over. I met him halfway and extended a hand. "How's it going, Paul. Thanks for holding down the fort. I appreciate it."

The man grinned and placed his other palm on my shoulder. "On ya, mate. Should I just hit the road now?"

"Hell no. I need a 2IC. And if we pull this off, I know the head chef at Beaudesert Hotel. I hear they're looking for a good sous. Let's get this party started, I say. What do you reckon?"

Behind me, Grace fiddled with her phone and Paul's speaker. Her eyes bored into mine, a sassy smirk lighting up her face. Then, "Livin' on a Prayer" blasted through the kitchen.

My playlist... Emotions shook me. She'd never given up on herself. On her project. This woman was something. When most people would have dragged me out by the balls for taking off in the first place, Grace was still Grace. Warm. Forgiving. Loving. A strange feeling wrapped itself around my insides. A mix of adrenaline, possession, and *safety*. I'd never belonged anywhere like this before.

"It's time for you to claim your lair, Chef." She grinned as she turned the sound down and nodded towards the madness.

I slipped two fingers in my mouth and whistled until every single body in the room had turned to look in my direction. "We're on a timer, so I won't repeat anything twice. Everything gets done my way, and I promise it'll be worth it."

Riley gathered his team and pointed at various stations before confirming our plan. "We've got all the prep under control. Then we'll take care of the sides, leaving the important bits ready for you big boys." He slapped my back and charged towards the sink full of lettuce leaves.

Grace rolled her sleeves up, palms out. "Tell me what to do."

I glanced around the room. The kitchen was filthy. Even a blind inspector would have failed our food permit. "Can you get all the dirty towels out to the laundry and find us some clean aprons?" She nodded, but before she moved, I added, "And after that, the only place I want to see you is in your change room getting ready for your big speech."

"Are you sure?"

I gently grabbed the back of her neck and pulled her towards me for a quick hug. Truth be told, now that I had her in front of me, I felt this incredible need to hold her.

Her fingers squeezed my forearm. "Really sure?" she asked again, hesitation in her voice.

I pressed my lips to her forehead, then tapped her on the ass. "Trust me. We've got this. Go!"

She giggled and dashed out, picking up a trail of dirty laundry on her way. Within a few minutes, the room was clean enough for a kitchen in the middle of a service. *Amazing what a little teamwork can do.*

A quick glance at the clock above the sink, and it was time to speed things up. I checked every station for progress, from the meats to the veggies steaming. I forked a piece of pork filet in red wine just as Paul watched me like a hawk. The slow-cooked meat melted in my mouth, the sauce a perfect blend of fresh tomatoes, herbs, and spices. I whistled as I sampled the first of our meals for the night. This one was ready to go. "Paul, my man... I'm impressed."

He beamed, pride reddening his chubby cheeks. Then he turned to his pan, his efforts doubling. If we kept this up, we'd definitely be back on track in no time.

A few metres away, Riley and Oliver took turns cooking different veggies: broccolini, cauliflower, pumpkin, leek, capsicum, and sweet potatoes all steamed nicely. I pricked them. When the sides came back cooked to perfection, I fist-bumped both kids. "Good lads. Now, find a Nutribullet and puree me some pumpkins and peas. We'll add them as background for presentation and final touches."

"You got it, Chef," the boys called out at the same time, pride in their tones. Within seconds, the blender whizzed behind me. Feeling lighter, I moved to the next station where two Polynesian fellows worked together on our fish dish. New Zealand hoki finished grilling under the heating light. A bed of mango salsa waited, ready to be added to the white flesh.

The older of the two turned towards me. "I lou nuu, o le auala lenei tatou te kuka ai ia."

Head tilted towards the younger guy, I waited for some form of translation. "My name is Osuelo. This is Ben," he greeted, before extending his hand towards me. "He said: this is how they cook fish in his village."

I glanced at the perfectly seared meat, light grey strokes lining the fresh fish. "Tell him that I'm grateful for both of your help. It looks great."

Ben grinned. "Ou te folafola atu o le a latou fiafia i ai, kuka."

Osuelo laughed. "Of course, they'll love it."

Confidence rocking me, I finished my rounds until all meals had been tasted and expertly plated, ready to be presented to the hundred patrons behind the kitchen walls. Satisfied we had it under control, I snuck out and caught a glimpse of the crowd eyeing Grace on the stage. When my sight connected with the usually casual woman, I froze. Mouth ajar, I shuffled to make room for my cock, now stirring in the chef pants. The slow, sweet burn had me on fire within seconds.

Fuck. It wasn't like she wasn't beautiful every other day. But God, as she stood there, in her tight little midnight dress, oozing confidence and sex appeal—Jesus Almighty— she was the hottest woman I'd ever laid eyes on. I closed my eyelids for a second, ordering my animal instincts to stand down. Finally, when they had, I retreated back into the kitchen where the front house manager was waiting with the staff on standby, ready to roll.

Excitement buzzed through the whole kitchen. Eight meal variances. All dietetics approved. Out of this world flavours. We'd achieved nothing short of a miracle in less than sixty minutes. *I'll be damned.*

When Riley pointed towards the music speaker, Sienna not far from him, I nodded. If ever there was a time to celebrate, today would be it. "We Are the Champions" thundered through the room and everyone cheered. I laughed, a new sensation running through me. As I watched my sister with Riley, a little voice by the name of Hal Cooper nagged at my subconscious. When it grew louder, I squashed the bastard, dormant pain and denial mocking me. "All right, guys, let's have a five-minute break, followed by another five for clean-up and then we'll start on desserts."

Within a few minutes, the kitchen was back in business. After making sure everyone knew their assigned roles, I plonked myself in front of a bunch of pineapples and cut them into wedges.

"What's your dessert?"

Without turning around, I passed a chunk of fruit to Sienna. "Grilled pineapples with Greek yoghurt sauce and pistachios."

She grabbed my offering, then leaned against the counter in front of me. "I'm so proud of you."

"You realise you're the *little* sister here, right?" I cocked an eyebrow, smirking at the irony. "But I'm proud of you too."

"Riley said they're loving the meals. Jarryd told him."

A weird calmness flooded me, my shoulders dropping. *Thank God for miracles.* "Did you ever doubt my mad skills?" I teased, and passed her another piece of pineapple. "Last one. Pretty sure that's not how commercial cookery is supposed to work."

She winked, then shoved it in her mouth and pushed herself off the counter, trekking behind me to join the other youths, no doubt.

"I love you."

I chuckled, and without glancing back, held more fruit to my side. "Stop distracting me, Shorty. I have a dessert to fini—"

"No. I love you."

An electrical current zapped me, a mix of panic and ecstasy as the voice registered in my head. *That's not Sienna.* Grace ambled in front of me, her gait slow. For a split-second, I didn't recognise her features, because her blue eyes were laced with something new. Courage? Angst? A cross between lust, love, and apprehension. Instantly, seeing her so vulnerable triggered me, and I grabbed her hand, pulling her closer.

I wish I could just say it back. It wasn't like I didn't love her—at least I thought I did—but life had taught me one thing: love wasn't enough. Every time I loved someone, shit happened. First Dad, then Mum, then Sienna. Acknowledging feelings to the universe jinxed us to get fucked around for good. I wasn't risking that with Grace. Especially without knowing what the future held with Cooper.

"Do you know how beautiful you are?" I kissed her cheek. "How hot and sexy?" I kissed her other cheek, and she giggled, pushing my chest away with one hand. I moved to the crook of her neck, murmuring deep into her collarbone. "You are the most resilient, self-assured, confident..." I nibbled at the flesh before I finished. "...woman I have ever met."

An awkward silence followed. When she tried to pull away, I tugged her back, and she clung onto my fingers. "Thank you for saving the day. Everything was perfect."

"Grace, you're the one who saved the day. That's just who you are."

The door burst open, and we both jumped at the shrieking that ensued, letting go of each other's hands in the process. April and the shrink stepped into the kitchen. He and I exchanged a curt nod, while his wife's attention was fully zoned in on Grace. "Oh my god. You did it!" April waddled until she had her best friend tucked between her arms and her massive stomach.

Jarryd followed and settled by the counter. "Good to see you back." The way he locked his eyes on mine said more than the words that came out of his mouth. Clearly, not everyone was as forgiving as Grace.

Try to run and tell Cooper, you fuckwit.

"Grace, the Honourable Mark Price would like to introduce himself," a voice called out from behind the door, and within seconds, both Grace and April had left the room.

Jarryd took a step towards me. "She's a good person. She doesn't deserve to be screwed around if your plan is to take off again."

Great. Way to ruin my night. I narrowed my eyes to slits. "Don't worry about me."

"It's not you I'm worried about." He snatched a piece of pineapple and tossed it in his mouth. "She's family, so you've been warned."

My grip tightened around the six-inch blade slicing through the fruits. "Get the fuck out of my kitchen."

In complete silence, Jarryd pushed through the door, leaving me alone with the thoughts running through my head. I pulled my shoulders back and took a calming breath.

The Cooper leach wouldn't go near her. Because Grace was my family now too, and there was no way I'd let another one of Hal's thugs get their hands on more members of my family.

No matter what it took.

Chapter 27
Grace

"We have been more than impressed, Ms Lawson," the federal health minister said, on behalf of his state counterpart. "I don't normally get invested locally, but Nutrify is just too good to be true."

Excitement and pure bliss sparked inside me. It consumed me. My mind. My body. My soul. After years of growing up in a loving family who couldn't afford decent food, this project meant more to me than anything else I'd ever done. Months of hard work, sleepless nights, eighteen-hour days, and fighting with myself to never give up—my moment was finally here. "It's my pleasure. There's a whole team of people behind this project, but we all share the same goal." I pointed towards the kids regrouping by Legacy's youth workers. "These kids come from difficult backgrounds. This is all for them, and other kids like them around the country." *Kids like me.*

"I'll leave this in the hands of my very capable colleagues in Queensland, but I'm hoping we might be able to chat more about a national expansion down the track."

My cheeks hurt from smiling. I shook their hands, grabbing their cards and promising an update on the commercial side of the project soon. Then, I collapsed onto one of the chairs, my fingers picking at crumbs on the deep burgundy tablecloth. Background laughter resonated in the hall. I waved at April, who was organising the kids for the night, and Riley, in charge of forming groups.

"Should I be worried about my sister?" Next to me, Avery pulled up a seat and settled. Fine lines marked his face, his white jacket covered in stains. He looked shattered.

"Absolutely not. They've hired a hall for the kids to bunk, and there're like ten youth workers supervising them all," I confirmed. Avery raised his eyebrows, the unspoken question lingering in the air. I chuckled. "Boys and girls are split, and both Jarryd and Riley are in charge of the guys. Other than a good movie or a trivia game, there'll be nothing happening with any of them tonight. Trust me on that."

The grooves on his forehead smoothed out. He shook his head, lips curling slightly. "I must sound like a psycho to you."

I placed my hand on his, our eyes locking. "Absolutely."

A spontaneous laugh came out of Avery's belly. Timid at first, but growing by the second. Judging from the way he bent over, a hand covering his stomach, he hadn't expected my comeback. From deep inside his chest came a shaking motion, and his abs contracted with every spasm.

I folded my arms, my poker face vanishing, and a giggle escaped my throat. "Didn't expect that, did ya?"

He settled, a finger wiping an invisible tear. "Nope. Can't say that I did." Catching our breaths, a few seconds went by while we watched the kids leave the lobby to enjoy the rest of their night. Avery's hand brushed mine. "It would be nice if everything was that easy, hey?"

"Being a grownup sucks sometimes." My fingers grazed

his back, until our pinkies interlocked. "But it's good some-times too."

His Adam's apple bopped. He swallowed hard. "Is it bad if all I'm thinking about is how hot you were on that stage tonight?"

Heat burned my cheeks. *Not as bad as me thinking about you watching me on that stage.*

I slowly rose to my feet and sashayed the metre sepa-rating us. Inviting me in, Avery spread his legs until I fit perfectly between them, then locked me in with his hands. I placed my palms on his shoulders, while lowering my fore-head to his. His fingers rubbed the tops of my thighs, circling as they edged towards my ass. I clenched my core, feeling myself dampen with every stroke. I inhaled him, like an addict looking for her next fix. "God..."

His grip on my hips kept me anchored to him. He pulled me in closer, his head dropping to my breasts. "You drive me crazy."

My hand crawled up to the base of his head, and I pushed his mouth deeper into my chest. He groaned, one hand now travelling underneath my dress to cradle my ass. I gasped when his fingers cupped my cheek and kneaded it. As if my moaning encouraged him, he shuffled on his seat and plunged his mouth into my neckline, nibbling at the flesh popping out of the cocktail dress, now threatening to burst. My moaning grew louder, and his body tensed in response. His dick stirred through his pants and my pelvis rammed into it, two magnets moving against their will. I dipped my face until our mouths connected, then pressed my tongue through his lips. He growled before gently biting my bottom lip.

Then, he froze, and the hands on my hips forced me back. "Wait." His lungs exhaled shallow breaths. "We keep this up, and I'm bending you over this table. I don't care who's watching."

Around us, a couple of waitstaff finished clearing the hall. When two giggly waitresses avoided my stare, I caved in and stepped back. Instantly, my body craved him, and I leaned on my chair, clenching my thighs while ignoring the painful throbbing between my legs. I closed my eyes, taking slow breaths. "Wow." Soft lips kissed the top of my hand, and I smiled, eyes still shut until my body stopped screaming inside. "Sienna's with the kids tonight."

"Mmmm." His tongue tasted each of my knuckles.

"Come up for a while," I rasped. When he nodded, we marched to the hotel elevator, my hand in his. As soon as the elevator door opened, Avery motioned me inside. I stepped in and pressed the button to our floor, holding my breath. New darkness flooded his eyes as he studied me. A shade of pink had my cheeks on fire. And filled with embarrassing lust, I immediately looked away from the mirror.

"You're hot," Avery whispered in my ear, one palm on the wall above my head, boxing me in. Deep, smouldering eyes looked back at me, his pecs moving up and down with each breath. And suddenly, the energy in the lift changed until we were both hanging on to one another, anticipation igniting the air. We were out of the elevator within seconds and tucked inside the hotel room a few seconds after that. The door slammed behind him, and he paused, his eyes devouring every part of my body. Desire consumed me, my legs threatening to buckle under my weight. I'd never felt so wanted before.

"Fuck," he growled, with a low rumble I didn't recognise. A desperation new to us both. Then, like he flipped a switch, Avery lunged at me, pinning my back against the wall with both my wrists held by one of his hands, while the other explored the skin under my dress. My calf locked behind his knee, granting him more room. As if given permission, he dropped my arms and hoisted me higher, his hands under my ass, my pussy rubbing against the hard bulge in his pants. "God, I have to have you," he grunted. "Tell me you want me too."

I cupped his face and forced his mouth to kiss me. "Shut up. We're not twelve. Fuck me already."

A light chuckle left him, quickly replaced by urgency. "I thought you'd never ask." His arms carrying me like I weighed nothing, he marched to the bedroom and lowered us both onto the bed. I tossed the pillows to the ground, shuffling higher so I could examine him better as he popped his jacket off. Under the white material, Avery's chiselled abs moved with every breath, his tattoos telling a thousand stories. Thick biceps flexed as he unbuckled his pants, and he trudged out of them in record time before hovering above me. "I think you're overdressed."

"I might be," I teased while raising myself on my elbows so he could unzip me. I shimmied out, the dress landing softly on the floor while leaving me in nothing but underwear.

A foot gently kicked my legs open, and Avery settled between. Then, he cupped my breast and kissed my nipple, a gentle lick giving me a glimpse of what heaven would be like being loved by this man. "You're so beautiful."

Heat drove me mad. Like a possessed woman, I clawed at his forearms, no longer able to hold the moans ripping from my throat. *God, let him take me.* I wanted him like I'd never wanted another man before.

His hands trailed up and down my thighs, and in a swift motion, my panties were tossed away. He stared into my eyes as his fingers teased my entrance. First, they rubbed my lips up and down, and then, spreading my wetness, they circled around my core until I threatened to burst. Mouth ajar, eyes squeezed shut, I begged for relief, my fingers digging into his shoulders. "Avery, please."

"Look at me." A certain authority had my eyes opened and locked on his within seconds. "I want to see you when I make you come." A finger plunged into me, and I moaned loudly as his thumb flicked my clit, then gently rolled it. Ecstasy built, my groin drenched, and when he pushed his digit deeper, I whimpered, arching my body into his. "Let go, Grace."

Oh god... A thousand electrical currents zapped me until every atom in my body was set alight, a mix of pleasure and pain. An earth-shuttering orgasm blasted my core, and I clung onto him like he controlled every bit of it. When my body returned to the surface, my mind racing and my breathing ragged, Avery gently kissed me on the mouth, his tongue swallowing the oxytocin oozing out of me.

"Are you ready for more?" he whispered in my ear as he leaned over, took his boxers off, and slid a condom on at the speed of lightning.

I nodded, my body unable to form words. He placed his hands on each side of my head and settled over me until his erection carefully lined up with my hungry pussy. Then, he grabbed on to my knee, lifting it up slightly and slammed into me as he groaned with each thrust. Shifting onto his elbows, Avery moved in and out of my core, faster and faster, his breathing matching mine. Another orgasm built inside me, and my body quivered, in sync with every one of his grunts. Finally, I exploded around him, my insides pulsing and gripping him until he collapsed on top of me.

"Fuck me dead." His voice was strained. Then he chuckled and kissed me on the cheek, before opening his arm to me. I snuggled against him, eyes closed, feeling safe for the first time in ages.

An hour later, as he dozed off, I studied the man asleep at my side, emotions swallowing me. I'd never felt anything like this ever before. Not the incredible sex. Not the warm pillow talk that followed. I kissed his bare shoulder, making sure not to wake him. "I love you," I whispered, my heart filled with so many emotions.

I just wish you could say it back.

Chapter 28
Avery

Last night, a version of Grace I'd never seen before had been unleashed. The woman had breathed fire through every one of her pores, but as we waited for our breakfasts to be served, in her pink little dress and white heels, she was back to being the professional—prim and proper—authority in the room. *My private little minx.*

"It looks fine," I said, my eyes scanning the décor of the restaurant and the dishes being served to other patrons.

"I'm starving." She poured us some juice.

My big Aussie breakfast was brought to the table. Across from me, the waiter delivered Grace's low-fat yoghurt, fruits, and English muffins. "Mine looks like the Devil's breakfast in comparison to yours," I joked. I pointed to the blueberries and sliced bananas with my knife. "Though those look juicy, I won't lie."

She popped a berry in her mouth, the corners of her lips rising. "You ain't getting my blueberries, Chef. Don't even think about it."

The bacon crunched under my teeth. Salty, fatty,

crispy. Just the way bacon should be. "Tell me, did you always want to be a dietician?"

Grace paused, cogs turning in her brain. Her fork clunked when it hit her plate. She left it there, her jam not making it to her muffin. "Yes and no. There's a story behind it. How much time do we have?"

"A little." I shoved some eggs in my mouth, wiping my lips with my napkin.

She took another sip of juice and pushed her plate away from her. "I come from a family of very hard-working people. My mum had two jobs; she worked at a servo during the day and packed shelves at night. My dad, he was a truck driver." I nodded, urging her to continue. I could see where she'd got her work ethics from. "I'm the oldest of three. A younger brother and a younger sister. Both quite nice." She took another gulp of her drink, this time, swallowing it slowly like she was deciding what version of the story to lay down. "I just don't want you to think anything bad about them, you know?"

Why would I do that? I put my fork down, waiting for the punchline. "Not at all."

Grace smiled, a smile that didn't quite reach her eyes. The pink in her face was long gone. "Short story, we were poor. There was never enough money for bills, so we had to sacrifice where we could."

"Most families do. Doesn't make them bad."

"No, it doesn't."

"But?"

She sighed, and I refilled her drink. Her fingers played with the condensation on her glass, tracing shapes until it was all gone. "Food is what we sacrificed."

Shit. I stacked my plate over hers, making room, and grabbed her hand. She gripped on to my fingers.

"Our diet consisted of toast, baked beans, and lots of water."

"I'm sorry."

She shook her head. "Please, don't be. I don't want any pity. We were loved and that's what matters the most." Making people feel better in shit circumstances, *that* was the shrink's job. Me, I barely managed to not get stabbed when opening my mouth, so I waited—in awkward silence —until she decided to talk again. "You know what people are like. Gossips and bloody wannabe saviours. They didn't understand, so my parents got a few visits from Child Safety, and we suffered the constant interrogations for the next few years until I could get a job and help out."

"That must have been tough," I said, wishing I could offer something deeper. Instead, I rubbed my thumb over the pad of her hand.

"Anyway, what better job than to design affordable food that tastes am-az-ing." Pink slowly crept back to her cheeks.

"Food's the bomb," I joked, the mood growing lighter.

"What about you?" She picked a piece of bacon off my plate and shoved it in her mouth. When I eyed her, she laughed, her index finger touching her lips and shushing me.

"I was a bit of a rebel. Dad was out of the picture since day one pretty much, and Mum, she was in and out of weird relationships. I left school in year ten to do a full-time apprenticeship. I was barely fifteen, so greed got the better of me, and I didn't do much for the next year. In all honesty, I was too busy getting drunk and high to care about finishing my cert."

"Why am I not surprised?" Grace chuckled, then handed me the last piece of bacon before she licked her fingers. "Eat it. I don't want to be tempted."

I grabbed it and tossed it in my mouth. "When I was in my twenties though, Mother Dearest got with her latest guy. He was bad fucking news. Fraud, drugs, dicey as hell. They took off one fine day, never to be seen again."

Her mouth dropped. "Seriously? Where was Sienna?"

I grimaced. "The kid was barely ten. Don't get me wrong, we were in good terms, but I'd had nothing to do with her for years. There's a fifteen-year difference between us. It's not like we grew up together."

"What happened?" Grace leaned forward, like she was watching the ending of a Hollywood blockbuster.

"The school called me. They'd dropped her off in the morning and never picked her up. I took her home, and before I knew it, she was glued to my bloody hip." I chuckled, the memory not that distant. What I didn't tell Grace was how hard the first couple of years were. From her tantrums, to her missing her old life, to her involvement with Hal Cooper's gang and what followed from there.

That's why we can't stay. No matter how much I want to.

I sighed. "I'd be lying if I said, given the choice, I would have picked this. But now that she's here, we're a package deal. I love her like my own kid." I stifled a cough, emotions building. Shame burnt the tip of the fingers still caressing Grace's hand, and like a coward, I let her go. I leaned back against my chair, a sick feeling boiling in my gut.

She flinched at the sudden disconnection. "You okay?"

No. "Yep."

She cocked a brow. "Something just happened. Tell me what it was."

A deep breath stabbed my lungs. I let it go slowly. I loved Sienna. I would take a bullet for that kid. But I was seriously falling for Grace. She was the best thing that'd happened to me in the last few years, and yet, I continued to betray her. "It's complicated."

"Because you make it so."

It was fucking cruel that I had to choose. *Maybe you don't have to.* Like a giant fist had punched me in the stomach, I froze, processing the batshit crazy thought skipping through my head. "Have you ever considered moving overseas?"

"Can't say that I have?" She tucked some hair behind her ear. "Why?"

Because it's the only way to give us a chance. "To get away from... things?"

She folded her arms across her chest, her head tilted to the side. "I think we've established a while back that there were *things* you should probably talk about. Why don't we start at the beginning?"

My fingers raked the top of my head a thousand times, like it would magically give me some answers. "Baby, if I could, I'd tell you." I downed some water before I continued. "I just want to keep everyone safe."

"I've heard this before," she deadpanned. "Let's be real, Avery, and cut the BS. You wouldn't be asking me about moving overseas unless there was a reason. Spill it."

"Wow. I didn't realise we'd moved into therapy territory."

"No, but I can read between the lines. You're about to take off again, aren't you?"

"I never said that."

She sighed, shaking her head. "Tell me I'm wrong."

You're not. A war between honesty and deceit, all in the name of self-preservation, raged deep inside my brain. Like two caged lions fighting to the death, my head and my heart bled until neither of them made sense to me anymore. *It doesn't matter what you do. You won't end up with her and a white picket fence. Who are you kidding?*

When the awkwardness stretched for far too long, she broke the silence, her tone beaten. "How can you keep doing this to me?"

"This isn't what I pla—" A tear fell on the table, and I shifted forward to reach her.

Avoiding my gaze, she jerked her hands away. "Don't." Her tone was cold, her pupils dark. I studied her, but all I could see was a stranger now. She'd slammed her heart shut; the woman who'd worshipped me like a god hid behind some big fucking walls.

Can you blame her? "Everything that happened between us, it was special."

She scoffed. "Listen, let's call it for what it was. A good fuck for the tough guy in transit." Our eyes met. Narrowed. A slight twinge of irritation zapped me as her voice dripped with ice.

"Seriously?"

"I can't help you if you don't wanna be helped."

My jaw clenched. "I don't need saving."

She grabbed a paper napkin, her fingers ripping it into tiny shreds as she blew a loud breath. "Pretty sure you're running away from yourself. For no good reason."

A jackhammer barged into my head at her comment, the invisible pounding thinning my resolve. My throat clenched, and I swallowed hard. *My reason is your BFF's fucking husband.*

I motioned the waiter for the bill. "I think we're done here." *Sounds like the universe laughed at you once again, you moron.*

She stopped me by the wrist before I could stand.

"Avery, it doesn't have to be like this. Don't ruin *us* before we've had a chance to even be."

Emotions drifted in and out of me like broken flags on a bad wind day. I sighed. "Just come with us. We can take Nutrify to Rome." My voice broke thin. God, I hated being so weak. "Let me love you there."

Another tear fell on her cheek. "I can't. I have my life here. Jarryd and April are my family now, and with the baby com—"

"Fucking Jarryd. Always in the way," I snarled, jumping to my feet. I dropped a fifty on the table and marched off.

"Jarryd is a good friend." Grace followed, her pace struggling to keep up with me. "What's your beef with him."

"Nothing. He's a god."

Planting herself in front of me, she yanked my chest hard, her palms flat. Her face was flushed, her eyes bright, and her breasts heaved with each breath. "Enough."

A couple of patrons looked our way as she yelled at me in the middle of the hotel courtyard. The betrayal stinging, I avoided her gaze. *You have no idea who you're choosing over us.*

A thousand volts of anguish tortured every fibre of my being. It hurt. An ache from deep inside, a buried pain bubbling up to the surface erupted in that instant. "Your precious doctor isn't perfect, you know?" I tossed my phone across the table. One of the many newspaper articles I'd found last night stared her in the face.

Psychiatry registrar accused of drug dealing to kids in care.

Grace paled. "How did you find out?"

There it is. The admission that the good doctor is nothing but a drug fuckwit. Mixed emotions slapped me. On one hand, I'd hoped I was wrong. For his family. But on the other, it made my job easier now. *That* was the connection to Cooper. The good doctor had buried his indiscretion well, but underneath the pretty boy façade, he was no different from the drug lord who'd ruined Sienna's life.

"Does it matter?"

"It does to me." She ran a hand over her face, taking a deep breath. "Listen, this is all past us now. It was years ago."

I scoffed, ogling her. "Dealing drugs to kids? Not a big deal?"

"It's not my story to tell," she murmured as we stepped into the hotel foyer. Her demeanour was flat, her glare cast down. "Please."

I caught Sienna from the corner of my eyes, her bag waiting by the door of yesterday's dining room. As if fucking staged, she followed Riley like a lost puppy, his parents sitting on the couch across from them, their cosy little setup making me want to claw at my eyes with a fork. "Not your story to tell?" I snarled, but before she could stop me, I stormed into the dining room, ready to get answers.

Chapter 29
Avery

I *'m done with the games.* It took a second for my brain to register the scene in front of me. It unfolded in slow motion, every bone in my body cringing, every neuron in my brain firing. But my limbs, they remained frozen in place. Sienna lounged on the hotel chaise, the bloody kid next to her, and across, the shrink and his wife. Laughing. Comfortable. *Happy.* When was the last time I'd seen Sienna genuinely happy?

A thousand shards of ironic glass shattered what was left of my heart. First Grace, now Sienna. I'd spent the last year trying to undo Cooper's damage, putting my own aspirations on hold to protect everyone, and instead of finally living the life in Rome, she danced with the devil's spawn. My breath hitched, my heart rate pounding in my chest like nails in a coffin. Mine. *You gotta be kidding me?*

"Can I have a word?" I barked, storming into the hotel foyer. Fists clenched and my jaw tight, my forearms twitched with every step towards the bastard. If he thought he was dragging my sister back to the underworld, he had another thing coming.

Jarryd glanced up, then pushed himself from the couch, nodding. "Away from them."

Tension increased in the room, only made worse by the complete silence suddenly drowning us. April narrowed her eyes—some weird question in the air—but before she said anything, Grace rushed to her side. "Why? Don't they know about your side gig?" I snarled. Based on the looks they gave each other, they did.

"He knows," Grace confirmed, goosebumps raised on her arms.

"Knows what?"

Grace tilted her chin towards Riley. When the kid noticed the gesture, he leaped to his feet, standing by Jarryd within seconds. *The kid's in on it too.*

April paled, a hint of panic spreading over her features. I took a step back, guilt flooding me, and unclenched my fists. Hurting families was Cooper's thing. Maybe Jarryd's too. But not mine.

"Relax, April. I just want a word with *him*."

"What's going on?" Sienna plonked herself in front of me. Brow arched, she looked older than her seventeen years. I prayed to God that I wasn't too late. If Jarryd'd got her back in with the gang, I'd have more than words with the tosser. When Riley grabbed her hand, dragging her behind him, I flinched.

"Go finish packing, Sienna." I pointed towards her suit-case by the door, my lips barely moving as I spat the words. No twenty-year-old punk would have more influence on my sister than me. Not after the last seven years.

"What's the issue, Avery?" Jarryd took a step away from April and the kids. "Why don't we leave the family to enjoy the day, and go chat in private?"

April clung onto his fingers and shook her head. "You're not going anywhere without me."

A weird feeling swam in my gut, confusion overwhelming me. How could she know he was a drug dealer meddling with kids and still ooze undying love for him this way? Something didn't add up.

The shrink placed a quick kiss on her cheek, one hand brushing her stomach, and added, "He just wants to have a chat. I'll be okay, baby."

"Dude, I'm telling you right now: we're having this conversation with or without them, but I'll be damned if I let these kids think you're God Almighty."

Grace spun towards me and placed her arm on mine. Her lip wobbled. "There's a lot you don't understand."

"Clearly," I deadpanned. The walls around my heart built faster than a Tetris tower. I could cope with the shrink being shady. No matter how pissed I'd be, I could cope with Sienna's teenage brain being roped into it again. But what I would not cope with was finding out that everything about Grace had been a lie.

Grace's shoulders shifted up and down, her fingers shaking against my skin. "It's not what you think. Please, can we just leave it at that?"

I scoffed. "How can you stand here and think it's all good?"

"Why don't you mind your own business? Just an idea," Riley growled, before turning towards his dad. "I'm done with this. April's not looking too flash right now. Come on, Jar, let's go."

My breath caught in my throat as Riley squared his shoulders and shifted on his feet. Behind him, April leaned against the couch, a hand on her back.

"Kid, let the grownups do the talking." When he took a

step towards me, I kept him in place with a firm palm on his shoulder "Last warni—"

Before I could finish, a blow shook me off balance, my head confused for the next five seconds. I turned to the side, ignoring the sting on my lower jaw. Jarryd braced himself, legs spread and shoulders pulled back. "You don't lay a hand on my family. That's just a friendly reminder." His tone resonated in the room. His eyes, confident, stared back at me.

"No, you'd just rather lay into other people's families." My fingers twitched, my lungs burning from the built-up anger of the last seven years, but right as I launched at him, he moved sideways and avoided the blow to his stomach.

"What the hell are you talking about?"

I raised my foot and slammed it down on his shin, before curling my hands and raising them to my face. "I'm talking about you dealing drugs to innocent kids."

He crouched into a fighting position. "What? You think you know me 'cause you read a press release from over six years ago?"

I matched his stance, the adrenaline fuelling my body like a junkie with his fix. "Now, the true colours come out. At least you've stopped pretending you're the good doctor."

His eyes turned black, then he charged forward, striking my ribs over and over like a madman unleashed. Each blow pounded into me as if his family's life depended on it. I leaned into him, our shoulders touching. *He's fighting for his survival. What gangster fears for his family like this?*

A small arm shoved in front of us, Grace pushed through our hard frames until her whole body was sandwiched between the shrink and me. "Enough!"

Rapid breaths drove my chest in and out, my vision blurred from the rush pumping through my blood. Behind

Grace, Jarryd was a mirror image of me. Consumed with rage and fear, his body readied to strike again, but the second April touched him, he melted against her.

"Look at me," Grace whispered, her hands around my face. "Just me." A version of her glared back. A mix of pain and frustration etched her clammy cheeks. Beads of sweat dripped from her forehead. "No more." Her voice was thin, her touch unsure.

Shame filled me. I hated the guy for what he did, but I never meant to scare Grace. Or the wife. "How can you be okay with him dealing drugs to kids?" I murmured into her collarbone, my arms grabbing on to her tight; a weird need to be loved by her overpowering everything else. I lost the will to fight. All I wanted was an end to the nightmare. Years of fighting Cooper's underground world, willing Sienna safe, for what? We were back to square one. "How can I protect you and my sister from yourselves?" I whispered, my throat so tight it fucking hurt.

Grace pulled my head into the crook of her neck. She was warm. A sweet smell enveloped me, and I let it blind me from the rest of the world like a coward. Her hand massaged the back of my head. "Shh... I've got you now. Just let me in."

I grabbed her tighter. "I can't make it end, no matter what I try."

"You've been doing this alone for way too long, Chef." Her lips pressed against the corner of my mouth.

"I need you." I turned my head slightly until my lips were on hers. A warm shiver ran through me as she cupped my cheeks and without hesitation, opened her mouth to me. Our lips locked, like a perfect puzzle, and she gripped me to stop me from falling over the edge, my mind going crazy.

Shuffling and murmuring in the background ended the

spell. I broke our kiss. Behind Grace, Jarryd leaned back on the couch as April pressed a cloth of some kind to his face. Next to them, Riley hugged Sienna. Her shoulders heaved, and he rubbed his hand up and down her back. *I must be in the twilight zone.*

"Can we sit and talk now?" Grace's fingers grabbed mine. I nodded.

Sienna spun around, her face wet, her breathing erratic. "You have to stop assuming the worst in people, Avery." Tears ran down her cheeks.

Drained, my brain not making sense anymore, I fell onto the couch, the cushion sinking with my weight. "Everyone's just confirmed he's a drug dealer, but no one gives a shit."

The girls exchanged a side glance. When Jarryd nodded, his eyes spaced out, Grace settled on the arm of the couch. She placed a hand on my shoulder. "He went to court for drug dealing. This was over six years ago."

I knew it.

The shrink leaned forward until his elbows touched his knees. "I was innocent."

"Right."

"He was." I turned towards the confident voice. Next to his dad, Riley glared at me, the pulse in his neck threatening to blow any second.

"Kid, I hate to say it, but you're all very cagey. I don't want my sister near it."

Grace dug her fingers in my shoulders, the tips easing me into silence. "Jarryd covered for Riley. On the court records, which I'm guessing is what you found, it looks bad. We know."

My jaw clamped. I'd spent the early hours of the morning going through the court records, followed by some sensationalized press releases indeed. And from where I sat, it looked pretty clear-cut. "Are you telling me that good old Jarryd is innocent, and all of this was to protect his kid from a slap on the wrist?"

Everyone in the room paused. They stared at each other, mouths open, like I'd crashed their secret party. *What am I missing here?*

I turned towards Riley, frustration shaking me, and pointed at Sienna. "You say you care about her welfare so much. If you do, give me more."

My sister wiped the tears off her face, and in one swift movement, spun herself towards her friend. Her bright complexion had taken on a ghastly tint. "Were you dealing drugs?"

He nodded. "My whole family was." She gasped at his admission.

"I did what I had to do to get him out of that lifestyle," Jarryd snapped before running a hand over his face. He leaned back against the sofa. His wife grabbed his hand. Maybe the shrink and I weren't so different in the end. Then again... *His whole family?* Confused, my head jerked from Jarryd, to April, then back to Riley. "I'm not his father for fuck's sake." Jarryd blew a hard breath.

"Are you telling me that you got charged with drug dealing just to protect some kid who wasn't even yours?" I tried hard to hide the scepticism dripping from my tongue. "Risking your licence?"

That made the man a psycho... or a saint.

"To save his life," April said, her free hand clutching the kid's wrist.

I narrowed my eyes at the whole lot of them. There had to be more. Something none of them wanted to give up.

Who would die for this? "Sounds like a shady deal, if you ask me."

A smirk crawled on Riley's face. Like he'd finally given up on keeping me out of the riddle. "You could say that." He scoffed. "My father's Hal Cooper."

And just like that, everything fell into place. Blood drowned my eardrums, Riley's words spinning in my head. Then, it clicked.

It wasn't a *what* that Jarryd had taken from Hal. It was a *who*.

Chapter 30

Grace

The colour drained from Avery's face. He dashed to the window, eyes staring in the distance, and every few minutes, he glanced back towards the teenagers like they'd turned into pumpkins. His face was unusually marked, deep lines running over his forehead and his pupils hollow.

"Well, it seems my father's reputation precedes him," Riley deadpanned.

April and I exchanged another look, the unspoken words begging me for some clues. *Don't stare at me, sister. I'm in the dark just as much as you are.* I shrugged.

Jarryd relaxed against the sofa. "Hal is a piece of work. I don't know anyone in South East Queensland who wouldn't know his name."

Sienna's wide eyes grew bigger with every glare from her brother. When he turned back again, I marched towards her and kneeled until our sightlines synced. "You okay, sweetie?"

She nodded. "Yep."

"You don't look so *yep*. What's going on?" When the

restlessness in her legs almost shoved me to the floor, I braced my hands on her knees, securing her in place.

Her head lifted slowly, and she swallowed hard. "Nothing. I'm just thirsty."

"I'll get you a drink." Riley pushed himself off the couch.

I pointed towards Avery still staring through the window. "Would you mind getting two?"

April shuffled to her feet, extending her palm out to him. "I'll come with you."

He pulled her up and they exited the room, leaving me and Jarryd studying the siblings, who appeared locked in some weird frozen state. As if he sensed it, Avery ambled over to us, settling in Riley's spot. "How long ago did this all happen?"

Jarryd's face twisted. "Depends what we define as *all*." He took a breath. "nearly seven years since the court case where I was charged with possession. But *Daddy* had his kids doing the dirty work for years prior to that. We just didn't know."

"That's so sad," Sienna's voice thinned. She wrapped her arms around herself, like a child pretending she wasn't afraid of the dark.

"It was." Memories of little Riley crying every time he lost a game of basketball flooded my heart.

"So, you're not dealing in any way, shape, or form?"

"Hell no," Jarryd snapped back. When Avery's wrinkles smoothed out in relief, Jarryd's tone softened, and he continued. "All I did was refuse to throw a fourteen-year-old kid under the bus, and that pissed off a lot of people."

Silence stretched on as April and Riley returned with drinks. Jarryd shifted, and April settled near him. On the floor, Riley leaned against the back of the couch, his legs out. When Riley'd finished his can, he turned towards the siblings and asked, "Do you know my father?"

"No." Avery's tone was clipped. Sienna paled, her head lowering. She played with the hands sitting in her lap, pulling her sleeves over her thumbs every few seconds. The kid was definitely uncomfortable. *Maybe it's her wild history that's triggering them both.* Avery smiled, a twitch pulsing in his neck. "I heard some stories about the bastard using kids to traffic drugs. Doesn't sit well with me."

"You and me both, brother." Jarryd brought his fist up to Avery, and my chef bumped it, the two men leaning back in their seats. Avery's shoulders dropped, and he glanced my way, his dimples showing slightly. *God, I've missed those.*

"What happened to you?" Sienna kicked Riley's thigh with the tip of her foot.

He chuckled before answering. "The same as every other kid in the family. When I turned thirteen, my brother got caught dealing, so he went to jail, and instead of getting in trouble, Hal was super proud."

"God, I hate the man," Jarryd mumbled under his breath.

"He made me take over for Trey, but I was going to the youth centre already by then, and I thought it'd be all right to leave the weed in the car while we played some basketball."

"Missed out on your twenty, and the privilege to load their gun..." Sienna murmured, one hand rubbing the other wrist, over and over, like a silent incantation. My eyes zoomed in on the girl. Something wasn't quite right, but I couldn't put my finger on it. *I can see why he's always so worried about her.*

Riley's eyes grew wide. "That's exactly what they did."

Sienna nodded before shaking her head, some Botox

smile replacing the weird expression she sported moments ago. "At least, that's what they do in movies, right?"

"Is this all in the past now?" Avery asked the guys, ignoring Sienna's weird joke.

Riley rolled his eyes. "It's never over when it comes to my old man."

"He'll come back. Maybe it's Trey's release from jail. Who the hell knows? But he can tell everything about our whereabouts. He knows when April's alone, and when Riley's in transit."

Avery's Adam's apple bobbed up and down. "Shit."

"You could say that." I rested my palm on his forearm to stop his twitching.

He placed a hand on mine, slight trembling resonating through my wrist, but he didn't make eye contact. "What's Hal's latest?"

Jarryd sat up. "Short version? I give him his son back or else..."

"Else being?" Sienna's tone was so low I could barely hear it.

"We don't know yet," Riley answered. "But I'm never going back. He can go fuck himself."

Avery's face hardened and he pointed to a quiet area by the bar. "Grace, could we catch up?"

There wasn't a soul in the bar at this time of day. Crystals clunked in the background, the waiter removing water marks from each glass like a mother wiping her newborn's face. Soft piano music played in the background, large fans humming above us. I grabbed Avery's fingers, and he latched on to me, a strange insecurity echoing through his touch. We settled on some café chairs behind a partition, my stomach filled with heaviness. Across from me, Avery extended his hand over the table, his palm open, and I slid mine into his. He relaxed, like it panicked him to lose the connection.

"You're not angry anymore?" I asked, my eyebrow cocked.

"I'm sorry." He rubbed his thumb over the top of my wrist. "I wish things were different."

"You're doing it again." I sighed, frustration nagging at me. It tickled my toes, zapped my fingers, and lashed at my stomach.

"There's a lot happening in my life. In Sienna's life."

"I know," I interrupted him. "If only I was willing to move to the other side of the earth for you, right?"

He pinched the corner of his eyes with his thumb and index finger. His head lowered. The wrinkles on his forehead looked like road maps in comparison to yesterday. He swallowed hard, and when he looked up, the weight of the world rested on his shoulders. Again.

Emotions railroaded me. Building from my belly and bulldozing through my heart, a need to protect this broken man had me hoist myself onto the table, my feet resting on the side of his chair, and he slid forward until his head rested on my thigh. He grabbed me, his arms snaking around my lower back, and I leaned forward, my chest hugging the top of his skull. As if he held on to me for dear life, Avery closed his eyes, his heart beating fast against my flesh.

My fingers ran over his upper body, tracing the outline of his tattoos and slowing down when they reached the temple on his shoulder. "I love you," I whispered into his ear.

He hugged me tighter. "I don't deserve you to love me."

I inhaled his smell. Musky. Deep. *Lost.*

A soft quiver shook his back. It only lasted a second, then he cleared his throat, burying his nose deeper into my pelvis. "I'm not a good man."

"Shh," I murmured. "I know your heart."

He jerked his head up and raised himself. With one hand, he lifted my chin, his eyes studying mine. His hands cupped my jaw, our foreheads touching. Gently, he pulled my face to his until our lips met. He kissed me. Softly. Quietly. *Desperately.* Like our kiss would feed him the strength to fight whatever storm was drowning him.

A hand crawled under my dress. I moaned when his fingers clawed into the tops of my thighs, heat spreading through my core. A strange need travelled from him to me, and I arched my back closer to him, until his tongue swallowed mine. He yanked my thighs closer, his pelvis ramming into mine, then his lips lowered to my neck, nibbling at the flesh. Goosebumps spread like wildfire. I took a deep breath, my heart rate pulsing through my core, and my hands travelled from his shoulders to his neck, pulling him closer with every kiss.

"Avery..." I murmured through clenched teeth.

He kissed faster, moving back to my mouth. "I don't want to talk."

"Someone could see..."

A cold breeze blew on my neck as he glanced behind the thick partition protecting us from the outside world. I missed his lips instantly. He shook his head, confidence oozing, and one hand moved back up to my breast, kneading it. Liquid pleasure travelled to my lower belly, and I clamped my legs around him, heat burning with every one of his touches.

"God, you feel so good." He slid me to the edge of the table and pulled back so his eyes could stare into mine. "I want to see your face when I taste you."

My mouth formed an O, words stuck in my throat, and I nodded, my core drawn to him like a magnet fighting a thousand steel doors. Slowly, he lifted my dress slightly above my knees. Then, with both hands, he pushed my legs apart before sitting down on his chair, his face resting against the inside of my thighs.

"I want you," he growled, before dropping a kiss over my panties. I jerked a finger in my mouth, and clamped on it hard, the moaning dying behind my digit. He smiled, dimples setting my ovaries on fire. "Good girl."

Fingers crawled up my inner thighs until they reached my underwear. He narrowed his eyes, and as if compelled, I lifted my bottom, letting him pull them down. He slid them off slowly, every movement sending a current through my clit.

I need you. I raked his shoulders with my nails, and he groaned when I pulled on his head, his tongue trailing my knee to my inner thigh, before landing on my mound. I shifted my hips closer, spreading my legs for him. As if the slow torture turned him on, he tapped my clit with his nose, inhaling before planting a kiss on it. Blood rushed through me, fire spiralling through every nerve in my body. "Avery..."

His tongue lapped my lips, opening them wider with each flick. I clenched on my finger harder, my body shaking from trying to hold it in. Wetness drenched me, and like he'd been starving, Avery licked my juices, small noises humming through my core. Then, he flicked his tongue over the full length of my slit, swallowing all I was giving him. I moaned through my finger, and his hands gripped my thighs harder as I squirmed under him.

"You taste amazing," he murmured, the vibrations sending me wild. Against my clit, a thumb flicked the bud, my insides growing tighter with every movement, and I brought my knee up above his shoulders. He chuckled. "You're so close already."

My toes curled as he pushed his tongue deep inside me. Warmth filled me, the nimble appendage moving against the pink flesh and draining it of all willpower. My breathing increased, my chest beating so hard it ached, and I whimpered, pushing his face between my legs. His tongue alternated with his lips in worshipping every bit of my pussy, driving me closer to the edge with each new exploration. When he pushed a finger inside my hole, stretching me slowly, I shook hard, my body lost to his wicked ways. It was thick. Firm. Confident.

A digit teased my G-spot while his tongue continued to lap at my clit. A blaze coursed through me as a sharp wave of pleasure squeezed my lower belly, and my body trembled, begging for relief. "I can't hold it anymore. Please."

The stubble of his jaw scraped against my inner thigh, and he thrust his finger in and out of me, pressure building while his thumb circled my clit faster. His baritone voice hummed inside me, drinking me as a volcano threatened to erupt. When it did, I buckled, my whole body quivering. A deep moan escaped me.

"Oh god..." I said, the orgasm splintering my body and mind. My head spun, the room suddenly appearing brighter.

He kissed both my knees as he rubbed my thighs. The motion settled the shivering overcoming me, then he stood, his arms enveloping me as I nestled against him. I breathed into his chest.

"I can't believe you did that," I said, heat warming my cheeks.

He hugged me tighter. "You deserve to feel good."

"It felt amazing." I smiled. "You're amazing."

He snuck his nose into the crook of my neck and took a deep breath. "You have a way of making me feel hopeful."

"But you still don't want to talk, right?" I teased, my tone lighter.

"Nope." He sighed before rearranging my dress, my panties now in his pocket.

Buzzing, I kissed him, my hands cupping his face. "Thank you for being you." I was his. Whether I liked it or not. No matter what his inner storm might be. He was a good man. Protective. Loyal. And I loved him.

"Thank you for being you," he offered back, dropping a last kiss on my swollen lips, and helped me off the table. Then, he extended his hand towards the hotel lobby.

What could he have done that would ever change this?

Chapter 31
Avery

Sienna tossed a shirt in the open bag on the floor, then grabbed another one lying on the bed by her side. "What do you mean you haven't decided what we're doing yet? I'm over this mental whiplash."

"You heard what I heard, right?"

Some pink tank top dropped to her feet. She picked it up and flung it with the rest of her clothes, then shuffled on the bed until her back lay against the headboard. She sighed. "I can't believe he's Trey's brother."

"And they're both Hal fucking Cooper's sons." I ambled closer to her and settled on the armchair. *Might as well. This looks like it'll be a lengthy discussion.* "Wasn't Trey your boy?"

She narrowed her eyes. "Yep. My first kiss."

"Not sure I wanna know." I extended my legs, my hands relaxing behind my head. "How long?"

"Between his two jail sentences, a couple of months?"

"How's he compared to the rest of the family?" It was obvious Riley wasn't cut out of the same cloth as his father. Maybe the rest of the family could be convinced to back off.

"He was nice, compared to Hal." Her shoulders shook in an exaggerated shudder. "Hal was scary."

A renewed sense of conviction zapped me. Cooper wasn't going near her again. That was final. I inhaled slowly, self-control fighting its way out of my mental fog. The thought of a thirteen-year-old alone with a gang—worse yet, being kissed by one of their deadbeats, a decade older than her—made me want to punch every wall in the hotel room. "What about Riley? Where does he stand?"

Her voice cracked, her chest moving higher. "We're just friends."

"At least *he* seems genuine," I grumbled.

She sneered. "Trey wanted me too much. He didn't give a rat's ass about my age. Riley, he's the opposite. Apparently, it would be *wrong*."

Riley was definitely taking on Jarryd's side of the family. I exhaled. As much as Sienna seemed pained, it was one less thing to worry about. "Is that because of the age difference?"

Not that four years was massive, but I guessed at sixteen, a twenty-year-old was getting up there, particularly given both their histories. She shrugged, her lips tight. "That, and something to do with *professional boundaries.* 'Cause he's a youth worker, and I'm just a kid... yada, yada, yada."

Relief eased the tightness in my chest. At least that was one Cooper I didn't have to picture in bed with her. "Is that what he said?"

She scrunched her nose. "No. But he might as well have. It's like he's trying so hard to be perfect and do everything above board. I guess, now we know why." He was trying to cut the gene pool out of his system. Eradicate the fucking Cooper out of his blood.

"Have you told Riley or Grace anything?" I leaned forward, my elbows resting on my knees.

She shook her head. "No! I would never."

"Good," I said, my eyes studying her. "They'd never forgive us." All the jobs I'd done for Hal to keep my sister out of his club played in my head. I forced the thoughts down, hidden in renewed shame. More recent memories flooded me. First, Grace nestled against my chest, then finding out Riley was Cooper's son, and worse, knowing Jarryd had been prepared to lose everything to protect his family too. I'd had it wrong all along, but until now, I hadn't cared who would go down in order to protect her. Firm knocks interrupted us, followed by the handle crunching. "Are you expecting anyone?" I murmured, yanking the base of the side lamp off the wall socket and grabbing it with both hands.

She shook her head, her eyes wide, and stood behind me. I flicked my chin towards the bathroom, and she dashed in. The door creaked open. Two lots of footsteps came closer. A voice crooned over the humming of the air-con. "Why are you being shy, Avery? Aren't we pals?"

I leaned back on the wall, my respirations pushing their limit. My knuckles grew white against the wood as I recognised the newcomer. My eyes darted towards the bathroom, Sienna's fucking toes peeking out from behind the door.

It's too late. My brain processed my options, the fight-or-flight urge pumping through my blood. If I tried to strike Cooper's gang, and missed, Sienna and I were both dead. I pressed a finger against my lips, and she pushed herself further back. Her toes disappeared.

"Who do you have with you this time, Hal?" I yelled from across the room, waiting for the sound of his voice to place him in the hotel apartment.

"Why don't you come and give us the tour instead of hiding like a pussy?" he spat.

Not even metres away. Judging from his tone, Cooper wasn't here to play games, and unless I had a Glock to splatter his brains across the ceiling, the only way I could protect my sister was to get him out of this room. I dropped the lamp and raised my hands, before stepping into the hallway and meeting Cooper face to face. "All right, Hal. I'm here now."

A long moment of suspense dragged in the air as neither of us moved. Then, Cooper's body tensed and he struck my face with his closed fist. Instantly, I fell off balance, shuffling back with the blow. I raised a palm to my mouth, blood staining my skin. "That's to remind you who calls the shots around here."

I clenched my jaw, my fists tightening. It wasn't a fight I could win with Sienna in the room. I pulled my hands down from my face, castrating all the manhood left in me. "I know, Hal." *Get on with it.*

"I hear you met my son today?" Cooper pranced forward, like he hadn't just right-hooked the shit out of me.

I shook my head. "Your son? I don't know what you're talking about."

The colour of his eyes darkened, and he charged towards me, sweeping low until I fell to my knees. Then he reached down, squeezing the back of my neck hard, and released a bunch of punches to my face, growing stronger—faster—with each strike. I winced in pain, biting my lip as I tried to stop the grunting from escaping my throat. If Sienna heard any of it, she'd come out and all bets would be off.

He stopped, a look of contentment spreading over his features. "It's so nice to catch up, isn't it, Chef?"

I spat blood on the other side of him, my face burning and my head spinning. "Always a pleasure."

Laughing, his enforcer reached down for one of the shirts on the ground and tossed it at me. "Clean yourself up, Chef. You're killing my appetite."

I grabbed it, the pink shirt turning crimson as I swiped it against my jaw. Something flickered in Cooper's eyes, and he spun towards his goon, a finger twirling in the air. Immediately, the enforcer drew his gun from his holster and shifted back on his steps.

"That's very pink for you, don't you think?"

Icy current froze my lungs, and I leaped to my feet, ignoring the pain drilling through my skull. *They know.* "I sent her away. She left two hours ago."

"Two hours ago, you say? Funny. The hotel CCTV says otherwise."

I nodded, fighting everything in me not to glance towards the bathroom. "Just tell me what you want, and we can all go home happy," I clipped. This had to end very soon, or they'd find her. Fear paralysed me.

Like he read it on my face, a new fury built in his eyes, and he stepped forward, kicking me in the kneecap. "Why do you keep lying to me, Chef? You've completely lost your will to fight, and we both know it's not like you to be so... *tame.* She's here. I can smell her."

The bathroom door sprung open, and the enforcer smirked as he pushed Sienna forward by her hair. "Look what I found, boss?"

Her hands locked around her ponytail to stop him from ripping it out. Her face, drawn into a grimace, stared ahead, and she whimpered as she passed me. Rage filled my gut, but dread kept me frozen in place. When the enforcer threw her onto the bed, I leaped forward but Cooper snatched me back, my arm now twisted at an awkward angle at the base of my spine. "Let her go. She has nothing to do with this."

Cooper pushed my chest against the wall, the cold metal of his gun pressing into me. "Actually, she has everything to do with this." He tilted his head towards her. "From one of my sons to the next. I say that makes you family, don't ya think, Sienna?"

Her sobs were muffled by the mattress. Sienna didn't answer. Instead, she squirmed as the tattooed machine dragged her closer to him.

"Get away from her!" I screamed at the bastard holding my sister down, bloody spit dripping from my mouth. "You touch her, and I'll kill you."

A hand tightened behind me. Then a click resonated in the room, the barrel pressing harder against my spine. "All I want is to reconnect with my bloodline. Nothing's wrong with that, right?"

"That has nothing to do with me," I barked, my shoulders pushing from the wall so I could keep my eyes locked on Sienna.

"Well, actually, it does." Like he read my thoughts, Cooper twisted me back with a kick to the underside of my legs, so I was now facing the bed on my kneecaps. He snaked his arm around my throat, the gun precariously settled between my shoulder blades.

Tears flooded Sienna's face, and our eyes met, my heart exploding in my chest. "I've done my part, Cooper. I've paid her debt. Now, let her go."

"Your debt is paid when you deliver what I asked for."

I clenched my jaw, pushing against the pressure on my neck. "I can't bring you a human."

The enforcer narrowed his eyes at his boss, a smirk

growing like they shared a sick connection. "Maybe we're talking to the wrong sibling, boss?"

Cooper must have approved, because almost instantly, the enforcer grabbed my sister's ankles and dragged her to the edge of the bed.

"Get your hands off her!"

Sienna froze when thick hands nudged her knees apart and travelled up the outside of her thighs, before disappearing under her shorts. He leaned forward, his chest pressing on hers. His face buried itself in the crook of her neck. "I'm as good as Trey, kid."

Darkness invaded me. Adrenaline overcame me. And rage possessed me until all I could see was the outline of the target framed by my mental crosshairs. I shoved my elbow back as hard as I could into Cooper's stomach, and with a grunt, he released his grip. Then, I extended my knee, catapulting my leg into his bastard of a sidekick's skull. His jaw crunched with the impact of my boot. Shock all over his face, he fell backwards, a chair collapsing under his weight. Blood seeped onto the hotel floor as his face was torn open, and I spat on it, a feeling of disappointment flooding me when a moan rose from his chest.

I tugged Sienna off the bed and pushed her back into the bathroom. Right as she disappeared, Cooper's gun cocked behind my head, and I froze, hands up in surrender. "I'd prefer us both be dead, over letting your fucking lowlifes touch her. So, go right ahead. Pull the trigger, Hal." Despair swamped me. It didn't matter how much I tried. There was no way out of this fucking nightmare. A part of me prayed he'd just pull the trigger and end it for us. "Do it, Hal. Just fucking do it."

"You're making this hard for yourself, Avery. All I need is a little help getting a one-on-one chat with my son. That's all. Surely, there're people in your life worth living for, right?"

A black cloud suffocated me further. Were there? The vision of Grace's arms rubbing my back earlier stopped me from begging Cooper to end me for a third time. I pictured her next to me, her invisible hand holding mine.

New steps entered the room. I glanced up, a pervasive pain shooting through me like a death sentence that didn't want to come. Within seconds, Black Tulip stepped around the body on the ground and hoisted the guy up. Then he lifted his chin towards me. "Need help with him too?"

"I think Avery's ready now, aren't you?"

"What do you need?" I exhaled. An invisible Grace cupped my face and kissed me. *Stay alive for us.* I inhaled her hair, the phantom smell giving me the will to fight. *One more day.*

"I want to know when Riley will be alone next. And where."

A shadowy Grace touched my chest, her small hand lingering over my right side. *I know your heart.* She smiled. Like she didn't care I served the Devil. Like I wasn't a coward. Like she'd still love me no matter what. "He'll be alone on Tuesday. Jarryd and his wife have an ob-gyn appointment at the H.I.P."

The gun pressed harder against my temple. "And where will my offspring be, all on his lonesome then, Chef?"

"He'll be home between two and three. At three, he picks up the small kid." I sighed, betrayal stinging just as much the second time. "That's when you'll get him."

The gun left my head, and I turned towards the drug lord. His fat smile matched the thick vest popping around his stomach. "Wasn't so hard, was it?"

A soul-shattering shame swam through my veins, my breaths frozen in despair.

Cooper swung his hand high, the gun shining against the hotel fluorescents. A piercing pain shot through my skull as the butt struck me with a resounding thud, the cold metal ramming my temple. Then, the room grew silent—Grace now gone and blackness invading me.

Chapter 32
Grace

The doorbell chimed, and I skipped to the door, opening it for April and her brood. "Welcome to my humble abode," I crooned.

April leaned over and kissed my cheek. "Thanks for having us for dinner. I'm looking forward to the Pictionary."

I motioned them forward, and she stepped inside, followed by Jarryd, Riley, and Lizzy.

"God, we haven't played this game in ages." Jarryd whistled as he hung his jacket on the back of a hook by the entrance.

"'Cause you're a sore loser," Riley teased him, landing a firm palm on his back.

Laughter filled the room as we ambled down the hall of the four-bedroom house. The tiles to the open kitchen felt cold beneath my feet. A soft, contemporary piano instrumental played in the background. It matched the fine décor I'd spent two hours arranging. After the intensity of the last few weeks, we all needed a pick-me-up night.

"Look at these." April ran a finger along the gold trails of a scented candle on the counter. Matching sets were spread throughout the kitchen. She brought it to her nose. "And it smells so nice. Lemongrass?"

The oven beeped and I turned towards it. Burgundy mitts covering my hands, I pricked the roast with a fork and pink juice erupted from the meat. Rosemary and thyme floated in the pan, their warm aroma further instigating my hunger. I removed the tray and rested the sirloin on the counter, then pushed the baby potatoes under the grill, shaking the pan hard a couple of times. "Dinner will be ready in twenty-odd minutes." I extended my hand towards the veranda.

We settled on the wicker chairs, and I served everyone some tropical punch, while Lizzy attempted to pass a plate of appetisers to her family. When she almost tripped, Riley grabbed the tray off her, tossed a mini quiche in his mouth, and put the food back in the middle of the table.

"Aunty Grace, me play with blocks? Please?"

April tucked a strand of her daughter's wispy blonde hair behind her ear. "Lovely manners."

"Of course, sweetie. You go have fun."

The little pitter-patters ran off and April finally relaxed against her seat. "God, I love the child, but she's just so full-on lately."

"You're almost at the end, baby. No wonder you're tired," Jarryd said, a hand rubbing her pregnant belly. He winked at me. "*You* tell her to stop working at that centre every day. She should be resting."

She rolled her eyes, her lips curling. "Don't try to get rid of me so quickly, hotshot. Lucky for you, you can tell all your little concerns to Dr Perry on Tuesday."

"Is this your last ob-gyn appt? You have to be closer than they reckon," I said. Judging from the size of her stomach, the swollen fingers, and how uncomfortable she looked in general, that little boy had to be due any day now.

"It sure is. Having to hear that doctor talk to my doctor about things only *he* cares about during the last appointment..." She chuckled. "...like whether my fundal height is consistent with Lizzy's pregnancy, or how high my normal protein levels are, does not interest me."

Riley popped another pastry in his mouth. "What interests *me*, though, is if I am still picking up the little monster from day care at three? Let me know, so I can move my music lesson on Tuesday?"

Jarryd nodded. "If you don't mind, and we'll get takeout on the way back."

I leaned towards April, our shoulders touching. "God, he's such a good role model, isn't he?"

She turned her head towards me. "I don't know what I've done to inherit him. He's a godsend."

"Ladies, stop giving the man so many compliments. His head will be too big for his shoulders soon," Jarryd teased. "Plus, I can't wait to try Grace's food. It smells amazing."

"Why don't you come and help me, doc?"

Jarryd and Riley followed me into the house. Lizzy dashed past us as we opened the glass doors, and she settled with her mother outside. I waved at them, then focused on setting the meat on the cutting board. Behind me, the boys arranged the roasted potatoes and broccolini on a dish.

"Any updates with you-know-who?" I lined up thin slices of meat on the plate in front of me. A day had gone by since our strange fiasco with Avery, and other than a quick reply to my text, I hadn't heard from him either.

Riley shook his head, swift fingers stealing a piece of meat from the tray, and he chuckled when my pretend smack missed his hand. He licked his fingers between words. "No. Which could be really good, or really bad. I don't know what's worse: my father's vicious stubbornness, or my brother's lack of scruples."

"They're both as bad as each other." Jarryd exhaled.

"It's a shame, because there was a time when Trey was decent." I sighed. A pang of sadness filled me as I stared at April and Lizzy cuddling on the outside couch. "I have to wonder who Trey would be today if we'd got him out at the right time too." I glanced towards the bunch of fresh herbs, but before I could reach for them, Riley'd passed them over to me.

"Sometimes I feel guilty about that." He sighed.

"Buddy, you have worked on yourself to get to where you are. Trey was out for a few years. He chose to go back."

Riley and I exchanged a quick glance. I didn't disagree with Jarryd's statement, but I had to agree with the kid too. Getting free from decades of family history, in the biggest bikie gang in the South East, was no easy feat. Everyone knew Hal Cooper. *Even Avery...*

Jarryd organised the green veggies, then ground some salt over the branches. "Perfection, Grace. As good as what your chef would have done."

"Ha." I chuckled. "I'm nowhere near as good as that."

"Almost."

I grabbed a paper towel and wiped the meat juice from around the plate, glad for the mundane action to stop the thoughts reeling in my mind. Avery was out of this world. He made me feel strong, sexy, and driven. With the man by my side, we'd killed the launch and received an offer twice as large as I'd hoped. Yet, there was a darkness within him I couldn't quite put my finger on.

Like he could read my thoughts, Riley asked, "I wonder

how he knows my old man." He leaned back against the wall, his ankles crossed.

Jarryd nodded. "I reckon he knows him, or at least knows of him pretty well, given how he flipped when he found out who you were."

A thousand pins and needles travelled from one body part to the next. I took a breath, overprotection for the man I secretly held in my heart buzzing to the surface. Avery's reaction *had* been intense. But, in all fairness, a lot of his reactions were weird at the best of times. Yesterday was probably just a mix of stress, angst, and family drama. "Everyone knows Hal. Let's be real, guys."

Jarryd narrowed his eyes, his head shaking fast. "Yeah. Nah. There's something else."

I straightened the meat on the plate again, following some invisible circle. "You're being paranoid."

He tapped the middle of his forehead with his index finger. "That's what you told me when I thought someone was spying on us at the centre, and it turns out I was right."

Riley hoisted himself on the side counter. "I like Avery. He's cool. But I agree with Jarryd. There was something off about how he freaked out. He froze Sienna with one look too. Like completely shut her off. That was mega suss."

My fingers tapped nervously on the bench, the tips beating rhythmically against the marble counter. Every second, my mind was trying to come up with good reasons to protect my man. He was lots of things. Arrogant, aloof, cold, mysterious sometimes even, but he was honest and caring. And I'd be damned if I allowed them to grill him in his absence, no matter how much I wanted to hide my feelings for him until we'd decided what to do with them. "What are you implying?" I snapped. "You're talking about my chef. *A chef* for God's sake. Not a secret agent."

Jarryd narrowed his eyes. "What do you actually know about him, Grace?"

Nothing. "Everything I need to know. He came highly recommended."

Riley tilted his head, his arms crossed. "By whom?"

"By the people who matter." My voice rose a few decibels. A mix of indignation and angst filled my belly. A dull ache twisted my insides as I tried to remember how Avery landed on my doorstep. The provisional tender documents materialised in my mind. Suddenly, I could see it like it was back on my desk a couple of months ago. The money, the proposal... and the condition that Avery would be the chef accompanying the massive endeavour.

Oh god... Someone wanted him involved. A sharp pain twisted my bowels, and I wrapped myself with one arm, the fire in my stomach burning. I must have looked faint, because almost instantly Jarryd was by my side, his fingers on my wrist as he checked my pulse. "You need to sit down," he said. "You're about to collapse."

I shook my head, but there was no point denying the obvious. Riley rushed and pulled a chair to the side, while Jarryd held on to my elbow as I fell back on the seat.

"What is it?" Jarryd asked, his fingers still on my wrist. With a flick of his chin, he motioned to the cooler. Riley poured some water and handed me the glass, then kneeled by my side.

You're being a complete idiot and making a scene. I glanced at April and Lizzy snuggled on the couch outside.

Jarryd's eyes followed mine and landed on his girls, light snoring resonating from the patio. His daughter used her mother's belly as a pillow. "Don't worry. They're out. She won't hear us if that's what you're worried about."

I brought a finger to my mouth, my teeth nibbling at the

nailbed. "He's not a bad guy," I said, my voice thinning. Despite my best efforts, my shoulders remained tensed, and the cramping in my stomach increased.

"No one said he was," Jarryd countered, his tone firm. "But if you know something I don't..." He glanced towards his adopted son. "...then you have to tell me, because I can't protect them with only half the information."

A tear escaped, and I wiped it quickly. Riley placed a hand on my shoulder, his fingers squeezing my muscles lightly. "Don't cry. Just tell us what's happening. Don't think you're alone in this."

I exhaled, forcing my shoulders down. *You're being a complete drama queen. There's nothing to know.* I ignored the gut feelings drowning me. After all, it wasn't like it proved anything. Avery had been Young Chef of the Year multiple times over the years. He'd won many awards. There were lots of reasons he could have been the first choice for the state members of Parliament investing in a project like this. But surely, as recommended as he came, he would have known everything about Nutrify. Been forthcoming. In familiar terms with the MPs we'd met a few times. And definitely not been in a rush to skip town not once, but twice, before he was even paid.

"Oh god..." I brought a hand to my mouth, my heart jumping in my chest. The stomach cramps doubled in intensity, and a wave of nausea hit me hard. He hadn't even known he came *recommended*. Jarryd pulled out a chair. His body square in front of mine, he leaned forward until all I could hear was the tone of his voice. Firm. Determined. Aware. I wasn't the only one putting the pieces together. And as much as I loved Avery, if he had anything to do with wanting to harm my friends, I needed to know. "I don't know how he got involved in the project," I cried, confusion swirling in my mind.

"What do you mean?"

"He was part of the tender. The offer came with the condition that Avery would be the executive chef. At the time, I was glad. Where else was I going to find a qualified chef like him?"

"And you didn't think to ask how that came about? Why him?" Riley questioned, his eyes wide.

"No. I didn't. He's got a thousand awards under his belt. I was glad for the help in finding him."

Jarryd smiled, but it didn't quite crinkle his eyes. "We don't mean to imply anything, Grace, okay? We're not blaming you. I think we're just a bit shell-shocked too."

I sighed. If I felt bad, I could only imagine how Jarryd and Riley might feel, with one trying to protect his family and the other one trying hard to stay out of his father's claws. I had no right to feel the way I did. And yet, that realization didn't change a thing. Despite it all, my brain could not comprehend how the man who kept making love to me with such depth could be remotely associated with Hal Cooper. There had to be an explanation.

"Okay, so let's summarise what we actually know, yeah?" Jarryd said, his head pushed back against his chair.

I nodded in surrender. "He came as part of the tender, but he didn't seem to know much about Nutrify. He's mega protective over Sienna and cagey about their past. He's been raising her since their mother took off with some Texan loser. And twice, he braced to skip town, before he even received his full pay."

Riley blew a hard breath. "It's a lot of money, isn't it?"

"He would have got some of it. Maybe half. But he would have left the other fifty grand behind though."

"Who gives up fifty grand without a good reason?" Jarryd raked a hand through his hair, the vein in his neck pulsing fast.

"Someone whose reason is bigger than money," Riley murmured, his eyes zooming in on the toddler still sleeping outside. Silence filled the air, my brain processing the unspoken words. My hand went to my mouth again, my chest convulsing as I dry-heaved and the nausea overwhelming me.

I'm not a good man... I don't deserve you to love me... I'll die protecting my sister...

"Sienna..." I said, my voice breaking between sobs.

"Looks like we found our spy," Jarryd grunted through clenched teeth. He stood, the chair dragging back against the tiles, and he moved to the sink to splash water on his face. "Fuck."

"Did Avery sell me out?" Riley whispered, his demeanour taking me back to the first time I'd met him as a child.

I broke down, nodding. "I'm sorry, Riley. I had no idea." I wiped my cheeks with the back of my hand. I bent over, my arm cradling my stomach, the psychosomatic pain now unbearable. I finally had the missing pieces of Avery's puzzle. I was nothing but a pawn in his game, and he'd used me to get to Riley all along.

Chapter 33
Avery

Ignoring my mangled reflection in the mirror, I dashed past and threw the last of our clean clothes gathered in the middle of the hotel room into our bags. The bruises on my face had deepened to bright purple circles, now masking the bags under my eyes. A yellow tinge marked my skin, probably my pores sweating the grog I'd drowned in through the night to dull my senses, both physically and mentally.

I hadn't slept in almost three days, but after yesterday's episode, I hadn't been able to eat or drink, and definitely hadn't stopped visualising Hal's enforcer all over Sienna. The only relief I could find strong enough to let me take my next breath was the sight of his fucking dislocated jaw pissing blood.

I clenched my fist, and when the fury bubbled up again, I punched the wall in front of me, the light fixture overhead shaking with the impact. Fresh blood poured next to the last lot. I opened and closed my hand, disappointment filling me when my fingers responded to movement. Open wounds seeped above each knuckle, my fingers looking like a gloved boxer's hand after a fight.

I'd lost direction. Hope. Drive. Pain drilled through me like a drunk swimmer in the middle of a rip in South East Queensland, and I raged against a universe that hadn't let me die when I should have. Because now, all I had left was a sixteen-year-old girl on the verge of losing it, and a mind that threatened to do something stupid.

My phone buzzed on the counter. I glanced at it, the burner I'd just given Sienna flashing on the display. Within a second, her message appeared, and I unlocked the screen with a swipe.

SIENNA

> I don't know why you thought I needed a girl's day. Charlotte is pissing me off with her gossip. Can I just come back to the hotel? We need to talk. Please.

Sending her away might have been piss-poor parenting, but Cooper would never have looked for her in a public shopping mall, and I couldn't hack my own emotions right now, let alone hers. Clearly, I'd not been handed the *Managing Emotions Guide After Watching Your Sister Almost Get Raped in Front of You*.

There was nothing constructive I could offer her when I could barely string a sentence together. I needed space to think. To plan our escape. To forget I'd tossed Riley in the lion's den. And pray to God Grace would forgive me.

> Just enjoy the shopping money. You need some new clothes, anyway. We're on the plane first thing tomorrow, and this time, it's for real. We're leaving this fucking nightmare, Shorty. For good.

Who are you trying to convince? Acting like it's all going to be fine. I shuffled to my backpack and felt the side pocket with the tips of my fingers. The small booklets were still there, our passports to a new beginning.

No fear, no lies, and no drug lord running our lives. I closed my eyes and took my first deep breath in hours. My lungs burnt with the cold air, and I exhaled softly. A new beginning is all I'd asked for. A safe place for Sienna to be a teenager, and a place where I could finally give her a good life. Hungry for hope, I swiped the gallery on my phone until the photos I needed loaded. The little Italian restaurant came up, the green and red logo smiling at me. Pasta of all kinds, wood-fired pizzas, and an assortment of desserts jumped out of the menu. I planned on making the owners an offer as soon as I settled. My life might have been over *here*, but that didn't mean I couldn't cook my problems away *there*.

The small flicker of hope took the edge off, and for a second, I almost felt my upper body again. I ran a hand along the back of my neck, the hard muscles relaxing at the touch. Then, when my body hated me a little less, I got on my feet to finish packing. Right as I was about to zip up the bag, someone knocked at the door.

My heart jumped in my chest, and I immediately grabbed the Shogun blade I'd stashed after yesterday's near miss. My knuckles paled against the handle, and unlike the day prior, if Hal came for us again, it would end with one of us bleeding to death on the floor. I slithered to the front door, the knife by my side, and peeped through the small hole above the hotel directory sign. A blonde head looked down, and in her hand, my menus from last week's launch.

Grace. My throat spasmed. A wave of heat overcame me. As much as I needed to see her, needed her touch, I didn't want her to *see me* like this. I looked like shit. Like a junkie gone wrong. She knocked again. "I know you're there. Just open the damn door."

I sighed before complying. "Hey," I said, my head checking both ways as I gestured her inside.

She scoffed. "Expecting trouble?" She did a double take when she noticed my face. The nurturing side of her was missing.

"Not at all." I pointed to the lounge and she stepped closer, settling on a thick chair across from me. I leaned forward and grabbed her hand. "It's good to see you."

She snapped it back. "Is it?" Some weird tension emitted from her pores. I had thought we were okay after our escapade at the café, but based on her tight lips and glassy eyes, she carried a chip on her shoulder.

It had to be about my fight with the shrink. "I'm sorry for yesterday. I didn't mean to be so touchy with Jarryd. It's been a long couple of weeks." I attempted a chuckle, but it fell flat when her body remained frozen in place.

"Why did you want to be involved with Nutrify?" she asked, her tone neutral.

This definitely wasn't about yesterday. I swallowed hard. Where the hell was she going with this? *Does she know?* "Sounded like a great project at the time. I was between jobs so I—"

"Thought why not? Is that it?" She finished my sentence, a touch a sarcasm pronounced with each word.

"It's a bit more complicated than that." I blew a loud breath. I hated lying to her, but what exactly was I supposed to say? This fucking nightmare just kept getting better and better. All because of some reckless attraction to a woman I was never meant to develop feelings for. The whole thing was meant to be a job. A job to get Sienna and me off the hook. Nothing more.

But you fell in love with the job, didn't you? My chest constricted, my breathing growing shallow. I forced myself to exhale slowly and flinched when I accidently bumped my cheek with the hand running over my face. *She knows.*

"You're making a habit of running into things, Avery. What was it last time, again?"

"Can't remember."

"Yeah, pretty sure you never told me what happened to your face back then, either." She crossed her arms, her eyes studying the marks on my body.

A minute of silence went by as we each avoided the other's glare while sinking into the hotel couch. Her breasts moved up and down with every breath, the navy top deepening the blue of her eyes. She crossed her legs, her perfect calves teasing me, a painful reminder of how they snaked my waist only a day ago. She leaned forward, her body moving closer to mine and her perfume triggering the memories of her in my arms. My heart stabbed me, and for a second, I remembered the Grace in my mind—the one who had held me together as Hal pointed a gun to my head.

I weakened and grabbed her hand, my voice thinning. "I just need to hold you for a minute."

She hesitated, but as if she needed it as much as I did, she allowed our fingers to interlink in silence. "You're drowning in your mess. You know that?"

I kneeled by her side, my forehead resting on her lap. "I don't mean to."

She cupped my cheeks with her hands, her eyes moist. "Your go-to is to shut me up by kissing me or fucking me, Avery. I'm not stupid. But right now, I need answers."

She pushed me back, and a coldness filled me as soon as

she let go. I stood and leaned against the wall, hands in my pocket as I waited for the verdict to fall. "Okay. Tell me what you need."

She might have got the hint that we were on the run again. Or maybe she'd decided to leave the country with us. My heart beat faster against my chest. Maybe she'd give me the strength to get through the next day or two, the will to leave Riley to deal with his father while ignoring my part in it all. Finally moving on to the next chapter of our lives.

I closed my eyes. A tinge of hope gripped me as I imagined Grace in my little Italian restaurant. *Our* restaurant. A cocktail in hand, bruschetta by the porch, and making love till sunset. But when I opened them again, Grace's face was stone cold. Paralysed by something I couldn't put my finger on. I pinched the bridge of my nose with my thumb and index finger, and urged her to continue, the despair of the last day or two clawing back into my soul. "What is it? Just say it."

Sweat pooled by her hairline, and she opened and closed her fists a couple of times before she blurted, "Are you working for Hal?"

Time stopped, her voice resonating in my head in slow motion. The wind knocked out of me like a kid being punched for the first time, I inhaled hard, processing her question and what damn answer I'd give her. I'd never lie openly, but telling her to her face I had hidden so much seemed like the death of our budding relationship. "It's not like—"

"*That.* But it's never like that with you, is it?" Her voice was strained as she stood and moved back a metre or two. "It's a simple question, Avery. Are you fucking working for Hal Cooper?"

I opened my mouth, the lie ready to slide out, but as I

looked into her eyes—the memories of her laughing at my dumb jokes, her competitive nature when making food, and the way she moaned when she came for me—I couldn't. "Yes."

Moisture brimmed her lashes, redness blotching her cheeks. She stared at me, tears falling freely down her face. "All this time, you were working for Hal?"

"I'm sorry." I cleared my throat, stopping the emotions from building in me too. I'd tell her the whole truth, but all it would achieve would be putting Sienna at risk while sounding like I was justifying my actions.

"You never cared about the project. You never cared about the kids." A sob broke from deep inside her chest. "You never cared about me."

I stepped towards her, the need to hug her—to take her pain away—unbearable. I craved her as much as a man could crave a woman. I grabbed her fingers, the contact my only lifeline.

She raised her hand and stopped me. "Don't come near me," she snapped. "How could you use me like this?" Her tone dripped like poison as her body tensed with every hissed word.

I moved back, giving her space. "Grace, it wasn't like that."

She screamed in the hotel room, the vein in her neck jumping out. "How was it, then? You freaking tell me how it was, because the way I look at it, you used me to do your job for the biggest piece of shit in history."

"At the beginning, yes, but that was before you and me—"

She snarled, her body shaking with rage. "What *you and me*? All this time... All your secret, coded messages as to why you couldn't love me back. Oh my god," she cried, "I'm such an idiot."

Panic overwhelmed me. My throat felt like sandpaper, and I coughed, my body rebelling against my betrayal. If only she understood, then maybe she would see I had no choice. "Grace..."

"It's not your turn," she yelled. "What about Riley? You don't think he deserves his new beginning? What about Jarryd and April? How long are they going to sacrifice their lives for the benefit of Hal Cooper?"

"You don't understand. Just let me explain."

"I don't need to hear any more stupid excuses, Avery. You had your chance to come clean so many times!"

She was right, and yet, it didn't make a bit of difference. I just needed a break from my life and fucking everything up all the time. "Can I please just hold you?" I whispered, my voice on the verge of breaking.

"You can go to hell," she barked, her hands shaking. When she noticed me watching her, she closed her fists and wrapped herself with her arms. "You used me. You pretended to like me, to care about me." Another sob shook her. "You let me get into you, into Sienna. For what? So you could get into Riley's life easier?" Her hands shot to her mouth, tears rocking her, and she steadied herself against the wall at her back. "All of it was a lie. The whole lot was a lie between bikies, who didn't care about anyone but themselves." Watching her like this broke me, and I fought my own throat tightening. I jerked forward and grabbed her. For a second, she let me. Her head rested against my chest, her hands fisting my shirt. "I love you like I've never loved anyone else, and it was all an act."

My heart smashed into a thousand pieces, because right there, I knew I'd hurt the only woman I'd ever loved. I only wished I'd been able to tell her before today. I held her tight, our hearts bleeding together. "It was never an act. I love you, Grace."

At the words, she raised her head, slowly, her blue eyes turning black. A dangerous aura possessed her, and she eyed the Shogun by the table. "Now, you love me?" She spat each word like they screamed an invisible threat, making sure I heard every single one of them. "You couldn't love me before, but right as you get caught snitching for Hal Cooper, putting kids in danger, and serving nothing but your own filthy and selfish purpose, suddenly you want to pretend you love me?" She shoved my chest with both her hands. "Don't ever come near me again, Avery Curtis, if that's even your real name."

"Grace, I swear to God, it's not what you think."

She shoved me again, this time with more force. "I don't care, Avery. We're done. You can take your lies, your herbs, and your goddamn playlist, and disappear from my life." Then, she marched towards the door, her face drenched with tears. "Pray to God that Jarryd doesn't hunt you down for this."

"I'm not who you think I am..."

She turned back, her palm gripping the door handle. "You were right about one thing though..." She shook her head, staring me down as she spat, "You don't deserve to be loved."

Chapter 34
Grace

"I understand," I said into the receiver for the third time today. "Unless I give you a timeframe in the next week, the office will reconsider the whole project."

The woman on the end of the phone continued to lecture me, her nasally voice making it really hard to remain professional. There was only so much I could manage after everything that had happened in the last few weeks. First, Avery taking off right before the launch, then being promised a budget twice its worth right at the last minute, and when everything seemed to be going for the best, finding out Avery was nothing more than a spy for Hal Cooper.

Yesterday, we'd broken up. Well, as much as a couple not officially in a relationship could actually break up. A mix of emotions flooded me. Anger at him for playing me all along, at potentially losing Nutrify for the second time, and at myself for missing him when I shouldn't.

That's right. We hate him now and that's final.

"Yes, I'll get back to you in the next few days with a plan. I'm just having some..." I cleared my throat. "...staffing issues, but as soon as I have found a new executive chef, Nutrify will be back on track. I promise you it's not worth losing sleep over. It's well under control." My tone was clipped. The secretary grated on my nerves, calling me every day like I'd run off with the money.

A thought sparked in my mind, and ignoring the woman's final warning, I logged into the banking app, checking the balance from last week's first instalment. Avery's second deposit of fifty thousand slept in the account next to mine. *He's still not taken that lot?*

Behind me, the front door opened, and April waddled through it. She waved at me, then put her bag on the couch, taking her wrap off with it. Then, she fell on a chair beside mine and waited for me to terminate the call. Within a second, the phone was on the kitchen table, my best friend smiling at me. "How are you, sweetie?"

I blew a breath. "Been better. What about you guys?"

She rolled her shoulders. "Well, like the boys said, now we know how Hal knew so much, and since Avery's gone, there'll be no new info being passed down the line, so there's that."

Shame drowned me for having brought Avery into their lives. If it wasn't for me, Riley would have been safer. "I'm sorry I landed you guys in the crossfire."

April shook her head. "Don't be stupid, Grace. You're a victim of Cooper's methods, just like the rest of us."

I grabbed her hand, emotions swimming to the surface. "Explain to me how it's you who is fighting with a bikie gang for your family, but it's me crying?"

She chuckled and squeezed my hand back. "Because the man you loved was part of the gang we're fighting against. And he is a dick for it."

"Ha. Thank you. I needed that perspective."

"Anytime." She winked at me. "By the way, how did it go with the Queensland office?"

"Urgh. They're being drama queens and demanding an update on the project. I told them all week that I was sourcing a new chef. I mean, why do they care, right? As long as we provide the meal plans and deliver the commercial licence, the rest shouldn't matter."

"I hate to say this, but someone must have been in on it at the office... to plant Avery in the tender in the first place."

It wasn't like I hadn't thought of that before. April was right. I just hoped that Hal Cooper had bigger fish to fry than looking to ruin my life any further. "I know. I hope it dies down and that I don't have to give the money back, now that we've spent a good chunk of it on wages and the launch."

She drummed a finger on the table. "Come on, let's think positive. Did you want to go somewhere... or watch a movie?"

I sighed. I just wanted to wallow in my misery. Cry in the shower, remember Avery's touch on my body, and swear at the universe for making me believe that I could be loved too. "I'm really not in the mood, sorry." My face scrunched, I forced a smile, hoping she'd take the hint and let me ugly cry in private.

"Do you have any old home movies? I'd love to see little Grace in action." She rubbed her belly lovingly. I appreciated the effort, but it was as clear as day that she'd come to babysit me rather than anything else. My eyes fell on the scar on her wrist, the memories of April's own battle shaming me. The girl had gone through so much more than I had, and yet, she always soldiered on. Pregnant to her eyeballs, she'd come to cheer me up. My heart swelled, tears glistening in my eyes.

"I don't know what I've done to deserve you, April." I leaned over and hugged my best friend.

"Show me your photo albums. God, you know all about my childhood trauma. Tell me more about yours for once."

I chuckled. "Oh god... Do we have to?"

"Yes, we do. We're gonna have a girly bonding time." She cocked her eyebrows and motioned to the comfier lounge across the room. "And this fat elephant will go and settle on the couch. You go and get those albums for us."

I caved, having realized that giving in to my best friend's maternal request was not the worst thing on the planet. A few minutes later, we were settled, photo albums on our laps, and I was showing her Grace Lawson's deep, dark, secret books. "That was me in year one." I pointed to a photo of a skinny little blonde kid, wearing jeans shorter than they should have been.

"Aw, you were pretty cute," April crooned, as her finger slid over the white frame of the picture. She turned the page and pointed to a different image. "Same year?"

I shook my head. "No. Same jeans."

When she narrowed her eyes, her head cocked, I answered the unspoken question. "Tough years, not a lot of money. I literally wore the same pair throughout most of primary school." I flipped the pages of the album, pointing at various photos of me, my jeans growing shorter and shorter. By the last one, they reached halfway up my calves, the t-shirt I wore faded.

April pursed her lips, surprise etched in her raised forehead. "Wow, I'm sorry. I hadn't realised."

I shrugged. "Don't be sorry. I was loved and cared for. We just had limited funds."

"I'm guessing dietetics and your love of good food isn't unrelated?"

"Good guess," I answered. "When food is a luxury, we quickly learn to make it last and stretch it out. And I was good at it, so it became my job. And the rest is history."

"How's your family now?"

I smiled, the memories of Mum's grin warming my heart. The first thing I'd done when we'd finished the meal prep with Avery last month was bring her one of each variety. She'd frozen them, labelling them preciously with days of the week, gratitude plastered all over her face. "They're great." *And I'll forever make sure they don't go hungry ever again.* "How's Grams? And Grandpa?" April's grandparents had raised her after her parents' car accident, and they'd been her cheerleaders at every event at the centre for years. Even I had started to consider them family.

"They're amazing. Not hating the city life as much as we dreaded. But speaking of, I was wondering if I could ask you a favour?"

I nodded. "Of course."

"They asked if they could come to the appointment tomorrow, 'cause Jarryd called in a favour from the head of H.I.P. and they're letting us have a 3D scan with one of the most recent pieces of technology in the country." She waggled her eyebrows. "And normally, I'd chastise him for it, but in all honesty, I'm excited."

I squealed, placing my hands on her belly. "Are you telling me that you guys are going to see this little one in 3D?"

She shook her head. "It's not just 3D. It's in colour, with life-size imagery on a giant screen. The machine is designed for super techy things but I don't get half of it, so I don't try to understand. And Riley asked if he could come too. So that's where you come in." She placed her hands in mock prayer.

"You want me to pick up Lizzie from day care tomorrow?"

"If you wouldn't mind."

Underneath my hand, my little nephew kicked hard. Both April and I giggled, right as I answered her. "I love picking her up. We'll play some fun games until you get home. You enjoy the moment, and make sure to bring me back some screenshots."

She checked the time on her smartwatch and shuffled to the edge of her seat when the numerals flashed. "I'll do better than that. I'll even bring you the video of it. But for now, I have to go. The spare key to the house is in the usual place, okay?"

I helped her up, her body rocking side to side as she waddled to the front door. We hugged, and within a minute, she'd disappeared into her car.

I continued to turn the pages of the photo albums. With every year that passed, more of my dreams and goals came through. On the last page, a scrapbook of a wish wedding decorated the cardboard—white, pink, and lavender colours flirting with the cut-out pictures I'd pasted there. According to the date scribbled at the top, I would have been thirteen. I sighed, my finger running over the edges while taking in the emotions still lingering in each word. Each photo. Each tiny sticker collaged around the wedding of my dreams.

My prince charming will love me more than anything on Earth. He will be beautiful, caring, and protect me from any villains. Our day will be the biggest, brightest, and most exciting wedding of the year. We'll have so much food that no one will need to eat for the next week.

My throat tightened at the last quote, and my finger shook as I traced each word like it would soothe the heart-break flooding every part of my being.

He'll never lie to me. No matter what, I will know his heart.

A sob escaped me as I tossed the scrapbook on the other side of the lounge, my arms cradling the pain in my chest. *Never lie to me...* Like Avery had done so many times, and I'd been stupid enough to believe there was something there, out of desperation to finally feel loved. I chucked the pillow next to me across the room, anger replacing the prior dejection.

Who did you think you were? Look at you. You're plain. Boring. Invisible. A guy like that was never going to settle for someone like you.

Ugly tears fell down my face, my lips trembling as my body crumbled back into itself. A guttural moan escaped my throat while my mind felt Avery's imaginary hands all over me, his lips on my forehead, his dimples calling me. I grabbed my phone and scrolled through the snapshots of us, our meals, our special moments. The pain increased with each fake memory. I stared at the photos of us fighting over desserts, a short video clip of Avery blasting The Cranberries in the kitchen as he cut onions at the speed of lightning, and what I thought was genuine emotions in his eyes through them all.

You were wrong. It was an act. Deep wailing resonated through the house, and I wiped tears and snot with an old shirt left on the couch before tossing it to my feet. Like a masochist begging for more pain, I pressed play on Avery's playlist, the one he'd made for me after he took off the first time. A variety of songs flashed up and down, but my brain stopped at the one he'd labelled: *In case you find yourself missing me.*

I'd never noticed it before. Hands shaking, I pressed play and "Wherever You Will Go" echoed loudly. Instantly, my heart sank, traitorous emotions sneaking into my mind and soul. Pain stabbed through every organ in my body, my head threatening to explode from the memories I'd never relive. Over the feelings I'd never be given a chance to experience again. All while the lyrics he'd chosen taunted me: *If I could, then I would... I hope there's someone out there who can bring me back to you... Through the darkest of your days...*

I hated Avery so much for what he'd done to me. But worse, I hated myself for being so weak that I'd missed all the signs, just because I was infatuated with the guy. His smile. His tattoos. His mysterious ways. Even his rough approach. He came with a persona that made me feel safe. Wanted. Like I mattered.

I listened to the song over and over until my brain shouted the lyrics like insults thrown at an adversary. Next, I hovered my thumb on the delete button, my heart pounding hard. *You were never safe, and you never mattered to him.* In an instant, darkness cooled me as the whole playlist vanished, followed by all of our photos and messages, until there was nothing left to remind me of him.

I closed my eyes and snuggled against the couch, allowing my gaze to trail the scrapbook photos scattered throughout the room. I ignored the half-ripped picture of my dream wedding, pretending to believe that one day, I really would be loved.

Chapter 35
Avery

Sienna looked around the airport, her childhood backpack bouncing off her shoulder. Her hair pulled back was a change, like even she had given up on normal life after this week. "Third-time lucky, right?" she deadpanned, as I loaded our suitcases onto a trolley.

I rolled my eyes. "Something like that." I felt for the passports in the side of my bag for the thousandth time, then checked the tags on our suitcases.

Mr Avery Curtis – Piazza Giuseppe Garibaldi 60. Pilastro. 43010. Parma.

Friends I'd met while doing a culinary summer school in France some years ago were picking us up. The couple was older, but they had a daughter Sienna's age, so I hoped it would help transition her somewhat. "You'll love it there," I said. "Vincent is an amazing chef and his wife, Maria, makes the best Aperol Spritz."

"Will we be staying with them for my birthday in five weeks?"

I checked the boarding pass for directions, then motioned towards the right counter. "We get the keys to our apartment next week, so probably not, but their daughter's your age so I bet she'll have a heap of cool friends to introduce you to."

"That's good," she said, conviction missing from her tone.

"I know it's hard, and it's unfair, Shorty. I feel the same. The guilt, the sadness, the wishing we didn't have to... But we're not safe here. You know that, don't you?"

She nodded, her lip wobbling. Tears filled her eyes, but she fought them and they vanished. A weak smile curled her lips. "I know. I can't stop thinking about everything though. What happened the other day with that guy, then trying to wake you up for ages... I thought you were dead." She swallowed a sob. "And I can't stop thinking of Riley, and what will happen to him when Hal shows up tomorrow. He might be his son, but I don't think he'll care... if Riley continues to reject their club."

My muscles flinched, the tension in my neck twitching. "I'm sorry this shit happened," I said. "I hate the whole lot of it, but all that matters to me now is getting you out of here."

"You know what happened to Trey's brother, right? Trey and Riley's brother?"

I shook my head. I'd been kept in the dark when it came to her fling with Trey. And Riley, until a couple of days ago, I hadn't even known he was Cooper's kid.

"Seth. I think he's younger than Trey, but older than Riley. He might be the next one right above Riley."

I narrowed my eyes. "Okay?"

"He didn't want to follow in Hal Cooper's footsteps either, and one day he went missing, but when he came back, he was all messed up."

When the woman at the counter motioned for us to

move closer, I waved to the couple behind us and they passed while I stepped to the side with Sienna. "What do you mean by messed up?"

She shook her head. "Like not himself. He'd been bashed, that part was obvious, but according to the other kids doing drugs with us, he'd been kept in the CTR for weeks."

My breathing sped up, my jaw clenching. *What have you sentenced Riley to?* "What's a CTR?"

She shuddered. "The Cooper Torture Room. Well, that's what we called it anyway, because it's filled with devices and weird electrical plugs. There's a small mattress, but I remember how it stunk in there so bad, and they're no windows. Just some makeshift toilet on the side and hand-cuffs welded in different parts of the room."

An invisible punch took my breath away, and I inhaled deeply, willing my lungs to settle. "You're telling me there's an underground torture room in that place that everyone knows exists, and yet no one does anything about it?"

"What was I gonna do? You've been there too. Even the cops are in on it half the time."

I closed my eyes, begging the universe for a way to disappear out of this fucked-up gang once and for all. But when nothing happened, I opened them, defeated. Sienna stared back at me. Her face had turned marble white and she bit her bottom lip, her fingers strangled around the strap of her backpack.

"He was in hospital for a while, and when he was finally discharged, he was in the psych ward for a month. All that Trey said at the time was that *little bitches get taught a lesson.*"

I'd seen the drug dealing in action, heard about the rapes and sex trafficking, witnessed the beatings and shootings, but never suspected that Cooper would have a full-blown torture chamber. *Who would rather torture their own kids than let them go?*

"Did anyone ever touch you?" My fists clenched as I hid the fact that my body was ready to blow. I wasn't sure how much more I could take. I stood near a precipice, hoping for the final kick to end it all as I waited for Sienna to answer.

She relaxed. "No one touched me. I was under Trey's protection, and he was adamant that he'd be my first." A shiver ran through me at the vision of a grown man fucking a thirteen-year-old girl. As if she read my mind, she added, "And you got me out before anything happened."

"Thank fuck for that," I growled.

She nodded. "But Riley won't have you to get him out. And what they did to the boys..." She inhaled deeply. "... was worse than the girls."

I raised my hands, my body pulsating with rage and panic. I couldn't save Riley and save Sienna at the same time. Watching some enforcer with his hands up her shorts wasn't something I could ever go through again. "All right, Sienna, that's as much as I can handle right now. I'm sorry we're up to our necks in ugly corruption, but torturing ourselves with it won't help anyone. I'm getting you out and that's it."

Back in the queue, Sienna and I waited in silence, until the hostess called us forward. Our passports checked, boarding passes stamped, and baggage loaded onto the plane, we made our way to the first-class waiting lounge. Deep grey recliners invited passengers to chill while a barista took orders for drinks of all kinds. Muffins, cakes, and other snacks sat in baking trays. Water bottles and cans of soda could be seen through the glass door of the mini-fridge, as businessmen read the latest professional magazines.

"Isn't all this expensive?" Sienna whispered in my ear as she played with the button on her recliner.

"Yep, but also more discreet. Do you want a drink or a muffin?"

She pointed towards a fat chocolate chip muffin and a can of Fanta. I grabbed one of each while I waited for my iced coffee, then settled next to her again.

"We have about an hour before boarding. Try to rest," I said, while I lifted the feet of my chair and closed my eyes to the sound of the classical music playing in the room. I drifted off, my body relaxing for the first time in days.

A voice called me from the back, but when I opened my eyes, we were in total blackness. Dark bricks surrounded me, moisture seeping through the cracks, and a metal banging drew my attention. I turned my head towards the noise, and a shape was curled up on the floor, one wrist handcuffed to the wall as soft wailing echoed in the filthy cave. "Help me, Avery," the prone figure cried.

I narrowed my eyes, which were now adjusting to the obscurity, my brain attempting to recognise the broken tone calling my name. I stepped closer, my boots swooshing on the mouldy concrete as the smell churned my stomach. I raised a hand to my nose, trying to block out the stench. The crying continued, the body seeking to hide its nakedness. As I stepped closer, I could tell it was a man, but based on the way his flesh moved when he shifted, he'd been starved and immobilised for some time.

"What's your name?" I asked him.

A metre away from his legs, a piss and shit bucket had been kicked against the wall. "It's me, Avery," the voice answered. "Riley."

I straightened, my feet refusing to move forward. "Riley? What happened to you?"

He looked up, his face beaten to a pulp and his flesh bruised. He'd lost weight, and sunken circles under his eyes made him look much older, a massive contrast to the juvenile body now on him.

"Stand up, Riley."

Leaning on the brick wall behind him, his arm wrestling with the handcuff holding him in place, Riley's legs shook as he pushed forward on them to face me. Blood dripped down his thighs, and he cast his gaze to the floor, ashamed, as his other hand wiped at the bright red gore escaping from his rear. He stumbled and I rushed to his side, the kid digging his fingers into my forearm. "Help me, Avery. Make them stop." Then he coughed, bile coming up and landing by my shoes. He wiped his face with the back of his hand.

My mouth opened, but no sound came out as I fought the nausea drowning my senses. My whole body shook as I held on to this kid, the life extinct from his eyes. A heavy door rustled behind us, and Riley cried as the lock creaked. He cowered at my back, his fingernails burrowing into my skin while marking words in blood on my forearm. Our eyes met and he smiled, a smile that froze me into place. It was dark. Vengeful. Not human.

"You know it's the truth, don't you?" he spat, pointing at the wounds he'd carved on my flesh. I looked down, my blood dripping and mixing with his, and my arm now tattooed with new words.

YOU DID THIS TO ME.

Icy air frosted my lungs, my heart rate skyrocketed beyond measure, and a sharp pain stabbed me in the chest.

Behind me, a hand grabbed at my shoulder, inaudible words floating in my ear. "Avery!" The hand shook me harder. "Wake up. We're gonna be late."

I jolted upright, my fingertips digging into the armrests. Sienna stared back at me, her mouth open, while a hostess rushed to mop up the iced coffee spilt all over the floor.

My sister leaned forward. "You tossed it on the ground and screamed blue murder."

An unbearable wave of sickness swirled in my gut, and I lurched myself off the chair, running to the men's room right on time to upchuck into the bowl. I steadied myself with a palm, sweat dripping off me like I'd been injected with heat straight to my core. *It's your fault. All of it is your fault.*

I'd always wondered if Cooper would kill his own flesh and blood, but the thought of what else he could do to Riley chilled me to the bone. Death would be more merciful. I cleaned up, then raced back to grab Sienna. I clutched her wrist, dragging her towards the boarding area. She tried to resist in vain. Instead, she yelled, "What are you doing? You're hurting me."

"We gotta go." I handed her the boarding passes and passports. "Sienna, sort them out. I just have to make a phone call. I'll be five." The phone pulled out of my pocket, I scrolled through the numbers until I found Jarryd's, then I pressed the dial button, my stomach churning with every unanswered ring. "Come on. Come on," I growled into the device, hanging up when the voice-mail activated. I glanced at the time flashing on the screen, my heart sinking with the realization. I had less than an hour before Cooper and his enforcers turned up to collect Riley from his house. I pushed the vision of him in that cave outside my mind and tried Jarryd's number again. No answer. "Fuck!" My fingers clamped around the cell, my throat like sandpaper.

Ringing the cops was out of the question while calling anyone but Jarryd was reckless. I closed my eyelids, a deep breath shaking my chest, my next move growing clearer by the second. I marched back towards the boarding gate, bracing for what I was about to tell Sienna. She watched me from a distance, her eyes narrowed at me and her lips flat. "What?" she asked.

I swallowed hard, my heart breaking at the thought I might never see her again. I loved this kid like my own, but if she ever found out I'd gotten Riley killed, she'd never forgive me. God, I'd never forgive myself. "You're getting on that plane alone, Shorty."

She dropped her backpack. It landed by her feet. "No, I'm not leaving you." Tears filled her eyes. "Why? What happened?"

I planted a kiss on her forehead. "I don't have time to explain. I need you safe, but I also need to do the right thing by everyone." Sienna. Riley. Jarryd. *Grace.*

"It's too late, Avery." She pointed at the passengers in front of us. "We're literally boarding now. Please don't leave me." Her voice screeched as she latched on to my arm. "I've got nobody else. Please come with me. We can start over. I promise I'll be good."

Behind us, a hostess ambled in our direction, a polite smile on her face. "Are we ready to board?"

"Yes," Sienna cried, handing the woman our passports.

I shook my head, ignoring the confused look on the hostess's face and shoved my passport in the back pocket of my jeans. "I promise I'll be there soon. Vincent will be at the airport to collect you, and you'll love Andrea. You'll be best friends before you know it. I'll call him prior to your arrival.

You have money and everything you need until you hear from me."

She launched herself into my arms, and I held her tight, sobs racking her much smaller frame. "You're my only family. I don't want to lose you."

I rubbed her back before handing her over to the hostess. The woman nodded, holding Sienna by the elbow and guiding her towards the terminal while murmuring reassuring words in her ear. Fear shook me as I wondered if I'd made the right choice, my fate now in a one-way lane. My sister stepped into the terminal, turned around, and blew me a kiss.

I smiled, calling out right as she disappeared, "You're not losing me, Shorty. You're getting your brother back."

Chapter 36
Grace

Keys. *Purse. Milkshake money.* I fumbled in my handbag, making sure I had everything I needed until I got home from April's tonight. A quick glance at the clock in my car showed almost two p.m. I had plenty of time to drive to Lizzy's day care before three.

Actually, you even have time to stop by the chemist to pick up some Nurofen. I felt better than yesterday, my mind slowly grieving Avery's betrayal while imagining us in a different dimension—a different place—and enjoying a much simpler life. It might have been make-believe, but it soothed me from the reality of knowing he was nothing but a backstabbing liar.

My ringtone snapped me out of my daze, right as I pulled out of my driveway. I grabbed the device, eyeing the name on the screen. I chuckled, then pressed the pick-up button on the console.

Geez, overprotective much. "April McKenzie... Do you not trust your best friend to look after your child for just a few hours?"

On the other end of the line, she teased, "It's April Williams these days, lady."

"Ha. True. But sometimes I have to remind you of who you were before the good doctor." I laughed along with her, grateful for our chronic banter.

"Have you driven past my house yet?" she asked, hospital machines beeping in the background.

"No, I've just left mine. Why? Everything okay?"

"Listen, you said you planned on taking Lizzy to Cold Rock, but I promised her she could use Gram's voucher next time she went, and that's twice I forgot to bring the damn thing, so if I forget again, she'll crack it. Any chance you can swing by my house on the way there and grab it?"

I shrugged, mentally saying goodbye to my chemist trip. "You realise I have money, right? I have no intention of getting the kid to pay."

The beeping in the background grew louder, as did April's laboured breathing. "Sorry, we're trying to find this high-tech room and we're lost." Jarryd mumbled something in the background, doors opening and shutting as they travelled through our old stomping ground.

"You worked at the H.I.P. for five years. How can you be lost?"

She sighed. "Because back then, we were good little allied health professionals and didn't visit the grown-up sections very often." She whistled. "But let me tell you, Mohan must have got a promotion because the place looks amazing."

I'd not stepped a foot at the Hope Island Private in ages. Since Nutrify had taken off, I'd had no time for consults at the hospital.

She continued. "Before I go... the funniest thing just happened."

I could hear her smile through the receiver. Contagion spreading, I grinned back. "Go on?"

"We just ran into Simon!"

"You gotta be kidding. What did Jarryd say?" Dr Simon Sarge was the H.I.P.'s Director of Social Work. He'd caused a great deal of grief for April and Jarryd back in the day. That, and he'd hit on her on more than one occasion. All in all, Jarryd hated him.

"Not much. They shook hands, Simon wished us the best with the baby, and he pretty much left. But god, that was awkward."

"Priceless." I chuckled before turning onto April's street. "I'm about thirty seconds from your house so I better go. Enjoy the futuristic scan and don't forget to show me everything." A goodbye or two later, I pulled into April and Jarryd's driveway. Grabbing my phone and my keys, I left the rest on the passenger seat, praying to God this voucher was exactly where April described it would be.

Junk mail stuck out of the letter box, and I grabbed it, shoving the papers under my arm as I fiddled with April's keys. I marched to the front door. The key instantly slid into the bolt, but instead of resisting the move, the handle turned, the door unlocked. *Weird. They must have forgotten...*

"Riley?" I called out as I ducked my head in. Maybe he'd changed his mind about going. His guitar lay against the wall. Untouched. I pushed the door completely open, my eyes zooming in on the muddy boot print by the buffet. *April will have a stroke.* "Riley! You're still here? I'm just after Lizzy's voucher." I stepped inside the house, eery silence enveloping me.

Don't be ridiculous. They rushed, that's all. I took a deep breath, focusing on what add-ons I'd have in my ice cream, and exhaled. Clearly, the stress of the last day was playing havoc on my head. I made it to the kitchen, a thousand pictures on the fridge, and opened the third drawer of the cabinet while following April's instructions to a T. Bills, phone contract, batteries, and even a couple of candles. But no Cold Rock voucher.

For God's sake, the kid won't even know if the voucher's real or not. I opened the pile of junk mail I'd brought in, shouting when one for the ice creamery popped up. "Ha. You'll do." The flyer folded in half, I slammed the drawer shut, then turned towards the front of the house, still on time to pick up Lizzie. Right as my foot hit the floor in the hallway, a sharp sting pulled my head rearward, and I screamed, my hands reaching for my hair. Thick fingers had me by the top of my skull, yanking me back towards the centre of the house. My throat constricted, and I struggled to breathe, shock slowing my reaction time.

"What do we do with her, boss?" a deep voice asked.

I closed my fingers around his wrist, hoping to stop him from ripping my hair out. The pain increased as I moved. "Let me go!"

The hand yanked my head harder, while another snaked itself around my neck. "Feisty little bitch, ain't she?"

Dark leather shoes stepped closer, their heels clicking on the tiles with every step. "Well, that's a surprise. You're not my son, are you?"

My heart sank. A wave of adrenaline paralysed me into place. *Hal Cooper.* "Let me go, please," I pleaded. To hell with my pride, I'd get that later. "No one's here. They've gone on holiday. They won't be back for a week." The lie came naturally.

"Look at me, young lady." Hal's tone left no room for negotiation. Behind me, the fist holding my hair dropped to my throat, and I clawed at the forearm now choking me. "It's never a good idea to lie to me."

"I'm not lyi—"

His open hand slapped me across the face. I screamed, heat radiating through my jaw. The arm around my throat tightened, and I coughed, air wheezing as I breathed in. Cooper crouched until he stared me in the face. Then, he grabbed my chin, forcing me to look him in the eye. "We both know you are. So, clearly, you know who I am."

I wrestled against the man holding me in place. "Everyone knows who you are." Cooper's sidekick chortled. "What do you want?" I pressed.

The thug motioned to the lounge room, and his goon dragged me there along with him. I flinched when one of my ankles twisted but ignored the throbbing as he tossed me on the couch. "Sit." It wasn't a polite offer.

I crossed my arms, fear setting in. The stories about the Cooper gang I'd heard from Riley and Jarryd weren't great. But they were tame compared to the ones they wouldn't share. My hand slid down until I felt the phone in my back pocket. Like an unused Joker, I hoped I'd soon get the perfect opportunity to call for help.

Be smart. It's not you they want. Play with their heads and get yourself out. "Listen, I'm not a parent, but I can only imagine how you might be feeling," I said, the saccharine tone almost believable. A fake smile plastered on my face, I tilted my head towards Cooper in sympathy. "I'm sure if you invited Riley to a family dinner, and slowly rebuilt the connection, he might—"

A boot thumping against the base of the couch interrupted me. "Shut up, bitch," the sidekick growled, his teeth showing like a rabid dog.

Cooper sighed, then stepped closer to me. His stomach

protruded above the leather belt holding his pants upright, the button of the crisp white shirt stretched by his size. The lounge shifted with his weight. "Grace." His finger pushed a strand of hair behind my ear. "That is your name, isn't it?"

I nodded, repulsion boiling through my blood at his touch.

Then, in an instant, he had the back of my neck crushed with his hand, pulling me towards him as his fingers imprinted in my flesh. "Don't ever bring up my sons again, you little bitch."

I whimpered, tears brimming my eyes. "I'm sorry." My hand curled into a fist at the pain, my mind slowly accepting my fate. This wouldn't end well. Fear stunned me as I realised no one would come for me. *I was no one's priority*.

The hand behind my head moved up to my hair, and he yanked it back until my throat was exposed. Then, he lowered his mouth, his tongue licking the throbbing vein hiding beneath my collar. I cried, my mind losing its grasp on hope and strength; despair and fear drowning me instead. *God, help me.*

"Where's my son?" Cooper barked into my ear, right before he bit my lobe, the shooting pain taking my breath away. His spit dripped down my neck, the warmth a major contrast to the shivering inside me.

"Argh," I sobbed. "I don't know. Please let me go."

"Maybe I should just leave you to get acquainted with Alexandro here, and then, *maybe*, you'll remember where I can find my son."

The rabid dog cackled, then leaned over the armchair until our shoulders touched. "I think that's a great idea, boss. She's on the skinny side, but I'm sure I can still make her squeal."

I flinched when his fingers brushed my breast, disgust sending a wave of nausea to my stomach. *Find a way. You have to get out of this.* Cooper had made it clear he was only after one thing: Riley. Maybe if I pretended to give it to him, he'd let me leave. Desperation flooded me with dicey ideas at best, but in the end, all I needed was five minutes alone to call for help. I took a deep breath, bracing myself for another blow if this failed. "No. Please. Riley's at a conference on the Gold Coast. Griffith University. He's there now. Until five."

Cooper and his lackey exchanged a look, hesitation in their eyes. Then the goon moved in closer, his arm around my shoulder, and he said, "You know what will happen if you're lying, right?"

I nodded, my body shaking against its will.

"What conference?" Cooper asked, his lips tight.

"I don't know," I cried. "Something to do with youth work." I brought my legs together and motioned down the hall. "Can I please use the bathroom? I need to pee." *Please say yes. I just need five minutes.* When Cooper waved his hand in the air, his obedient beast lifted its arm to set me free. I shuffled to the edge of the couch and jumped to my feet, the phone in my pocket now heavy. "Thank you."

Limping to the bathroom, my heart racing, I locked the door behind me and turned on the faucet. Right as I was about to dial ooo, Riley's voice echoed in my head: *Half the cops are in on it.* Tears ran down my face, my vision blurry, but I managed to pull the phone out. A sob escaped my throat when Jarryd's number went straight to voicemail. I hit the sink with my palm, ignoring the pain shooting through my fingers, and tried to slow down my breathing.

"Hurry up, bitch," the rabid dog called from the lounge room.

I racked my brain for what to do next. I scrolled to Riley's number, but stopped short of calling him. Telling the kid that *unless he turned up, his father might kill me* sounded like something Cooper would want me to do. No, I needed a grownup with some experience with the drug lord, who might care enough about me to want to help. *Avery.*

I closed my eyes, ignoring the self-talk bashing me with reminders that Avery never cared about me: *He used you. He doesn't love you. He's gone.*

"Do I have to send Alexandro to fetch you, Grace?" Cooper yelled from a distance.

"I'll be a minute. I'm almost done," I yelled back, my voice trembling and my heart laughing at me. In my darkest hour, I still hoped for the man I loved to save me. I scrolled to his name, fear crushing my spirit, and I pressed dial, the handset as close to my mouth as possible. He answered on the second ring, traffic resonating in the background. *He's driving.*

"Grace, I'll explain everything soon. I have to find Riley." Avery's tone was tense. Worried.

I sobbed into the phone. "Riley's with Jarryd at the hospital." Hiccups interrupted me. "Cooper was waiting for him at the house."

"Where are you right now?" His words were clipped.

"At their house," I cried into the phone. "In the bathroom, but they're right outside the door."

"Fuck!" Avery yelled into the phone. Then his voice slowed right down. "Listen to me, Grace. I'm coming for you. Hang in there. Just—"

The crunching of the door interrupted us, and the fibre-board splintered like a toothpick. Next to me, wood debris collapsed in on itself, hitting me in the process. I shrieked, the phone dropping by Cooper's feet. His hand connected with my face, and I screamed as I fell back. My skull hit the toilet bowl, pain shooting through my brain, and for a second, everything went black.

When I opened my eyes again, I was back on the couch, a gun pointed at my head while Cooper rocked on April's chair with my phone against his ear. "One second late, and I put a bullet in her head," he snarled, then he flung the device across the room, the screen shattering and bits of plastic and metal scattering the floor. An evil smile lit his face, my mind struggling to comprehend why. Dizziness and nausea overtook my senses, the throbbing in my ankle and head only making it worse.

Then it hit me. *Oh god.* They hoped I'd ring him. "You knew..." I cried, my palm covering my mouth.

Cooper rose to his feet, and after one look, Alexandro tossed him some thick tape. Cooper fiddled with the roll, ripping a large piece, then settled in front of me. His grin deepened, his pupils darkening. "I've been playing this game much longer than you, Grace." He forced the tape over my lips, whacking my mouth hard in the process. I whimpered. "I was hoping for Riley. But you're giving me better. With Avery, I'll get my son *and* the dead man who took him from me."

Chapter 37
Avery

Panic had my stomach in knots, my heart rate spiking with the adrenaline now fuelling my blood. Cooper had Grace. *My Grace.* Her sobs, combined with the screaming as the bastard grabbed her, had me losing focus on the road. *I'll kill him.*

A minivan almost hit me, and I swerved just in time to avoid a collision. A quick glance in the rear-view mirror, and my lungs exhaled when the family appeared oblivious to the near miss. I pushed my foot to the floor, running through a red light, and didn't stop until Williams's house was around the corner.

Focus, Curtis. You need a plan. My hand tightened against the steering wheel, my knuckles pale. There was no fucking plan. All I had was the blood rushing to my head, the rage possessing me, and the determination to do all it took to get Grace to safety. Nothing else mattered.

I grabbed my phone, swiped to Jarryd's name, and texted him.

Cooper got Grace at your house. On my way there. Check your emails.

I veered onto the lawn in front of their home, jolting forward as my tires hit the curb. I bolted to the front door still hanging ajar. I pushed it quietly, sliding through the open kitchen. A couple of rooms away, deep voices mumbled. I scanned the room until my eyes landed on the knife block, and I pulled a few until I settled on a sharp paring knife. I slid it through my belt.

"I'm coming in, Cooper." I stepped into the lounge room, my hands in the air.

The man was sprawled on a rocking chair, his feet extended like a Russian king. Across from him, Alexandro— one of his favourites but not the most vicious of the Cooper enforcers—mirrored his boss. My eyes searched for Grace, angst building. As if he read my mind, Hal pointed to the shuffling behind his goon. "Is that what you're looking for?"

Instantly, Alexandro moved back, and Grace appeared. Bound and tied. Bloodied and bruised. *Jesus Christ...* Shock and fear sucked the life out of my breath. It hitched, my eyes unable to leave the vision in front of me. This wasn't my Grace. This was a broken woman, terror and tears floating in her gaze. My protective instincts kicked in, and a surge of adrenaline added to my determination to get her out. "I'm here now. She can go." Alexandro snickered in response. I jerked my head towards him, my jaw clenched. "I'm not talking to you, fuckwit."

Cooper straightened. "Not a good way to start, Curtis."

I took a step closer and both Cooper and Alexandro jumped to their feet. I raised my hands where they could see them. "Relax. I know the drill. Let's just get the girl out so we can talk amongst men, yeah?"

"That's not how it works, and I think you might need another reminder as to who calls the shots here."

I'll kill you slowly and love every minute of it. "I just want to make sure she's okay, and then we can talk business." I took another step, but Alexandro threw an arm in front of me, blocking my way. I turned towards Cooper. "I'm gonna check her, and then I'm going to back up slowly. Right, Cooper?"

He nodded once, and his man dropped his arm. I rushed forward, grabbing her face with my hands as I inventoried her visible injuries: a bite mark blotted the top of her neck near her ear, both her cheekbones were bruised, blood seeped from her nose, and red fingerprints were scattered on her arms. When my palm cupped her jaw, she leaned into me, tears flowing. With my mouth tucked in the crook of her neck, I murmured into her ear, "I love you. I'll get you out, I swear."

Her breath increased, and she blinked, her body tensing as Cooper grabbed me by the shoulders and threw me across the room. My back hit the coffee table, and I winced when the blade hidden in my pants pierced my skin.

"What a lovely little scene," Cooper mocked. "Almost like you didn't use her for business."

Alexandro laughed, then in one rough motion, ripped the sticky tape off Grace's mouth. Her face tensed, and she recoiled at his presence. Visions of his body lying in a pool of blood kept me controlled, and I inhaled, forcing the breaths to keep me focused. On target. "Your beef has nothing to do with her, so let her go and let's talk."

Cooper's eyes darkened, and he marched towards me, determination in his stride. Right as I was getting back up, Alexandro kicked me behind the knees, and I fell, on time for Cooper's fist to bust my lip. Behind us, Grace screamed, but Cooper and I kept our eyes locked on each other. Despite my head spinning, I recovered quickly enough to avoid the next kick from his guy. Fury and shame saturated me. It was one thing getting beaten by a gang on a regular basis. It was another to have them do it in front of Grace, like I was some sort of ball-less coward.

You'll fight back when she won't have to pay for it.

"Don't hurt him," Grace yelled, her voice dry, before she broke into a coughing fit.

I narrowed my eyes, my lips flat. "How long have you had her gagged?"

Alexandro shrugged, his nonchalance tipping my rage over some imaginary cliff. I spun around, and in a split-second took a swing at him, my fist landing on his nose. My knuckles popped, or maybe it was his nasal cavity. I didn't care either way. He dropped, blood gushing out, and brought both hands to his face. "You broke my nose, you fucking bastard. You'll pay for this."

I spun again, relaxing my fighting stance just in time to see Cooper lower his phone. *Fuck. Now you've pissed him off.* Within seconds, footsteps barged into the house, and Black Tulip and a couple of other massive guys had us surrounded. If I didn't get Grace out soon, she'd really get hurt. I swallowed hard, fighting the need to lay into them. With Sienna safe, a weight had been lifted off my shoulders and I craved restitution for what they had done to us. But first, I needed Grace out of their crosshairs.

"Well, if that's not my future brother-in-law," a voice droned amongst them. A couple of the other guys laughed.

I turned, recognising the fuckwit. Instantly, I saw red, my hatred for the family barely keeping me breathing. "You can forget about Sienna, Trey."

He ambled towards me, then fell back onto the couch

next to Grace. "Why is that, bro? She and I are a perfect match."

"Because you're ten years older than her, and she's out of the game," I spat.

Grace's eyes widened. "Sienna?" she murmured, loud enough for Trey to twist himself towards her.

A vicious smile curled his lips. "Sienna was our most hopeful recruit, until this wannabe daddy agreed to pay her debt."

A deal with the Devil I was still obligated to make good on almost four years later. Her mouth formed an O as she put some of the pieces together. "They blackmailed you," she said to herself, her voice thinning.

Trey rolled his eyes. "Oh my... so dramatic." He whipped his head around until he completely faced her. "Now, you're a smart woman. Am I not someone you'd like to have in your corner?"

She narrowed her eyes, studying me from a distance. Then, she addressed Cooper. "You're nothing but a piece of shit. How could you use a kid like that?"

He growled, but before he could get to Grace, his son had his arm around her, shielding her from the older man's assault. "Relax, Pops," he said to his father. "Let me be the ladies' man of the family." He kissed Grace on the cheek, and my whole body strained as my fingers felt for the blade behind me. I waited to see what his next move was. He loosened his posture, crossing his legs on the upturned coffee table in front of them. "See, Sienna was quite happy with her lot in life. And she and I..." He waggled his eyebrows as he said it. "...got along dandy. So why big bro, here, chose to be my old man's bitch in exchange for her supposed freedom... *that*, I have no clue."

I clenched my jaw, my nails digging into my fists.

"Because she was thirteen," I growled. "A life with you was a life in jail, drug-fucked and running from one kill to the next."

Cooper snapped his gun out of its holster and pointed it towards me. "Okay. That's enough. I'm tired of all this dramatic reminiscing. I want Riley, dead or alive."

Grace gasped, and Trey pretended to shudder. "Pops, you're scaring my new lady."

Cooper cocked his gun as he took a step towards me. "Get me my son here, or I'll blow your brains out."

Adrenaline rocked me as I stared into the barrel. "You don't scare me anymore, Hal. Four years of this shit and it keeps on giving. There's always more, isn't there?"

"I don't scare you?" His voice dripped with the unspoken threat. "What about this?" Slowly, he turned on his heels until the front sight was aiming straight for Grace's head. Trey grabbed her by the biceps and pushed her forward, so his father had the perfect angle. "I wonder if you love this one as much as you love the other one?" Hal sneered.

Grace whimpered and shut her eyes tight. She clasped her hands, soft sobbing moving her chest up and down. My heart bled, acceptance lodging itself in my brain. "Grace, baby. Look at me."

She lifted her head slowly. Our eyes met. Hers filled with fear, mine with resignation.

I spoke to her softly, like we weren't standing in a room with thugs pointing guns at our heads. "I love you. Don't ever forget it."

She squirmed against Trey, and he gripped her harder. "Don't do it, Avery. Please, don't."

A weak smile formed, my heart suddenly naked with all my feelings, emotions, even my fears laid bare for her. I loved this woman. I had loved her from the beginning, but I'd been too stubborn to admit it, and now that I could lose her forever, I wanted her to know. "Drop the fucking gun," I pronounced each word slowly, staring Cooper in the eye. "Or I will end you. You, your son, your bikie gang, and everything you care about."

Cooper flinched, clearly not used to being stood up to. Around him, Trey and the enforcers waited for instructions, guns cocking right, left, and centre. Alexandro lurched at me, and I moved to the side, avoiding his blow. He collapsed on the already-splintering coffee table, and I kicked the base of his back. He grunted. He turned around, his fist aiming for my stomach, but I locked the back of his elbow with my arm, the enforcer screaming as his bone crunched. Then, I pulled the knife from my back and stabbed him in the stomach.

Grace screamed again, her voice like white noise now. All I could focus on was the number of bodies I'd have to drop to end this nightmare. Right as I went to pull my blade out of Alexandro's gut, my arms were pulled back, and a kick to the underside of my knees had me on the ground. Four biceps held me, my own blade now at my throat.

Cooper whistled, then marched towards the men weighing me down. "I'm impressed, Curtis." He grabbed the blade off the guy holding it and pressed the metal harder against my neck. Warm drops drizzled down, and I tensed at the sharp sting. He sighed, shaking his head. "It would be so easy to end you." He stared at the knife like it held the answer to all his problems. "But you have been one of my best enforcers, Curtis. I won't lie."

"Don't hurt him!" Grace screamed, trying to get out of Trey's grip to no avail. "Please, let him go."

"If only you just accepted what you're good at." Cooper

pressed the blade harder, the bite of its edge worsening. "I would welcome you back in the fold. You and Riley. Back home where you belong."

I closed my eyes, seeking to stop the visions of Grace sobbing in Trey's hold. A part of me hoped Hal would just press harder. End it. Once and for all. But as I opened my eyes, my woman in another man's arms, her pain and fear screaming in my head, I resigned myself to the only thing I could do to save her. "She walks off, and I'll join your club."

Chapter 38
Grace

W e had it wrong. We had it all wrong. My mind froze at the image of Avery on his knees, a knife to his throat, pain and desperation in his voice: *She walks off, and I'll join your club.*

"Avery, no," I screamed, my throat burning. Trey's fingers dug into my biceps. I ignored the pinch, pushing him away with my shoulders. "Let me go," I warned, my jaw tight.

"Cooper, is that a deal?"

Hal pursed his lips and handed the knife to the man behind him. "It sounds very attractive, Avery, but you've tried to skip town a few times with this last job, so I'm a teeny bit worried you might have the same idea."

"If you let her go right now, I'll give you my word." Avery's tone was flat, and my heart broke at how blind I'd been. I'd never put the signs together, and worse, I'd assumed he was working for Hal and loving the perks, when really, he'd been putting his life on hold for years to protect his sister. *And now you.*

Cooper signalled something to his men, and they let

Avery go. He got up, tears of blood dripping from his throat before disappearing under his shirt. He snatched the knife from the guy behind him, and in one stride, he was by my side, my wrists suddenly freed. My chef's pupils turned jet black. They screamed fearless, scaring even me. As soon as Trey registered the twitching in Avery's jaw, his fingers tensing against the blade, the kid took his hands off me, and Avery grabbed my palm, pulling me off the couch and towards the front of the room.

Warmth filled me at his touch. He locked his fingers with mine, his grip tight. His pulse jumped through his wrist, and fear settled when our heart rates synched. Once we'd crossed the room, Avery stopped a couple of metres away from Cooper and his men, shielding me behind him. I clung onto his forearm, my chest against his back. "I'm going to let her go now," he said to Cooper.

I grasped his hand tighter. "I'm not leaving you here with them."

He turned slightly, his eyes remaining on the thugs. "Baby, you have to go. Please. Just go."

My forehead rested on his back, my hand shaking in his. "I love you. I can't lose you again," I cried.

He squeezed my fingers and exhaled. "I'm sorry for everything. I'll never stop loving you, no matter what happens." Then, he forced his hand away from mine. "Find Sienna when all is done."

A cold sweat drowned me, and my brain fogged at his words. My mouth dried, sentences struggling to form in my throat. "No. No way. You'll look after her yours—"

Avery turned around, authority emanating from his eyes. I swallowed hard, my brain begging to have misunderstood what he *wasn't* saying. He cupped my face, his pupils glistening. "I love you, Grace Lawson, but you're leaving."

I closed my eyes, a sob jolting me, and I let go of him. "Finally," Cooper snapped. "Get rid of the bitch or I will. We have business to discuss."

Avery remained stoic, nothing shifting within him. His breath steady, his body immovable. I stepped away, a thousand shards of despair, fear, and grief stabbing at my heart.

Then I saw them. First shadows, then their faces. Cold. Confident. Ready. Riley and Jarryd followed by all the guys from the launch. A dozen men marched in their footsteps, weapons of all kinds tucked in their belts or holsters. Like a pack of wolves, they advanced together, not leaving a single member behind.

I gasped. Avery's lips twitched, a smile flirting with his eyes, and his shoulders dropped. Cooper jumped to his feet. "What the fuck is this, Curtis?" His pupils dilated when he noticed his youngest stomping in.

"My last job for you, Hal. I'm delivering your son. Like you asked."

Riley and Jarryd joined Avery's side. The three men, shoulders squared, exchanged a glance, and Jarryd nodded towards my prodigal chef, some unspoken message conveyed. "I'm here, Hal. Isn't that what you wanted?" Riley spat. A darkness I'd never noticed lined his features. A vein pulsed hard in his neck, and he crossed his arms, legs spread as he faced his father for the first time in seven years.

On the other end of the room, Trey sided with the drug lord, the brothers staring at each other next to their chosen families. "Riley." The eldest of the two thrust his chin up.

My face blanched at the greeting he tossed at his younger sibling. Envy crossed Trey's features, and my spirit sank with compassion for anyone stuck with Hal Cooper from birth.

"Hi, Trey. Out of Jail?"

"No thanks to you. But lucky for me, my girlfriend came to visit once or twice before you got your claws into her."

Riley's face hardened. "She was never your girlfriend."

Trey stepped forward. Cooper grabbed the kid by the shoulder, stopping his progression. Riley's older brother clenched his jaw and continued speaking from his father's flank. "I'll decide when she's no longer my girlfriend, and I'll get her back in the club. If you like her so much, I suggest you come home."

Riley's hand clenched, but he relaxed when Jarryd murmured something in his ear. "Neither of us are going to get near her. You're nothing but trouble, and..." Emotions passed over his features, like a curtain he refused to drop for far too long. "...no Cooper will taint her. Not even me."

Trey cackled. "Come on, brother, you're gonna try to make me believe you'd choose to stay away from her, just to prove a point?"

"I'll never touch her if it guarantees that she's safe from you and this fucked-up family. She's dead to you, Trey," he hissed. "And if she has to be dead to me too, to make sure this happens, well, so be it."

Like he'd once again grown bored of the games, Hal whistled in the room, and everyone turned towards the loud pitch. He pointed at his men and barked, "End this now."

One of the enforcers, the one with a black tulip on his forearm leaned into Cooper. They nodded, then their guns cocked with the ends directed at Avery, Jarryd, and Riley. I threw my fist in my mouth, biting it until all sound had died inside my throat. Behind the trio, Avery's chefs and friends brandished their own weapons, and everyone in the room froze at a standstill.

"You see this ending well, Hal?" Avery warned.

"There're five of you. Twelve of us. At best, we walk out. At worst, we all die. Your choice."

Cooper sat back on his chair, the rocking resuming. He stretched his legs out, the lines of his forehead smoothing. "You're insulting me, gentlemen. You think I've got to where I am," he said, his voice growing louder, "by letting pretty little boys intimidate me?"

Then, as if triggered by a secret code, Cooper's men charged towards the group. As soon as Avery, Jarryd, and Riley noticed the shift, they crouched into fighting stances and braced for the frontal assault. Like he'd waited for the opportunity for way too long, Riley met Trey halfway. They moved together like mirror images of each other, their resemblance now striking. Trey threw the first punch. Riley moved sideways, his knee landing in his brother's stomach.

Not far from them, Jarryd faced the tattooed enforcer, the tension palpable. Based on the blood on his lip, he'd received a blow to the face. Then, when his opponent least expected it, Jarryd had the guy in a head lock, his fist laying into his side, the enforcer grunting.

A couple of metres from me, Avery motioned for Cooper to take him on. I gulped, all my fears turning into a ball of dread in the pit of my stomach. The grin on Cooper's face transformed my angst into fury. I was beyond enraged. My tears vanished as I willed Avery to end this once and for all. Cooper's expression grew blank. Not afraid. *Yet.* But visibly shocked. Like he'd not expected to find himself off his throne for the first time in a decade. My hand lowered from my mouth as I refused to be paralysed anymore, and I narrowed my eyes at the bastard as he approached the love of my life. *He will end you.*

Cooper paused, then rushed forward until his whole body strangled Avery by the waist. Avery elbowed him in the gut a thousand times as he was freed. His muscles flexed, his eyes flickering, inviting his enemy to strike again. A filthy, smug smirk lit Cooper's face, obliterated by Avery's right hook to his jaw.

All around, chaos drowned us. Screaming, grunting, and the sound of broken furniture being tossed as Avery's crew fought with the gang members. Blood dripped from all sides, and I snapped my eyes shut, frustration killing me. Every emotion I'd ever felt bubbled to the surface, boiling like a volcano ready to erupt. Memories of the last three months flashed in my eyes: fear, pain, despair... *love*.

I hissed with rage, no longer willing to sacrifice what we could have, at the hands of the piece of crap in front of me. Hatred encompassed my mind. Determination settling in my soul, as Avery wrestled with the man who'd destroyed everyone's life. And I knew, without a shadow of a doubt, that I would do anything it took to protect the ones I loved too.

Next to me, Riley elbowed Trey in the mouth, and the eldest brother fell, his gun flying across the room. As if in slow motion, I watched the weapon bounce against the floor, right before I launched for it. The metal felt heavy in my palm. Bracing both hands on the textured grip, I held it tight. Secure. A month ago, I hadn't been able to protect Avery from his demons. But today, I would.

I stepped towards the turmoil, my arms steady. Avery's eyes met mine before the barrel was flush against Cooper's head. For a second, he froze, and there was a minute of dead silence as I screamed, "Enough!"

Cooper stiffened as the gun cocked. Glances were exchanged, hesitation saturating the room from all sides. "Let me take the gun, Grace." Avery slid next to me, and his hands replaced mine. He shoved it further into Cooper's temple. "While you're in a cooperative mood, I want to strike another deal with you."

"I'm listening," Cooper hissed.

Jarryd and Riley moved forward so they could face him as they spoke. "I received an interesting email today. Can you believe it, Riley?" Jarryd said.

Riley crouched in front of his father. "Yeah, I was as stunned as you were. Four years of perfect intel on the Cooper gang: where they've been, what they're planning, names, dates, places. I mean, if that doesn't get us something, I don't know what will."

From a distance, Trey yelled, "Like you'd do that to your own flesh and blood?"

"Here's what's gonna happen, Hal. I'm gonna make sure this info gets buried deep somewhere, where no one will ever find it. All I ask in exchange is that you mind your own fucking business, and we mind ours." Avery waited for a response, the gun not moving an inch.

"How do I know you'll stick to your word?" Cooper spat between clenched teeth.

My heart rate intensified, my body and mind awaiting the drug lord's decision. Then Riley leaned forward, looking his father in the eyes, and said, "You'll know, *Dad*, because we share blood, and honour is the only good thing you've kept all these years. You have my word if I have yours."

Cooper pushed to his feet, his gaze never losing sight of Riley. A grin formed on his face, pride filling his eyes. Avery lowered the gun. "There's my son," Hal said as he squared his shoulders. "Right there." Then he turned around, pointed towards the door, and just as quickly as they'd arrived, the thugs were gone, Avery's crew following in their footsteps.

"Oh my god. I thought I'd lost you." My body crippled by tremors, I lurched myself into Avery's arms.

He gripped me tight, enveloping my waist as he kissed me. "God, Grace Lawson... I love you so much."

I sighed into his chest, inhaling him like it was the first time. "Don't ever do that to me again."

Another kiss blessed my lips, and I leaned into the soothing feeling. A couple of throats cleared behind us, and I blushed as Jarryd and Riley extended their palms to my chef. They embraced. Like brothers who'd finally found each other. "I was getting worried for a minute," Avery teased.

Riley chuckled, a hand running over his thick black hair. "Just in the nick of time, hey?"

"I appreciate everything you've done today, Curtis." Jarryd ignored the phone ringing in his pocket. "And I'm sorry we didn't have you figured out."

The ringtone went off again, and when Jarryd ignored it for the second time, a text beeped loudly for his attention. I chuckled from Avery's arms. "Can't catch a break, can you?"

Jarryd rolled his eyes, the message loading as he paled. Then he said, "April's having the baby."

Chapter 39
Avery

Grace stiffened in my arms. "What? As in, right now?" Jarryd nodded, the colour further draining from his face. "It's just started, but if it's anything like Lizzy's birth, God..." He raked his hair. "Today of all days!"

I extended my hand again, and Jarryd shook it. "Can we do anything in the meantime?"

He blew a breath, his eyes scanning the bomb field around us. "If you're serious, I wouldn't mind an actual house to come back to, with an exhausted wife and a new baby, before Lizzy gets dropped off by Grams in the morning."

Grace tilted her head, a grimace growing on her face. "I have a feeling that April wouldn't mind either." Then, she mock punched him on the shoulder and said, "Go. What are you waiting for?"

He chuckled, excitement building, and nodded towards Riley. "I'll take you to Grams, and we can all meet back at the hospital when our boy makes his grand entrance." Jarryd and Riley dashed out, leaving Grace and me in the middle of the mayhem. In each other's arms.

"I think I'm still in shock," she whispered, her fingers digging into my forearm, like she was afraid I'd run off.

"And I'm in awe of you." I cupped her face, my eyes plunging into hers. "I can't believe how kick-ass you were today. I owe you our lives."

She shook her head. "It's your quick thinking that got us out in the end. And the double-spy move? Clever. You're a genius." Heat warmed her cheeks. Her lips curled, and she moved forward until they touched mine. I inhaled her scent, the smell of fear fading away slowly, and allowed her to penetrate my pores until her soul had settled within the depths of my existence.

Our tongues touched, dancing to the same tune. Celebrating the reprieve. Memorialising our open hearts. Being able to tell Grace I loved her was a new feeling, but God I cherished every part of it. My chin rested on her head, and she tightened her arms around my waist.

"How will I ever let you go?" she murmured against my chest.

I chuckled. "You don't have to ever let me go again, Grace." A kiss landed on her forehead.

"Other than long enough to clear this house."

She pried herself from me, small lines forming at the crease of her eyes. "Hmm. Any chance your crew is available for a bit longer?"

Gaging from the commotion on the side of the street, the answer was yes. A good thing, given we'd kicked ass big time, taking half the house down with us. But with all these guys around, we'd have it cleared before the bundle of joy showed his face.

"Congrats, man." I placed my palm on Jarryd's shoulder. He glowed from head to toe. Behind us, the women fussed over the little blue ball in April's arms, Grace's clucky eyes making me want to fuck her right then and there, every time she cooed at the tiny mewing coming from the boy.

Jarryd followed my line of sight. "I know that look." He chuckled.

I raised my hands in the air, panic teasing me as I realized the depths of which Grace and I had fallen so fast. "Wow, don't even kid about that, Williams. All this is—"

"New? Fucking unbelievable? Nothing you ever thought could happen to you?"

My throat tightened. "Sounds like you've been where I am, brother."

He nodded, love oozing from him like chocolate sauce in a warm lava cake. "You bet. But let me tell you one thing: Resistance is futile. They have our balls for good."

And our hearts. I shook my head, the visions of Grace holding my child dissolving in my mind, and asked, "Any updates from Cooper?"

Jarryd's face darkened slightly. "Nothing for me. Trey messaged Riley though. I think, deep down and as messed up as it is, they have history."

"Any *history* in that family is a concern."

"I agree. But he asked me to trust him, to let him handle them. So, I guess I have to."

"Well, you know where to find me if Cooper starts anything."

A curt nod flashed before he continued. "Tell me about Nutrify, then? You're in for good?"

I smiled, unable to hide from my fate any longer. "She's already got it all planned out. I bet she's emailed half the state with updates. I think it's fair to say that wherever she goes, I go."

In the distance, Grace glanced at me. Her blue eyes shone through the whole room, her smile warm enough to roast the whole of Antarctica. She tapped her heart with one fist, then extended her hand towards me before opening her arms to the little boy.

"Like you ever had a choice." Jarryd laughed. "Welcome to the family."

Epilogue

Grace
12 Months Later

The Parma sun kissed me in all the right places. I sunk into my sunlounge, the Puccini in my hand begging me to take another sip. My lips pressed around the straw, and I sucked on the mandarin-flavoured drink. "Muffin, at this rate, we'll need to open a bar too. You've become a cocktail god."

A hand travelled up my thigh, settling right at the seam of my swimmers. "I'll offer you a deal," Avery murmured in the crook of my neck. "You make love to me like you did this morning, and I'll whip you up a thousand of these."

I chuckled, my fingers kneading the back of his head, and I kissed him, his lips suddenly tasting like citrus too. His tongue invaded my mouth, and my nipples hardened at his touch. I pressed my legs together, heat stirring in my core, and he laughed, his hand teasing me over my bathers.

"No. Don't close your legs. I like them spread. Wide."

My eyes opened, my lips lifted, and I winked at the man standing in front of me on the balcony of our holiday haven. Avery's natural olive tone had taken on a darker complexion from two weeks of gallivanting in Italy. The lines on his face, which had marked him over the last couple of months, had smoothed out, and he sported a relaxed aura I'd not seen on him before. Or maybe it was just the amazing European sex.

I traced his stomach with my index finger and his tight abs twitched. I followed his happy trail and he grunted, his shorts stirring at my touch. I waggled my eyebrows, a grin stretching my cheeks. He launched forward and tossed me over his shoulders. I squealed.

"That's it, baby. You're going back to bed where you belong." In one stride, he'd crossed into the apartment and lowered me onto the mattress, his body descending with mine. His mouth teased my collarbone. "God, you smell so nice."

Soft kisses trailed my chest, starting above my breasts. Slowly, Avery opened his mouth, his lips caressing the mounds before sucking at my nipples, and instantly, I grew wet. My hands landed on his chest, my fingers massaging his flesh while his tattoos danced with the movement. My calf locked behind his knee, and I tugged him closer to me. "I could have you on top of me forever, Avery Curtis."

His pelvis pressed into mine. "That makes two of us." Then, his fingers grabbed the top of my thigh and he lifted it until I fit perfectly, like we were somehow two pieces of the same puzzle.

"What time is Sienna coming?" I murmured, my eyes closed.

"As soon as she decides to say goodbye to her friends." He chuckled. "Stop distracting me with my sister."

I rubbed my palms over his shoulders, and his muscles flexed as his hands travelled my body with more intensity. "Just checking that she doesn't do an *Avery* and take off before our flights back home tomorrow."

We hadn't heard much from Sienna in the last couple of months. Riley had heard nothing at all. Hopefully, returning to Australia would help with settling her tumultuous emotional development after years of unresolved trauma.

Avery pulled himself away, a tiny frown drawing a line between his eyebrows. "She better not. We still have so much to do before *Bello A&G Italiano* launches next month."

Nutrify had taken off and turned into both a self-sustaining and profitable venture, and while it would always be my baby, opening a family restaurant was also something I looked forward to. Lodged in the beautiful Sanctuary Cove, our new endeavour promised to be out of this world. Like my chef.

"The plates and paintings arrived this morning," I said between soft murmurs. "And the Italian exports should be there by the time we land."

His kissing escalated, and my breath quickened under his touch. "They better have got me the real deal. I won't cook with shitty ingredients." His fingers travelled to my side, teasing my ribs.

A laugh exploded from my chest, and I rolled us both until I was straddling him. "You are such a cheat, but two can play that game." I closed my fist and rubbed hard on the underside of his chin.

He wrestled beneath me, a chortle brewing deep within

his belly, then grabbed my hands and landed a kiss on my knuckles. "Okay, I surrender. I'll change Scotty's nappies next time we're on duty if you let me love you now."

I winked at him, then leaned over until I could taste his breath. His mouth opened. It welcomed mine. Our heart rates spiked with each stroke, and I moaned, eyes closed, as his hands rested on my ass. "God, I love you," I murmured to the universe.

In one swift motion, he had me underneath his naked body, my swimmers tossed to the ground. He raised himself on his elbows, our chests touching. And with a devilish grin, his knee nudged mine. My legs widened and our eyes met, the energy in the room shifting. Then, he lined himself up, his hardness teasing my core. "Are you ready for me?"

I exhaled, my heart swelling. "I am now."

And with one thrust, Avery took over my body, mind, and soul.

The End

Dangerous Love

Check out the next page for a SNEAK PEEK of Dangerous Love
Book 3 in The Hope Island Series

Available on **Amazon**

Love may just be the most dangerous game of all.

RILEY

If history has taught me anything, it's that blood's definitely not
thicker than water, whereas my profession as a youth worker,
helping troubled teens affected by crime, seems to only further
solidify that belief. However, it's hard to cut your familial ties
when all your mistakes stare back at you in the eyes of the woman
you're not meant to love. She was too young, and ethically
speaking, our relationship would have been taboo at best. So I
shoved those feelings down, convinced I was doing the right
thing. Especially for her. That is, until the past comes calling
back, threatening both the life I've worked so hard to build and
the woman I've tried to forget.

SIENNA

After a less-than-stellar upbringing, despite the best efforts of my
big brother turned guardian, I've tried to stay out of trouble and
make new friends. Better friends. But how do you ever recover
from the type of wounds that just won't stop bleeding? How do
you move on from rejection, when it's reflected back at you from
across the dinner table? That's easy. You don't. Instead, I've
avoided him, his family and even my own. All in the name of self-
preservation. Little did I realize that the strongest emotional walls
can come crumbling down, when I once again find myself face to

face with the worst of my youthful indiscretions. Avoidance no longer a viable option, can I trust him to protect not only my life but my poorly stitched heart?

Sometimes love is worth a little danger.

Trigger Warning: *Mentions of suicide, past and present emotional traumas, treated and untreated mental illnesses as well as histories of sexual assault.*

Chapter One

Sienna

The Wi-Fi at the Hope Island Coffee Hub might as well have been dial-up. It sucked. I disconnected and reconnected the network on my laptop, hoping the messages from Evelyn, my therapist from TeleCare, would stop lagging. Having secret sessions at the back of a coffee shop was bad, but having time to answer my own questions, compliments of the shitty technology, was worse. At this rate, I might as well stop selling her my soul every Saturday morning and deal with my crap privately.

> EVELYN
>
> Why was this week particularly bad, Sienna?

I sighed, my fingers cupping the mug of hot chocolate between my hands. The small white marshmallows undulated every time I blew cold air on the steaming beverage.

> The wedding date has been set.

EVELYN

> I see. Sounds like you're not looking
> forward to that?

Nope. My brother Avery and his fiancée were finally getting married. They'd been together for three years, and I loved Gracey, so this was definitely not a case of replacement mum syndrome. Though, living at home was a bit weird now that Avery was all whipped and in love.

I took a sip of the hot liquid, my whole body warming up as I worked on dropping my shoulders before Evelyn lectured me on the benefits of muscle relaxation again.

> I'm gonna have to see him at the wedding.

The chat window brightened, the three little dots working their way on the page. I closed my eyes, surrendering to the internet lag, my mind wandering to the last time I'd seen Riley. It had to have been right before my gap year in Parma. Right before he told me there would never be anything between us, because the measly four-year age difference made him some form of freaking predator.

EVELYN

> It's been three years. Tell me what would
> make it difficult for you, Sienna?

Frustration poked at me. God, I hated how much I'd cared about the guy. The last thing I wanted to do was revisit how ashamed I'd felt when he tossed me away. I took a deep breath, my fingers banging on the keyboard.

> He let us get close, almost kiss. He let me develop feelings for him, and then turned around, all self-righteous, and told me that I was too young for him. Too vulnerable. Like he'd suddenly signed up for some ethical club I wasn't good enough for.

The bubbles on the screen resumed.

EVELYN

Good enough?

I swallowed hard, my throat tightening. My fingers shook as they hovered over the laptop.

Are you even trying to work on yourself, Shorty? Avery's voice drilled through my ears. I pictured the line between his brow as he lectured me outside the Gold Coast police station on Wednesday night. A tear fell down my cheek as guilt flooded me. I was a spoilt little bitch. My brother had raised me for the last decade, paid my debt to Hal Cooper, risking his life through the whole ordeal, and I still couldn't act like a normal person.

> I'm sorry. I'm not being very helpful. Avery has been amazing to me, and I shouldn't be so negative about my lot in life.

A smiley face emoji appeared on the screen, followed by Evelyn's usual nurturing spiel.

EVELYN

> Good job for the reflection, Sienna. I like to remind all my patients that we're not responsible for what happens to us, but we are responsible for what we do about it moving forward. You had a tough childhood. You didn't have a father, your mother deserted you when you were just a kid, and you found yourself hooked up to the biggest drug ring in the state at age thirteen. From what you and Avery described, getting out of it was not a small feat, and so at the time, being rejected by Riley when you needed to feel loved left you with a scar. All we can do is reflect and try to heal it. It sounds to me like the first step to this might be getting ready for the wedding. Focus on Avery and Grace's big day, while making sure it doesn't get spoilt with any drama in the meantime. Because the truth is, Sienna, Riley's in your past. Just let him go.

Hard to ignore him when they all work together and eat at the same table five days a week. Between Grace and Avery's Nutrify, and Jarryd and April's Youth Legacy, avoiding Riley had pretty much alienated me from both centres and family gatherings for the last three years.

I wiped another tear off my cheek, glad that this session wasn't face to face. There was something about being able to hide behind my screen that allowed me to share the ugly parts of my mind. The parts I'd never felt safe enough to share with anyone else. It cut deep that, in order to protect my heart, I'd had to remain invisible. In the end, I missed them all. I'd missed being involved with Bello A&G Italiano as it grew, but the worse part—the part I didn't want to admit to anyone—was that I missed him.

> This is what I want too. To make sure they have the best day ever, and that I don't ruin it by crumbling down, all because I have to face a guy I thought I loved when I was sixteen.

EVELYN

> Good on you, Sienna. That's a great attitude.

The chat room minimized itself in the right corner of my screen as soon as the second browser was opened. I clicked on the Facebook link, amazed at the fact the hyperlink hadn't combusted at the rate I'd stalked it since the wedding news.

Riley Williams. Twenty-three. Senior Youth Worker- Youth Legacy- Gold Coast.

My heartrate galloped as my eyes landed on his profile photo. Shirtless, sunnies, a guitar in his hands, some mysterious smile as he leaned against a wall on the steps of the Surfer's Paradise pedestrian walkway. God help me. I thought the guy was hot when he was half the size, but now that he sported broad shoulders, perfect abs, and a smile to kill, he was all eye candy.

I switched to the chat window and answered my therapist before she wondered where I'd disappeared to. And telling her I'd graduated to the Riley's stalker category was not an option.

> Thank you, Evelyn. One day acting normal will be natural, I swear.

EVELYN

> It sure will. One day, the scars won't hurt as much, and we'll look back on this and smile.

That might have been pushing it, but the woman was nice, so I didn't want to burst her Pollyanna bubble.

> What's my homework for this week?

In all honesty, Evelyn's homework wasn't horrible, and it really helped despite my ambivalent moods.

EVELYN

> Let's continue working on the gratitude journal. Add the WWW exercise to it.

> WWW?

> What Worked Well today. Find one thing each day that worked well and show gratitude for it. Nice and easy, right?

I sent her a smiley face, before confirming our appointment for next week. Then, I closed the chat room window, Riley's blown-up photo taking up my screen. The photos kept coming as I scrolled down the page. The beach, camping, music rehearsals. I narrowed my eyes at one of his most recent shots. Some event at Avery's restaurant, Riley wearing a Bello A&G Italiano cap as he performed on the make-shift stage. A girl stared into his eyes, her hand on his chest.

Ugh. She looks like a fan. A desperate attention seeking groupie. Some weird jealousy teased me, the completely unjustified and irrational type, and I scrolled faster, running away from the image. My fingers hovered over the next music video, a home recording—judging by the converses and dickies shirts scattered through the room.

Riley rested on a bed, one knee bent, the other leg straightened with a guitar hugging his middle. His black hair was a little longer than I remembered, the locks falling over his forehead. He smiled at the camera, his brown eyes twinkling in invitation.

Hands shaking, I pressed play, guilt flooding me for officially turning into a lurker. Soft guitar music sounded through the speakers, the notes seamless as he relaxed against his headboard. He closed his eyes as his pick slid across the fret. A feeling of peace and comfort filled me as I let Riley's music wrap around me silently. I took another sip of my hot chocolate, my own eyes shut as I allowed the unrest to leave me for the first time in a long time. Then, his voice accompanied the gentle thrumming, a husky melody singing lullabies to the universe. Goosebumps crawled up my arms as I processed the lyrics, my throat tightening at the emotions building in his tone.

For the world around us, she was just a child.
But for me, she was my special girl.
Beautiful. Smart. Loving.
It wasn't fair to me.
It wasn't fair to her.
If only the world would let me.
I could have told them she wasn't just a child.

A deep breath drowned my lungs, my chest compressed with sadness, and I turned the sound down until Riley's voice was just a whisper in the busy coffee shop. I reached down for the wedding invitation sticking out of my bag, and opened the fuchsia and dark-grey cardboard in front of me. The fancy fonts tossed a stern reminder of the inevitable, and I slid my finger over the silver lettering. The twenty-first of March.

I had less than one month to prepare for Avery and Grace's big day. A month before I'd face Riley Williams again.

Chapter Two

Riley

As soon as my new song was announced, clapping and whistling replaced the screeching of cutlery on plates, and a mix of excitement and apprehension filled my stomach as I settled on the stool behind the microphone. I cleared my throat, my fingers picking at the guitar until the chords surrendered to my directions, and like a mother's lullaby, soothing notes filled the private room of *Bello A&G Italiano*. The crowd quietened.

Just let your mind float. Like every other time.

The waitresses resumed their duties in the background, and the dining room settled. I wet my lips, ready to let the lyrics of the song tell their own story, my heart in sync with its tempo. As soon as the words left my throat, I was drawn to my own paradise, the one I hid in when things got too... *complicated*. And peace filled me, like it did every Friday night since I started performing for Avery and Grace six months ago.

Although I'd only been playing for a few years, it'd

become natural, and it gave me an outlet I looked forward to, outside of my work at Youth Legacy. Something just for me. Something precious. Something I could guard deep down in my heart without anyone having to understand the turmoil that came from being born a Cooper.

When my last melody for the night was up, I relaxed against the low back of the stool, my shoulders dropping in complete ecstasy as everyone cheered. I didn't care what anyone said. This felt better than any hook-up ever would. No matter how hot the blonde in front of me looked in her little red number.

"Thank you for another great night." I wiped the sweat off my brow with the back of my hand, addressing the patrons in the restaurant. "You guys are just awesome."

When the clapping died down, I pulled my guitar strap above my shoulders and jumped off the stage. Miss Little Red Riding Hood waited for me, her wide smile showing perfect white teeth.

Two weeks in a row, stud. If she's not into you, I don't know who is.

"Hi." Her eyes travelled up and down my body.

"Enjoyed the show?" I had to admit, for some reason, the guitar attracted women like bees to a big freaking jar of honey.

"I loved it. Awesome new song too." She took a step closer, her teeth biting on her bottom lip.

"Thanks. Means a lot." My gaze landed on her mouth.

She took another step until I could feel her breath by my ear. "Can I get you a drink? You must be thirsty." She placed her hand on my forearm, ignoring the beads of sweat dripping off me.

Go clean up, you animal. You reek. Then, you can have your after-party reward.

My lips curled. I smiled at the vision. This Little Red Riding Hood naked under me wouldn't be a bad way to end the night. "I tell you what? Give me fifteen, and I'll meet you at the bar." I pointed to the counter on the other side of the restaurant. She blushed, her fingers lingering on my arm for an extra second, then sashayed her way there. I watched her perfect heart-shaped ass sway through the room until it disappeared, then I made it to the staff area.

I pushed the door in, my guitar under one arm, sheet music under the other, and exhaled as the air-con in the staff room cooled me down on the spot. I dumped my stuff on the small couch right before I fell back on the seat, sprayed myself with deodorant, and swapped my shirt for a clean one. Then, I closed my eyes, relaxing my head against the cushion, and waited for the post-show butterflies to die down.

"A little bird told me that we're already bursting at the seams for your next gig."

Freak. My neck spasmed as I jolted on the couch, my eyes scanning the room for Avery's voice. When I spotted him by the bench making a coffee, I straightened, my ankle resting on my other knee. "When did you sneak in?" I chuckled.

"Another great night." Avery whistled, his spoon stirring the hot liquid. "You're becoming a local talent, kid."

A grin formed on my face, a mix of excitement and surprise. I loved my music and I loved performing, but I was still pretty green in the scheme of it. As much as I tried to act all humble, it was a big deal. "It's crazy, hey?"

He nodded. "You're just good at it. Maybe the pretty boy looks help too." He smirked.

I tossed my dirty shirt at him, and he avoided it just in

time. "Hey, don't blame me for still having the youth you don't," I teased.

My shirt landed back at my feet, Avery's laughter resonating in the room. "At the expense of wisdom, kid. Trust me, I'm still ahead."

Behind our regular claims for alpha status, I loved Avery. He'd been a great mentor, and I was grateful for the opportunity he'd given me here. "Thanks, man. For everything. I still can't believe how much I'm loving this."

"A good thing, because we're booked out on your Fridays for the next three weeks."

"Wow." I took a deep breath, working on accepting my good karma. The last few years had been mayhem. Between Jarryd's trial and Hal recruiting Avery to bring me back into the fold, so many people had got hurt because of my family, but for the first time in my entire existence, my life was mine to steer. Career, music, and peace. I loved where it was headed. "You know I'm grateful, right?" I scraped the guitar pick against the top of my thigh as I continued. "You've become the closest thing to a big brother I could have ever asked for."

Avery sighed, a half-smile on his face at the words *big brother*. He settled on a seat next to me. "You're a good kid. Everything you got, you worked for it, so don't give me any credit."

Silence filled the air while Avery sipped on his coffee, the elephant in the room growing by the second. The guitar pick scraped at my leg a little harder now. *Apologise for using the word brother. Tell him you didn't mean it.* Buzzing stirred in the pit of my stomach at the guilt I'd carried around for the last three years. *Just freaking ask him about her.* I took a settling breath, my heart rate increasing at the thought, then our eyes met. I sighed. "How is she?"

Avery ran a hand over his face, lines deepening on his forehead. "I actually wanted to talk to you about her."

I cocked an eyebrow. Until now, the topic of Sienna had remained in unspoken territory ever since the standoff between us and my father. "It's not like you to volunteer information about her."

He huffed. "You're my last resort."

Panic spread at rapid speed. Something must have happened for Avery to bring her up to me. Even worse if I was his last resort after breaking her heart. "Is she okay?"

"She's alive and safe, if that's the question."

I exhaled, my chest sinking. Sienna was known for her impulsive moves, and nothing was ever off the table with her. The look on his face wasn't relief though. "But...?"

"Something's off with her. She's isolating herself and there's nothing we can do to change her mind. Even Grace only gets polite nods."

"Why me?" I narrowed my eyes. Last time I checked, they'd all told me to back the hell away from her, considering how fragile she'd been through the whole ordeal.

"She needs a friend, Riley."

My mouth dropped open, confusion coursing through me. "You might recall that we all agreed that I'd back off to keep her away from Cooper and any repercussions from my impasse with my brother?"

"I remember," Avery said, his tone neutral.

"And that my refusal to give in to what I really wanted was admirable, especially while she was a minor and I was her youth worker. You remember this part too?"

He nodded, his lips flat. "I wouldn't be asking if we hadn't tried everything else, Riley. But you're both adults now, and I'm not asking you to get into anything other than a friendship. We all know you can't touch her."

I rolled my eyes. "Right. A friendship." I marched to the fridge and grabbed myself a water bottle. Once my throat had cooled down, I added, "Have you ever tried to be friends with someone you had feelings for? How do you think that'll go? Come on, let's be realistic here."

"She needs us and there's no one else, Riley."

I clenched my fingers around the water bottle, my knuckles whitening. "Do you suddenly not care about my weekly contact with my bloodline? No part of you worries about putting her back in Hal's crosshairs? Because I sure as hell ain't prepared to have any goddamn Cooper around her. Not even me."

Avery paled a bit. "Jarryd's pretty confident you guys are on top of any bullshit he might be sprouting. Maintaining the happy family pretence is what's working to keep him at bay."

"I just want to be ten steps ahead." I sighed as visions of my brother filled my mind, like heavy rocks sinking to the bottom of my conscience. "And I'm worried about Seth. He's not doing too good."

Avery sneered. "No wonder. I think your fucking father might have something to do with that."

"Exactly. So, forgive me for not wanting a woman I care about to be exposed to it. You know how I feel about her," I growled. "She's your fucking sister, man."

"I trust you with her."

I shook my head. "Trust me to do what? Not feel anything for her, or not touch her? To make sure I'm the right balance of nice, so I get her back to you, but not too much so that I break her heart again?"

"Yes."

My water bottle missed his head by a short distance. "Go to hell, Avery. I'm not God."

"I know that. But you have professional skills that will mitigate any boundary issues."

"As in, making sure we stay in the friend zone, right?"

Avery's voice thinned. He ran a hand over his buzz cut, thick lines crinkling the corners of his eyes. "Riley, don't make me beg. I need her to snap out of whatever the fuck this is and come back to us. And all she needs is a little guidance from you."

I shook my head, some weird uncomfortable feeling tingling through my limbs. Surely, this couldn't be what I thought it was. "Let me translate this. You're really asking me to get into some pseudo-friendship again with your sister, a girl you all banned me from being with, so that I can steer her in the right direction before she does more damage to her life?"

Avery's biceps twitched, and he shifted in his chair. It had to have taken some balls for the guy to bring this up. "Riley, cut me some slack. There was a time when you cared about her."

I closed my eyes, a deep breath settling me. *I never stopped.* "Okay, so just to be clear. She's not doing too good, and you reckon me reappearing in her life like the good old days might help her?"

Avery's shifting increased, and his jaw clenched as he answered, "I'm asking you to find out what the issues are and help her problem-solve them... the right way."

A deep laugh brewed in my stomach, and when it escaped, it rang out in the room, the irony not lost on anyone. "Avery, you realise we're talking about your sister, right? Sienna? The ice queen who won't do anything she doesn't want to do?"

"The one and only." Deeper lines appeared on his face,

and he slumped on his chair, the wooden frame creaking under his weight.

I softened. The guy didn't need any more stress by the looks of the road map marring his flesh. I cared about Sienna more than I'd ever admitted to any of them. I wanted to help her. I wanted her safe. But this was playing with fire, and he'd have to be brain dead not to see how his plan could go awry. "How does she feel about that?"

He flinched. I studied the change in his demeanour, and when he avoided my eye contact, I asked again. Avery was as straight as they came, but he'd made a living playing two sides to the same coin, and I wasn't born yesterday. The cogs ticked in my brain as I processed Avery's odd request. Then it clicked. *You gotta be joking?*

My mouth gaped, the realization not unlike an odd déjà vu. What Avery asked of me was to spy on his sister. Bring her back to him like a perfect little coincidence, and then go on my way.

"She doesn't know, does she?"

He exhaled loudly. "Don't make me beg."

I shook my head, my hands raised up in the air. "No fucking way. Nuh-uh."

Avery uncrossed his legs and leaned forward, his hands cupped into a ball. Sweat glistened at the base of his skull as he spoke, his tone desperate. "I would never ask you to do anything unprofessional, unethical, or otherwise. Riley, you're the only person who could get through to her while you guys were friends. But since she's been back, she's exiled herself completely. She won't come to any family events, just in case you might show your face, and I need her to get over this."

Over me. My brain fuzzed with this conversation, and I shook my head, begging for five seconds of reflection time.

Am I being her friend, or am I helping her get over things between us? "You wouldn't be asking me unless there was more to it." I rubbed my palms over my thighs. "Am I helping her, or am I turning her off from the memory of us so she can start coming to your social gatherings?"

He deadpanned, "Do they have to be mutually exclusive?"

I raked my fingers through my hair, my heart thundering against my chest. Sienna was an amazing girl. She was kind. Honest. Caring. And right now, she needed a friend. Because as much as Avery's request might have been... unique, it wasn't right that Sienna missed out on all the Legacy family bonding just because I hadn't managed business and pleasure right once upon a time. It'd been my fault. I'd liked her as much as she'd liked me, but she had deserved better than what any Cooper could have given her. My shoulders dropped, their weight feeling like a thousand bricks. I wanted to be there for her. I really did. But what I didn't need was the risk of reigniting feelings and finding myself ten steps backwards, right when life was finally looking up.

Feelings from her or from you? "You can guarantee me that once I find out what the issues are, you will make sure she gets the help, and we can all heal moving forward?"

"You have my word." Avery extended his hand towards me. "Just be her friend and find out how we can help her."

My fingers shook all the way up, like hesitation had set through my bones. *All you have to do is be her friend. No strings attached.* "And once we know what's up, you'll take it from there and really help her?"

"I'll go to my grave fighting for Sienna, Riley. You don't even have to ask."

My hand gripped his, and I shook it. "All right, Avery.

I'll reconnect with her because I care, but if I can't find anything out, or worse, if I'm hurting her somehow, deal's over and you'll just have to help her the old-fashioned way. Fair?"

Avery's forehead smoothed out, and he leaned back against his chair, somewhat of a smirk replacing his earlier frown. "That's all I'm asking."

I closed my eyes, exhaling deeply, the mixed emotions drilling through my gut. It had been years since I laid eyes on Sienna and a part of me did want to help her. It was in my job description. But the other part screamed at me to run, and not to fuck up the stillness in my life right as it finally settled. "How do you suggest I start?" I asked, resolve crawling in.

Avery stood, confidence returning to his face, and marched towards the main dining room. "I have to get back to work." Then, right before he pulled the handle, he added, "I hear she likes to hide at the Coffee Hub."

I nodded. "Got it."

The exit door pushed ajar, I unlocked my car from a distance and jumped into the driver's seat. I started the motor, desperate to climb into bed for the night. Alone, any thoughts of Little Red Riding Hood long gone.

If you would like to read more, get your copy of Dangerous Love on Amazon.

Also by SK Mason

ETHICS OF THE HEART SERIES

Beautiful Enigma

THE HOPE ISLAND SERIES

Forbidden Promise

Reckless Attraction

Dangerous Love

Glossary

Tender - An Australian Government application to get funding for community projects or government jobs.

White Goods - Kitchen appliances including but not limited to fridge, microwave, oven ect.

Tradies - Tradesman like electricians, plumbers and carpenters.

Navara - Australian Pickup Truck.

Airtasker - Website to hire people for small jobs.

2IC - Second In Command.

Servo - Service Station or Gas Station.

Windscreen - Windscreen or Windshield on a car.

Acknowledgments

A massive thank you to the 2 women who made this possible. My PA Natasha and my editor Kat. There are no words to express how grateful I am. This book is yours. Your baby just as much as it is mine. I am beyond grateful xxx

Thank you for taking a chance on me and reading a little piece of my heart. You the reader is why I write and I really hope you enjoyed my book. If you enjoyed it I hope you will consider leaving a review on Amazon, Goodreads or Bookbub as that helps authors like me grow and be found by other readers.

Lots of Love, Sheridan xoxxo

About the Author

I began writing stories in primary school, stories I would sell to my maternal grandmother, and stories she kept forever. Now, my paternal grandmother, an avid romance reader, would let me read her Harlequin collection over every summer, and soon my books took on a romance turn of their own!

Fast-forward thirty years later and SK Mason was born. A romance lover with a passion for "happily ever after" and pretty groovy ethical twists. In "real life", I mingle in the health sector, so don't be surprised that most of my books are inspired by these fun and intense settings.

When I'm not writing, I'm spending time with my family in Australia. My children are my life and together we cook, swim and ride our bikes. Life doesn't get better than that!"